PRAISE FOR
THE HOUSE OF DISCARDED DREAMS

"On one level, this is a reflection of ancient fairy tales and legends; on the other, it's a perfectly straightforward tale of finding oneself in a bizarre world. Either way, Sedia's prose is a pleasure, her story a lovely place to have spent time, even with the horrors her characters face."—*Booklist*

"A moody feast of the fantastic, dreamy, surreal, just the right fusion of thematic depth and unbridled creativity that I'm always looking for."—David Anthony Durham, author of the Acacia Series

"With *The House of Discarded Dreams*, Ekaterina Sedia has written a satisfyingly complicated coming-of-age novel where "adulthood" isn't about leaving fantasy behind. In this beautiful, surreal story, a young biologist discovers that dreams are as meaningful as empirical research."—*io9*

"Sedia crafts a tale of magical realism that explores the connections between culture and identity as well as the nature of reality and dreams. Humor and metaphysics blend in an elegantly written story of a woman's quest for her true home."—*Library Journal continued*

"Nothing could prepare me for the power of her latest, *The House of Discarded Dreams*, presenting the absolutely strange in the same lucid prose as the everday, even when dream threatens to detail off into nightmare."—*Locus*

"A unique fantasy that combines urban legend, creatures, and magic to give a fresh take on colonialism and the dilemmas that children of immigrants face."—Nnedi Okorafor, author of *The Shadow Speaker* and *Zahrah the Windseeker*

"Lyrical writing and rich imagination compensate for loose plotting in this quirky, joyous fantasy, as Sedia shows how competing natural and supernatural worldviews can enrich each other."—*Publishers Weekly*

THE HOUSE
OF DISCARDED DREAMS

BOOKS BY EKATERINA SEDIA

The Alchemy of Stone

Heart of Iron (forthcoming)

Paper Cities: An Anthology of Urban Fantasy (edited)

Running with the Pack (edited)

The Secret History of Moscow

THE HOUSE
OF DISCARDED DREAMS

Ekaterina Sedia

PRIME BOOKS

THE HOUSE OF DISCARDED DREAMS

Prime Books
www.prime-books.com

ISBN: 978-1-60701-228-3

To Bill and Tait, who made this book possible

Chapter 1

VIMBAI KNEW THAT IT WAS GOING TO BE ONE OF THOSE DAYS the moment she shuffled downstairs, her socking feet blindly finding their way on the carpeted steps. Her eyes still half-shut from sleep but her nose already picking up the oily smell of freshly roasted coffee beans, she smiled just as the raised voice of her mother cut into her mind. Vimbai stopped smiling.

Ever since she was a child, she had not liked these days, when her parents fought first thing in the morning and the rest of the day came out all narrow-eyed and lopsided, devoid of the usual sense of balance and rightness in the world. Not that those were ever serious fights—the normal spousal squabbling, Vimbai supposed; nothing bad, and most families had it far worse. And yet these fights made her feel exposed and vulnerable, betrayed in her sanctuary and given to the mercy of strange hostile elements.

She slipped into the kitchen, her eyes wary now, looking from under the lowered eyelids.

"Don't squint," her mother said. "Do you want any breakfast?"

"Just coffee," Vimbai answered, and momentarily envied her mother's accent. The words, the familiar English words that melted and mushed in Vimbai's mouth, came out with startling sparkling edges, as if they were just born, unpolished by the world, rough and fresh and solid.

She sidled up to the table—they always ate their meals at the table, and even breakfast was a family occasion, an extra opportunity to either bond or hurt each other's feelings.

Her mother shook her head but poured Vimbai a large steaming cup. "You have to eat breakfast."

Vimbai's father made a sound in the back of his throat, a mild sound that seemed to serve only to remind them that he was also present and perhaps could offer opinions on breakfasts and other matters but was too absorbed in his thoughts to vocalize them.

Vimbai looked out of the window, at the familiar suburban street and the red leaves of maples that grew in this sandy soil through some miracle of gardening and landscaping. "How are you doing, dad?" Vimbai said. "Long day today?"

He nodded. "Double shift," he said. "You?"

Vimbai pursed her lips and blew on the surface of her coffee, wrinkling it like smooth brown silk. "Three classes today."

"You're coming to school with me?" her mother asked.

"Maybe," Vimbai answered. "If you're not working late again."

"You can go to the library," her mother suggested.

"Or I can take my car and drive home." Vimbai tried to keep her voice neutral—when her parents fought first thing in the morning, it was not wise to annoy her mother. If Vimbai was not careful, shit would go down and both her and her father would get it—not that they didn't deserve it, Vimbai admitted to herself. After all, why shouldn't she get in trouble every now and again?

Mother rose, pushing her chair away with a hair-raising squeak. "Fine. Suit yourself. Carpooling is of course too much trouble and inconvenience. Who cares about global warming anyway?"

"Mom." Vimbai cringed. "Don't be like this."

As Vimbai had grown older, she had realized that the arguments and the problems she had with her mother were not unusual—in fact, she suspected that teenage girls who did not get along with their mothers outnumbered those who did at least three to one. It did not make her feel any better, and she still wished—selfishly, she would be the first to admit—that her mother paid more attention to Vimbai than the news from abroad, or to the Africana studies and who set the agenda there. She wished that she would pay as half as much mind to Vimbai's problems and worries as she did to the white men trying to hijack her department.

Mother shrugged and left, and Vimbai and her father traded looks.

"What brought that on?" Vimbai said.

Her father shook his head. "Everything, darling. Be nice to her—she's having a rough time. Her department and all that. Stress."

"You have stress too." Vimbai drank her coffee, sizing up her father from the corner of her eye. He was always so much more subdued, so willing to make excuses and make peace and sacrifice, always minimizing his own fatigue and heartbreak. It's not important, darling. Such a slight man, his eyes so sad and kind. She did not know how to tell him.

"It's all right," he answered. "You get used to it; you get used to everything."

Vimbai shrugged and drank her coffee, considering all the things she never wanted to get used to; at the same time, the habitual guilt stirred—her parents had been through so much, it felt downright selfish for her to complain about anything at all. And yet, if the experience was all that mattered, wasn't hers just as valuable? All she knew was that she had to get out of here, before she became the same as her mother.

Her father was a nurse down at one of the Camden hospitals, and whenever she visited him or picked him up after work, she felt shamed for her sheltered life, reasonably devoid of suffering. This one wasn't a university hospital, and the emergency room always overflowed with gunshot wounds and overdoses, with beatings and burnings and other godawful things. Vimbai did not know how he could stand it, how it was possible to get used to things like that.

"You seem pensive today," her father said. "Hope we didn't upset you."

"Of course not," she said. "I was just thinking . . . am I getting too old to live at home?"

The words just poured out, mushed by habituality. Her parents never spoke like that, all their words considered, even in the heat of an argument. Even when they fought in Shona, even though she understood little of what they said then.

He put down his newspaper with the picture of Barack

Obama on the page folded over. "Why would you say that? You know we don't want you living on your own."

"Just thinking." Vimbai finished her coffee in a few quick gulps. "No reason. Do you think Obama could really win?"

Her father shook his head. None of them thought that he could—the country is not ready, her mother said. He is black and not really American. He was like them, the unsaid words crowded. They would never accept people like us. We are to remain on the cultural margins of multiple worlds, abandoning one and never entering the other. Even Vimbai felt that though she had lived in New Jersey most of her life—she too was on the margins. What hope was there for her parents then, and how would they cope if she was really to move out? And yet, how could she not?

VIMBAI DECIDED TO SKIP CLASS. IT WAS THAT SORT OF A DAY, and missing a lecture on invertebrate zoology seemed only fitting. What was there to learn that she couldn't find out by walking along the shore, the dirty hem of foam curling around her bare ankles? She stopped to crouch over a dead horseshoe crab and to stare at it for a while, then to flip it over and count its limp little legs, jointed and pale and slightly obscene. She flipped it back on its belly, as if the dead crab's dignity needed preserving.

The beach was deserted—just gulls and terns circling overhead, waiting for the tide, just sandpipers endlessly chasing after the retreating waves and then running away from them, just the surf and the sky, the tang of October bursting through the iodine smell of seaweed and the ocean to singe the back of Vimbai's throat. Just the wind and the promise of winter, when the beach will be gray and dead, a giant whale flank colonized by silent invisible life under the leaden clouds.

These beaches of the barrier islands lining the eastmost side of the continent like the crook of a mother's elbow had been so good to Vimbai—they nursed her through the first years here, they sustained her through school that had seemed so endless and was now over; they whispered the answer to her when her mother had asked if she considered a college major yet. Marine biology, Vimbai had answered and never lost her temper as her mother lectured that marine biology was not the same as swimming with dolphins or whatever other romantic garbage she thought Vimbai was imagining. Invertebrates, she said, the word that wondrously summed up all the fascinating transparent things that the tide left behind thrashing in tiny pools. I want to study invertebrates. Anything, she wanted to add, but your Africana Studies, anything but that continent you—both of you—carry inside; what was the point in ever leaving if you were going to bring it with you? Instead, she babbled about horseshoe crabs that were declining in number thanks to their use as fishbait and to the pharmaceutical companies who drained their blood to make vaccines.

Oh, the blood draining, the *wazimamoto* and the colonialism; as much as Vimbai resented the Africana Studies, her mind was its own little storehouse of legends and stories and memories not quite her own, she didn't think—but *wazimamoto*. The vampire, the white man who came on a medical truck to steal your blood. She learned the story from her Kenyan babysitter, an old woman who was so dark and shrunken she seemed to smolder. And her mother's verbal annotations—Vimbai could never get away from those. And then the books, anything that her mother could find translated, anything African. And yet, Vimbai's alliance was to the horseshoe crabs, the ones who were in real danger of having their blood stolen.

The sand under her feet—bare, her sneakers tied by their shoelaces slung over her shoulder—felt wet and solid, tamped down by the waves. Seaweed and driftwood, the usual refuse of the Atlantic, studded the solid sand surface and Vimbai wandered along, her sharp eyes looking for signs of movement of any critter left behind by the waves. She was skipping class, but let no one say that she did not study.

It was time to return to the car and drive back to school; before the inevitable, Vimbai went for a quick skip across the dunes—the signs and wire fences warned that any such behavior was illegal in the nature preserve, but Vimbai knew that the migratory birds had left already, and the rangers rarely visited the beach in October, so there was no one to witness her impropriety. She ducked under the wire slowly undulating in the wind, and staggered across the warm loose sand that sucked in her feet and stuck to her skin. The thickets of low shrubs and occasional grass patches clung to the sand with admirable, if misguided, determination; the scattering of yellow flowers surprised her—nothing was supposed to be flowering at this time of year, at least in New Jersey. Then her attention snagged on another dead horseshoe crab. It lay among the flowers, belly up, with something bright and white clutched in its stiff little legs.

It was a piece of paper with a fringed edge, of the kind usually sported by homemade ads. None of the pieces with the phone number on it was torn off, though, and Vimbai crouched over the dead crab and its white piece of paper as if it was an exotic chimera composed of animal and inorganic parts. The paper lay blank side up, and Vimbai tried to guess what was on its other side and how it got here. It could've been blown here by the wind, after being torn from whatever wall or bulletin board it had previously graced; it could've been thrown from a window of a passing car, speeding on the way to or from the town, a sleepy place after August but screaming and bustling in the summer, in contrast to the quiet nature preserve of the beach and its environs.

Vimbai wrested the piece of paper from the clasping pincers and turned it over. The ad was handwritten in a generous loopy scrawl, and it took her a moment to decipher what it said. "Roommate wanted for house in the dunes. Own bedroom and bathroom, separate entrance. Very reasonable rent plus one-third utilities. Any pets except fish." And the phone number.

It was true that Vimbai had thought about moving out—but the thought had remained soft and amorphous, hiding in the long creases of her pillow and only surfacing with any determination in that half-asleep state at nights and mornings. The ad had brought the thought into daylight, and as Vimbai walked back to her Saturn parked in the small paved lot off the only road that bisected the island, she thought, why not? House in the dunes and a very reasonable rent sounded quite appealing, and she had never owned any fish. She decided to call as soon as she found herself near a phone with decent reception and away from her parents' superior hearing.

THE THOUGHT OF THE HOUSE IN THE DUNES WAS PUT AWAY AS soon as she reached the campus and stopped by her mother's office to say hello and to check on the latest drama. There was always plenty in the Africana Studies, the most current being her mother's threats to complain and quit after the program appointed a white man as a department chair; the said chair busily set about redefining the agenda, and Vimbai's mother would simply not stand for it on general principle.

She was in her office, looking run down even though it wasn't even lunchtime yet.

"You okay?" Vimbai asked. "Sorry you're not having a good day."

"I'm fine." She looked up from the sheaves of paper strewn on her desk, memos and attendance reports and student essays mixed into a terrifying entangled mess that threatened to consume any mortal's sanity with its sheer size and complexity. "Another meeting, and after that I just have to grade."

"Don't work too hard," Vimbai advised.

Her mother only shrugged in response, not bothering to pretend that she would even consider such foolishness. "And you should probably go to your next class."

Vimbai left the office marveling at her mother's ability to sniff out any shirking of one's responsibilities, no matter how otherwise preoccupied she was. And she had been preoccupied—ever since the new department chair, Dr. Bouchard, was appointed, Vimbai's mother seemed to know no rest. Even late at night, she paced the hallway, sometimes muttering to herself in English and Shona; Vimbai could hear her voice through her closed door. All the more reason to move out, Vimbai thought.

She arrived to her class late and slunk to the back, to take sporadic notes of plants' inner workings and to brood. The tubes inside the plants formed neat organized patterns Vimbai enjoyed sketching; it felt almost like doodling rather than studying, and her thoughts flowed along with wavy lines and pooled in quiet oases of shading, neat little areas of cross-hatch pencil strokes.

"This is nice," the girl on Vimbai's left whispered, peering into her notebook.

Vimbai remembered the girl's name—Sarah. They were in a few classes together, and Sarah had irritated Vimbai on several occasions with her pre-med student's obsessive anxiety. "Thanks," Vimbai said with a little stingy smile.

Sarah smiled back, apparently oblivious to Vimbai's disinclination to make friends. It always puzzled Vimbai, this implied certainty some people possessed that their attention could not possibly be an imposition.

Vimbai turned the page and took more thorough notes than usual to indicate that she was not going to participate in any conversations.

Undeterred, Sarah waited for her after class. "Boring, huh?" she said by the way of striking up a chat.

Vimbai shrugged. "I like it. I like anatomy." She took a tentative step away.

Sarah followed, and there was really no good way of escaping her in the long straight hallways, made all the more desolate by the poisonous shade of their green paint. "You have any more classes today?"

Vimbai nodded. "African American Lit," she said.

"Oh," Sarah answered. White kids never knew what to say. "How is it?"

"Why don't you take it and find out?" Vimbai suggested with more vehemence than she felt.

"I don't think it's for me."

"Why not? You know all there is to know about it?"

Sarah shrugged. "I'm just not interested."

Of course she wasn't. Vimbai remembered her mother's frequent complaints that the white kids never took any classes at the Africana studies, that they always assumed that black equaled special interest. As much as Vimbai hated to agree with her mother, she had to in this case. But she didn't argue with Sarah—the fatigue was overwhelming, the sense that she had had this conversation and this argument too many times before. "Whatever," she said. "I have to go."

It wasn't true—her next class did not start until an hour later, but she was not in the mood for explaining herself. Another thing her mother complained about—the constant necessity of explaining oneself, of answering questions. "People are just trying to be nice," Vimbai used to argue when she was much younger. "They're just showing interest."

"Showing interest," her mother had replied, "would be bothering to do some research on their own rather than pestering people with questions. Don't you see? Even when they're nice, they're placing a burden on you. Just wait and see how quickly it gets on your nerves."

Vimbai sighed and headed for the library—it was usually empty during the lunchtime, and in the stacks it might be easy to avoid Sarah or any other overly talkative classmates who would be eager to burden her with their interest or socializing.

The library was located in the new building, adjacent to the science labs. It had tall narrow windows running all the way from the high ceiling to the tiled floors, and Vimbai liked the way sunlight striped the stacks, while others hid in the shadows, light and dark interspersed in regular narrow slats. She headed for the shelves draped in soft shadow, meandered between then into the unexplored library depths hiding reference materials—newspapers from the sixties and the seventies, artifacts no intrepid explorer would be likely to sift through—and sat on the floor, her back resting comfortably against the cloth-bound sheaves of papers. The air smelled of dust and air-freshener, mixed with Vimbai's own scent of warm skin and salt, and she curled up in this quiet welcoming ambience.

Unlikely to disturb anyone, she dug through her book bag and found her cell and the crumpled sheet of paper from the dunes. She dialed the number and almost chickened out and hung up when the female voice said "Hello."

"Hello," Vimbai answered, keeping her voice low out of the old library habit. "I'm calling about the house . . . in the dunes."

"We still have a room," the woman said brightly. "The rent

is two hundred bucks a month, and you will share with myself and Felix—he has the third bedroom. Interested?"

"I'd like to see it first," Vimbai said.

"Come by tomorrow," the woman said, and dictated the address.

Vimbai wrote it down and promised to stop by.

That night, she dreamt of sea and whales. The whales floated on the silvery ocean surface like balloons, and water from their blowholes rose and fell like the fountains in Longwood Gardens. The whales sang in surprisingly soft voices, a rhymed children's song Vimbai could not remember when she woke up; but as the dream retreated, she kept smiling—the whales were a good omen.

Chapter 2

No wonder the rent was so cheap—the house was in a woeful state of disrepair, its wooden siding bleached by the ocean winds to the color and consistency of driftwood; the street on which it nominally stood proved to be a cul-de-sac, almost concealed by the sand blown off the dunes that surrounded the house like waves. The surf pounded the beach nearby, and Vimbai suspected that the house wasn't condemned only because of pure oversight, since it clearly violated several zoning laws and the next good storm would likely flood it. Still, she could not deny that she was thoroughly charmed.

She lingered for a while on the porch, cracks between the boards wide and gnarled like fissures in dry clay. She thought she caught a palimpsest of motion in the shadows under the porch, a quick shift of light and a change in the quality of the cool dusk. Some wildlife was bound to nest there, and for no good reason Vimbai hoped for a den of the tiny dwarf foxes that still lingered in the barrier islands, despite the constant expansion of the tourist towns and vacation homes. The foxes who begged by the roads, their red tongues teasing and wet between their sharp teeth; a whole nest of tiny pups, Vimbai imagined, cuddled together in the somber secretive darkness under the porch.

"Do you want to see the rest of the house, or are you content with the crap under the porch?" a female voice said next to her.

Vimbai straightened, smiling. "I thought I saw something under there."

The girl who stared back at her smiled too, then laughed. "Of course you did." She was taller than Vimbai, and gave off an air of good health and clean strength. She wore a somewhat unseasonable yellow tank top and bleached cutoffs that exhibited her long strong legs to great advantage. She shook hands with Vimbai. "I'm Maya. We talked on the phone."

Vimbai nodded, her fingers trying to hold their own in Maya's strong grip. She shook hands like someone who liked to show strength from the beginning, but Vimbai did not think her threatening. If anything, Maya reminded Vimbai of herself, in her need to establish dominance from the start. So she squeezed back as hard as she could. "I'd like to see the rest of the place, if you don't mind."

Maya smiled more, released her grip, and turned away giving Vimbai a chance to wince and mouth 'ow' while shaking her hand.

Maya motioned for Vimbai to follow, and stepped through the banged-up screen door much molested by the elements into the kitchen that bore traces of recent but unthorough cleaning. A few plates dripped in the rack, and the linoleum floor shone with fresh traces of water. The windows let through the pale light, and its diluted quality testified to the fact that the panes had not been washed in a long while.

Formica counters, bottles with bleach, and a patchy geriatric refrigerator sighing in the corner.

"It's modest," Maya said, noticing the trajectory of Vimbai's gaze, "but it works."

Vimbai nodded and followed Maya to the sunroom or perhaps the den—there was a TV and a concave couch, which at the moment cradled the languid form of a very young and very white man who Vimbai presumed was the second housemate.

"This is Felix," Maya said. "He's quiet, so pay him no mind."

Felix offered no opinion on the matter, and Vimbai dutifully turned her gaze to a couple of mismatched chairs that huddled by the wall, as if not quite believing their luck in having been rescued off a street corner on a garbage pick-up day, and a stern wooden table, covered in slicks shaped like pizza boxes. Good student living, familiar from the visits to Vimbai's study group buddies off campus. A sense of hastily put together and transitory space, with a modicum of effort to make it one's own and yet not to get attached. A ficus slowly dying in its way-too-small pot by the window where there wasn't enough light.

"The rest is straightforward," Maya said. "Bedrooms are upstairs, and then there're bathrooms and closets and shit. You want to see it, or do you want a beer?"

Honesty born out of living at home for all her life, under her mother's hawk-like gaze, compelled Vimbai to say, "I'm not twenty-one yet."

Maya shrugged. "I don't card. Don't worry, if you're in no shape to drive, I'll tell you."

"Okay then," Vimbai said. "I guess I want a beer," and only then realized that she had forfeited her right to the rest of the tour.

"I want a beer," Felix said from his trough on the couch, miraculously brought to life by a single phrase.

This outburst of verbosity encouraged Vimbai to give him a closer examination. First thing about Felix that she—or anyone, for that matter—noticed was his hair. It wasn't merely long or big; it undulated. The color of it was darker than black, a pure absence of light, so dense that no individual strands were visible. Occasionally this alarming hair reared up like tongues of flame, and then ebbed, calmed, and returned to its peaceful slow and hypnotic movement.

"I know," Maya said. "It's like a fucking lava lamp." She had returned from the kitchen bearing three golden long-necked bottles, and handed one to Vimbai. "It's even better with beer."

Felix sat up and extended both hands to take his, a motion that Vimbai found childlike, almost animal-like. For the first time, Vimbai got an unobscured look at his features.

Felix could've worked as a model for a Raphaelite painter specializing in cherubs—he had smooth porcelain skin and a small perfect mouth that seemed painted on—if it weren't for his eyes. Gigantic and fierce, with jaundiced whites streaked strongly with fat red capillaries, they rolled in his head with quiet fury, quite independently from one another.

Vimbai took a long swallow of her beer. She was aware that staring like this was impolite, but there was just no helping it when faced with Felix; fortunately, he seemed to neither mind nor notice—although the exact direction of his gaze was impossible to determine.

Maya pushed her gently toward one of the armchairs, and took the other. They did not speak a while—Vimbai staring, Felix preoccupied with his beverage, and Maya apparently giving Vimbai a chance to decide whether Felix was a sight she was willing to behold daily. Maya sat in the armchair that used to be burgundy, but currently hesitated between pink and gray; the original color survived only in the piping of the armrest over which she slung her legs carelessly, showing Vimbai the pink soles of her bare feet. Her black curly hair had been freed from the scrunchie that had held it together, and sprang up like a halo to rival Felix's.

Vimbai smiled and took another pull. "I like it here," she said. "It's a nice place."

Maya nodded. "And I," she said, "I would like my other roommate to be a girl, and a black girl at that. His pale ass," she motioned at Felix, "is plenty for me."

Felix grinned and bobbed his head, as if acknowledging a compliment. "There are forces in the world," he said cheerfully, and drank.

"Yeah yeah yeah." Maya waved her hand in the air. "Whatever." She turned her attention to Vimbai, a smile hiding in the plump corners of her mouth ready to come out as soon as Vimbai gave a signal. "So, what do you think?"

Vimbai shrugged and nodded, and found that her tongue had grown fat and lazy. She had had alcohol before, and half a beer never had this kind of an effect on her—no, it was this house, the languorous strangeness that colored the air despite the mundane furnishings; it was Felix and the black hole of his hair, Maya's sharp gaze and quick speech. The house in the dunes pulled her in, and she imagined herself sinking all the way, deep beneath the waves of sand where it was quiet and golden, blue shadows of the trees above dancing—or perhaps it was the ocean with its still forests of kelp and bivalve shells scattered about on the wavy sand bottom, shells empty like open hands. She imagined picking up one of these shells and whispering into it, her eyes closed, her weak hand pressing the pearly concave surface to her lips. Another shell to her ear, whispering in the susurrus of the sea, talking in monotone, come back, come back, baby, come back home.

And then her own lips, her slow tongue shaping words like stubborn clay, I'm sorry, mama, I'm so sorry. The sea between the shells a distance, pounding of the surf, the impossible separation by many tons of dense and cold water. Two continents, too far apart to ever hope for reconciliation.

Vimbai pressed the phone receiver to her ear, the voice of her mother so far away, so defeated and alone. "Mom?" Vimbai whispered.

Only the static of the ocean answered, the empty static in the shell of the phone like a small ghost trapped in the wires.

IT CAME OVER VIMBAI WHENEVER SHE STAYED IN THE HOUSE long enough. Being trapped in amber, in ocean water, in time, in distance, suspended and separated finally from everything in the world. She used to dread her mother's reaction, what she would say if Vimbai decided to move away from home; more than that, she feared her father's resigned and unconditional support. Now, she could only whisper faintly into the phone, her lips salty and barely moving, I'm sorry, mama, I'm so sorry. She did not let them help her move; her separation, this carving herself off from the rest of her family, had begun.

Maya blamed the strange effects of the house on Felix, on the gravitational pull of his hair; Felix did not argue. Vimbai thought that it was the dunes, the underwater singing of the horseshoe crabs buried in the sand for the winter; the shifting of sand, the lapping of the waves, the eroding processes that ate away at everything, that made land part of the sea and carried the sea over land, the same forces that pulled Vimbai away from everything her parents were. At night, she listened to the whistle of the wind in the rigging of the old house and its creaking moans, the lapping of the tides, unable to sleep. And so it went.

VIMBAI LIKED TO SIT IN THE KITCHEN IN THE MORNING—SHE made coffee and waited for Maya to come downstairs. Maya, always fascinating and evasive, a strange thing in herself, something that needed to be puzzled out and unraveled. Even though Vimbai was not sure why she felt that it was her job to unravel this enigma wrapped in a striped bath robe, she looked forward to the moment when Maya stumbled downstairs, her eyes half-closed and her nostrils flared in anticipation of the hot, clear coffee; there seemed to be few things in life Maya enjoyed more than that first cup of coffee in the morning.

"Good morning," Maya said and poured herself a cup.

"Thanks for making coffee—before you moved in, I was the one making it. Felix always sleeps late."

"Sure thing," Vimbai said. "I enjoy making it—I get up early anyway."

Maya made a face. "Whatever possesses you to commit such silliness?"

Vimbai considered the question she wanted to ask and then discarded it—there was simply no polite way of asking Maya about the way she spoke, about her carefully cultivated non-regional accent, without sounding offensive. She sighed and gave up on the idea—her mother was right: Vimbai, even though she was born and raised in New Jersey, was still a foreigner to most African-Americans, oblivious as she was to fine distinctions of speech patterns and code-switching. She was informed that she was not getting it when she was still in high school, and she was ashamed to admit that she had made little progress in the matter.

Instead, Vimbai poured herself another cup of coffee. "How do you like working in Atlantic City?" she asked.

Maya barked a short strained laugh. "What's not to like? Casinos surrounded by a ghetto. Land of contrasts, as it were. Plus, it's a good place to bartend, really—men are too preoccupied with gambling to hit on you. Which is, you know, a good thing. Like Martha Stewart."

"I've been at the casinos a few times," Vimbai said. "With my mom, mostly. She does some research there—her specialty is urban folklore, and there's a ton of it in Atlantic City."

"But not in the casinos."

"No. We went there for the buffets."

Maya laughed. "Oh my god. Those are such freak shows."

Vimbai's upbringing urged her to argue, to insist that all people deserved a claim to dignity and respect, and ought not to be called freaks. But she remembered these pale and lumbering shapes, their faces slack and remote, their eyes permanently dilated in the artificial semi-darkness. They seemed to live in the casinos—at least, Vimbai had never seen them anywhere else; they seemed shy underground dwellers, sliding softly through their habitual dusk with white porcelain plates heaped high with pasta salad and ribs, their only break from the life of sitting on a high stool and pulling a lever and putting shiny coins into a large Styrofoam cup, their lives augured by the fast-spinning cherries and lemons in tiny transparent windows.

"I know what you mean," she finally said. "Are the bars any better? I bet you have stories."

"You bet right," Maya said. "See, the casino bar is a great place—people come there when they are not gambling or eating, and that usually happens when they just lost a shitload of money, and cannot gamble anymore but are afraid to go back home. Some celebrate when they win, some are just there to hang out, you know? But it's always the losers who are interesting. This is why I remember them the most, I guess."

"Oh?" Vimbai smiled and refilled Maya's cup. This solicitousness felt natural to her, warm. "What's so interesting about them?"

Maya patted Vimbai's hand in gratitude, making her blush a bit. "I don't really know, but I guess this is when people are . . . honest, I guess. They know they've been beaten, and they are out of tricks for a while—they really know that they are fucked. And yet, there's this thing when they try to tell themselves that it's not that big of a deal. I don't know how to explain it, but it's like if they cannot lie to themselves about what happened, they start diminishing its importance. When they are honest, they almost have to be deluded, you know?"

Vimbai considered. "I'm kind of getting it, I guess." She wasn't really sure that she was getting anything, but she wanted Maya to like her so badly. Vimbai suspected that the spell of the house that lulled her so much tried to tie her not only to the house, but also to its inhabitants. Otherwise there didn't seem to be a reason for her to feel so invested in what Maya thought of her.

VIMBAI ATTENDED CLASSES, DUTIFUL BUT DISENGAGED, caught in the slow molasses of movement of time and the sucking embrace of gravity. The world came through muffled, and only the house and the dunes and the ocean remained real. Winter was coming, and there was a first dusting of miserly snowflakes scattered almost invisible on the frozen sand one morning in November.

That day, Vimbai stepped onto the hoary porch and saw that the very character of the dunes had been transformed— they lost their fluid, mutable aspect and even though they remained the same in appearance they now stood motionless, seized by the ice within, trapped into immobility.

Vimbai's bare toes curled instinctively, cringing away from contact with the cold boards of the porch (which, as her investigations had shown, harbored no nests of adorable foxes). She hugged her shoulders and stared at the leaden water, visible between the dunes, barely puckered by waves. Her fingertips grew numb, and the hairs inside her nose grew stiff with frost, singed with the smell of ozone. Still, Vimbai lingered in her robe, thinking of her mother—the first serious frost always put Vimbai in that frame of mind. As long as she could remember, it was the time when her mother grew pensive and quiet, and when pushed given to reminiscence. It was in November that Vimbai's parents left their home and came to the U.S.

Vimbai strained to see over the water—it just seemed impossible that the entire continent could be hidden by the curving razorblade cut of the horizon, bleeding now the first red streaks of dawn. Her breath formed tight white clumps in the air, like the memories of the still invisible clouds overhead.

Her mother had to regret *something*—and Vimbai suspected ever since she was little that her mother still, twenty years later, was not convinced that she had made the right decision. How could one know something like that, how could one not agonize over how life would've turned out if one had made different choices? Even Vimbai, with her sheltered existence and precious few choices with any consequences, wondered. Those were small things, insignificant perhaps, but she wished sometimes that she had chosen differently.

She breathed open-mouthed on her fingers, numb and discolored by cold, and thought about that kid, the little ten-year-old whose name she never learned. She was in high school then, old enough to largely ignore the kids playing in the elementary-school yard she passed on her way to classes. She walked alone, absorbed in her thoughts, and paid no mind to the persistent cries emanating from the schoolyard. The word that jettisoned her out of her preoccupation was 'lion'—not the sort of thing one heard often under such circumstances.

"Go hunt a lion," a largish and very pink boy shouted. "Go back to Africa."

Vimbai stopped and stared at the small black kid in ill-fitting white shirt and khaki shorts, backed up against a set of monkey bars. A few other children surrounded him in a tentative semicircle, not quite backing up the assailant but not dissuading him either. Non-committal, waiting to see how things shook out. Little vultures.

The small kid said nothing and just swallowed often and hard, as if trying to dislodge the words stuck in his throat.

The pink boy advanced half a step, and the semicircle drew up on itself tighter, the kids smelling blood now, just a moment away from taking part.

"Leave him alone," Vimbai said.

The pink kid turned to look at her; she still remembered the expression of contempt in his eyes. Without saying a word, he returned his attention to the cornered kid in the white shirt. "Go hunt a lion," he said again, with rather more force, as if challenging Vimbai to climb the fence and kick his plump behind.

Vimbai looked at her watch; she was already running late, and kids did this sort of thing all the time. "Stop it." She raised her voice to be heard over the rising hum of the other voices that had decided to join in.

Her stomach had ached when she turned and walked away.

In her darker moments, like that day watching the cold ocean over the frozen dunes, she wondered if she somehow upset her karmic balance that day, if everything that ever went wrong since then was the result of her failure. She had wished she would see this kid again, but no matter how many times she walked past the elementary school, he was not there.

Vimbai winced at the pain in her feet the moment she shifted her weight, and she hobbled inside, trying to remember how long it took for frostbite to develop. "Not clever," she mumbled, "not clever at all."

She decided to call her parents, just to tell them that she remembered what was important to them, and that she cared. Her roommates still slept, given to late hours and disorganized lifestyle; Vimbai would have disapproved if it didn't mean that in the morning she had the house all to herself. She walked in slow mincing steps, letting the sensation and accompanying pain revitalize her toes, to the phone—an almost extinct rotary affair, gleaming with slick black curves and the soft creamy ivory of the rotating disk. She picked up the receiver and listened for a while; she was puzzled by the static that inhabited the wires of the phone—it seemed haunted, like the rest of the house, alive with blurred disembodied whispers, and Vimbai thought that if only she listened carefully enough, she would be able to discern the words and the sobbing laments of the little ghost.

The static ceased just as she hovered on the brink of understanding, and the phone beeped and inquired whether she needed assistance from the operator. She sighed and dialed the number.

And once again it was as in a dream, with slow cloying molasses weighing her eyelids and her lips, as she whispered that she was sorry and that she loved them.

"Vimbai, are you all right?" her mother said. "You always sound so tired. Are you getting enough sleep? Are you staying up late?"

"No," Vimbai said, and then, "yes."

"Vimbai..."

"I am getting enough sleep. I'm not staying up late. I just miss you."

Her mother remained quiet for a while. "You can always come back home," she finally said.

"I can't. I have a lease."

"At least, you can visit. How's Saturday for you? I'm making stew."

These words coaxed a smile—Vimbai was unreasonably attached to the bland beef stew and rice, the food so generic it could be hardly counted as traditional. "Okay," she said. "I can make Saturday."

"Good," Vimbai's mother said. "It is decided then."

And then her voice faded, and the ghost in the wires spoke—clearly, for the first time.

VIMBAI WAS NOT SURE HOW MUCH TIME HAD PASSED—SHE slumped on the floor, her frozen feet forgotten, the receiver pressed hard to her ear, listening to the stumbling, simpering words that poured out. She did not dare to ask any questions for fear of the ghost in the phone falling silent, spooked away by the fleshy human voice. So she let it talk, clutching the receiver with desperate force, afraid to loosen her grip and let go of the mystery inside it.

The ghost was not a ghost at all, or so it claimed—it claimed to be a psychic energy baby, birthed in some ethereal dimension, and pulled into the phone by the powerful magnetism of phone signals. It remembered with perfect clarity how it came to be—remembered coalescing from the reflecting membranous surface of the world, streaked with reflected light, humming with surface tension under the pressure of emptiness underneath. The Psychic Energy Baby found form among the emanations of people's minds and the susurrus of their voices, it found flesh in the shapes their lips and eyes made, the surprise of 'o's and the sibilations of 's's; its skin stretched taut like a soap bubble, forged from the wet sound of lips touching; its thoughts were the musky smells and the breath of fresh bread. Its fingers spread like ribcages, and its nerves twined around the transparent water balloons of the muscles like stems of toadflax, searching restlessly for every available crevice, stretching along cold rough surfaces. Its veins, tiny rivers, pumped heartbeats striking in unison, the dry dallying of billions of ventricular contractions. And it spoke, spoke endlessly, it spoke words that tasted of dark air and formic acid. It could speak long before it took its final shape.

And when it happened, when all the sounds and smells and words in the world, when all the thoughts had aligned so that it could become—then it found itself pulled into the wires, surrounded by taut copper and green and red and yellow insulation; twined and quartered among the cables, rent open by millions of voices that shouted and whispered and pleaded and threatened, interspersed with the rasping of breaths and tearing laughter. It traveled through the criss-crossing of the wires so fast that it felt itself being pulled into a needle, head spearing into the future while its feet infinitely receded into the past, until it came into a dark quiet pool of the black rotary phone, where it could reassemble itself and take stock.

When Maya woke up and came downstairs, she found Vimbai still sitting on the floor in her robe, the silent receiver in her hand, her face buried in her knees and her shoulders shaking with sobs—not grief-stricken but merely shaken and amazed beyond words.

To Vimbai's surprise and gratitude too deep for words, Maya was neither skeptical nor disbelieving when she heard the tale of the Psychic Energy Baby. "It happens," she said. "Don't you have classes to go to?" Maya's shift at the casino's bar did not start until eight p.m., and she left the house late.

Vimbai shrugged. "Who cares," she said. "There's that thing in our phone. I think it wants to get out."

"Of course it does," Maya said, her rich voice acquiring a soothing tone as if speaking to a cranky child. "Don't worry, we'll get it out. Just as soon as Felix wakes up. Come on, I'll make coffee."

Vimbai sat at the kitchen table as Maya went through the ritual of brewing coffee. They didn't bother with grinding whole beans, and Vimbai was getting used to the taste of coffee that came out of the can or a more fancy bagged variety—when it was Vimbai's turn to shop, she went for shade-grown and fair trade, more out of habit than any conscious choice. This is what her mother always bought. The clinking of the carafe and hissing of steam, the smell of coffee felt comforting, and with every passing minute Vimbai was more and more willing to believe that the Psychic Energy Baby was just a product of fatigue, cold, and bad reception.

The coffee bubbled and poured in a fragrant stream, and Maya sat down. "This ought to wake Felix up," she said. "He'll get that baby out of those wires. Poor thing."

"How?" Vimbai said. "What is Felix going to do?"

"What he always does," Maya answered. "You don't think he earns rent money by sitting around all day, do you?"

"I don't know what he does," Vimbai answered, and poured herself a cup. It warmed her hands and instilled a sense of serenity.

"Well, I'll tell you. He's a freelancer. Only what he does, no one else can. He separates things."

"Oh?"

Maya laughed and drank her coffee. "Things you can't see, like that baby in the phone. Felix says, they sometimes contaminate the things you can see, or the other way around."

"People pay him for it?"

Maya nodded. "Uh-huh."

"Like exorcisms?"

"Not those, the Catholics do them. Felix does more simple

stuff. Like junkies with invisible insects under their skin, or amputees with phantom limbs."

"He amputates phantom limbs?"

"I suppose he does. In any case, we'll see what he can do, huh?"

Vimbai nodded. Somehow, the fact that Felix had an unusual occupation was easy to accept, and once accepted, any strange occupation seemed as reasonable as the next one. So if Felix made a living untangling the invisible babies out of the phone wires, what business it was of Vimbai's? Who was she to judge? She felt only intense curiosity, and the weakest pang of guilt for missing her classes.

Chapter 3

———

FELIX STUMBLED DOWNSTAIRS JUST BEFORE NOON. HIS terrible eyes were mercifully closed, and his hair hung into his face in tangled clumps. Vimbai gasped—the long strands didn't just obscure parts of his forehead, but rather seemed to consume them entirely. His face seemed streaked by darkness, fractured like a tiger hidden in shadows. Her encounter with the Psychic Energy Baby had jolted her enough to realize that what she assumed was hair—had no other option, really, but to assume that—was a conglomeration of darkness, of absence of light; a black hole, emptiness of outer space, a jagged nothingness. It spilled over Felix's face, threatening to consume it and retreating when he tossed his head and smiled at Maya.

"Can I have some coffee?" he said.

"Of course," Maya said. "Help yourself."

Felix raked his insane hair out of his eyes, and his hands disappeared in blackness up to their wrists; he extricated them somewhat hastily, and his left eye rolled to look upward with a troubled expression.

Vimbai tried to think of a question to ask, but came short. She could only round her eyes and shrug at Maya.

"Felix," Maya said the moment Felix took his seat by the table. "Vimbai found a ghost in the phone wires, think you can get it out?"

40

"It depends," Felix said and winced at the too-hot coffee. "Does it want to come out?"

"I think so," Maya said. "Well?"

Felix blew into his mug. "What kind of ghost is it?"

Vimbai finally found her voice. "It's not really a ghost," she said. "It's a psychic energy baby."

"Did you Google it?" Felix asked. "Don't think I ever heard of one."

Vimbai brought her laptop downstairs, but the results were disappointing. Psychic energy baby turned out to be one of the very few things Google had no insight on.

"All right," Felix said. "It's in the phone now? I guess I'd better take a look."

It was the most words he had said since Vimbai moved in; in fact, he sounded remarkably coherent. It prompted Vimbai to blurt, "This is not really hair, is it?"

"No," Felix admitted. "I'll explain some other time."

Maya and Vimbai followed Felix to the hallway where the phone huddled, forlorn, on its dusty shelf. Felix picked up the receiver and listened for a while, his bloodshot eyes rotating quietly in their sockets in opposite directions; Vimbai found that he looked thoughtful.

"Just static," Felix said.

Vimbai sighed. "Just listen."

Felix did. He listened for a long while, slouched against the wall, and the thoughtfulness started giving way to boredom, but then there was crackling in the receiver, and he startled upright. "That's a Psychic Energy Baby all right," he said, covering the mouthpiece with his hand.

"Will it ever grow up?" Maya asked, and bit her fingernails in excitement. "Will it be a Psychic Energy Adult?"

"How should I know?" Felix glared a little, both of his eyes managing to simultaneously focus on Maya. "The thing is unGoogleable."

Vimbai cleared her throat. Her head swam, and she felt as if in a dream, able to do and say anything. "Seriously, what's with the hair?" she said.

Felix shrugged. "Not now." He grunted and picked up the phone, leaving the phone jack connected so as not to lose touch with the Psychic Energy Baby. Both Vimbai and Maya held their breath and each other's hands; Vimbai imagined that participants in a spiritualist séance would feel the same mix of disbelief, giddiness and fear lurking just under the surface as they did right now, watching Felix work his magic surrounded by peeling wallpaper and creaking floorboards, a black rotary phone the focus of his attention.

Felix thrust the phone into his hair; Vimbai whimpered a bit as the entire squat plastic box plus its dangling cord and the receiver were swallowed by the darkness. There was no way for it to fit—there was no way Felix could thrust his arm into his hair almost all the way to his shoulder, as narrow tongues of emptiness licked it, trying to pull it in. For a moment, Vimbai imagined Felix being sucked into the black hole of his hair and disappearing in a recursive black dot, but he managed to pull away, his hand still gripping the phone.

"That ought to do it," Felix said. "I hope."

Maya reached for the receiver and listened to the recorded

incantation that suggested dialing 0 for the operator. "It's gone," Maya announced. "Where is it?"

"It's in my hair," Felix answered, as if referring to a moth or some other harmless but annoying insect. "Hold on."

Now both of his hands disappeared into his hair up to the elbows, and moved about energetically. Vimbai though that he looked like a man reaching for something slimy and nasty in the garbage disposal—his face acquired the same apprehensive expression as it did every time he had to touch his hair. Vimbai used to think that her own hair was unruly, but it didn't even come close to the existential horror of Felix's.

He finally grabbed a hold of something and pulled— judging from his wincing and the restless motion of his hands kneading some invisible dough, that something was either slippery or reluctant or both. A few times his arms were pulled back in and struggled out again, the resisting prize still hidden from view.

There was a shriek and a wail, and Felix grunted as he pulled out the wriggling shape.

"Yep," Maya said. "It's a Psychic Energy Baby all right."

VIMBAI HAD NOT VISITED FELIX'S ROOM BEFORE—IN FACT, she used to avoid thinking about Felix, because even after she had lived in the house for a while, she found that he didn't quite fit into her usual thinking patterns. He was the oddly shaped piece of a jigsaw puzzle that didn't seem to belong anywhere, and probably had tumbled here from some other, entirely different set, but there he was.

And there she was, following him and Maya up the stairs

to the small bedroom at the end of the corridor. A not very mature "Keep Out—High Voltage" sign guarded the door. This is where they carried the Psychic Energy Baby; it wailed, distraught, and struggled and seemed to resent the unfamiliar surroundings and the lack of the binding (yet directing) phone wires. Vimbai half-regretted ever bringing it to Maya's attention.

Felix's bedroom was surprisingly clean and tidy—the bed neatly made, books on the shelves, the desk amazingly free of piles of paper and stray objects such as found their way onto Vimbai's. The only thing that was out of ordinary was the row of phantom limbs lined against the wall—there were hundreds of feet and legs and hands and arms, all cast in the same transparent substance as the Psychic Energy Baby, visible only by the curving of the reflected light stretched taut like a soap bubble.

"They are all . . . yours?" Vimbai said.

Felix nodded, his eyes rolling in rhythm with the bobbing of his head. "Well, they used to be somebody else's. But once you detach a phantom leg or arm, the owners don't want them. So I keep them—not like I can throw them away."

"How do you . . . " Vimbai posed, thinking of ways to better formulate the question. After some hemming, she gave up any hope of sophistication, and hoped only for coherence. "How do you do these things?" she pointed at the limbs and the baby that still lay transparent, cradled against Felix's narrow chest.

Felix seemed to have only a tentative hold of the ways in which his hair—or a small universe that orbited the dome of his skull, whatever one wanted to call it—worked; he understood it only enough to exploit it. The universe which he explored like a blind man would, by touch alone, contained primarily clean socks, a few household objects, and a desiccated head or two (he promised to explain the heads later as well). Also, it seemed to work as a prism of sorts—except that if a prism could split a beam of light into its component wavelengths, Felix's hair split any entangled objects into their components, be they material, spiritual, or both. Felix discovered it by accident, when he was quite young—a neighbor's kitten crawled into his 'do, and got separated from its voice—the disembodied meowing haunted the house until they moved.

"So you could separate a person from their soul," Vimbai said.

"If you believe in souls," Felix answered. "I suppose. But then the person would be dead, wouldn't it?"

"Oh for crying out loud," Maya interrupted. "Yes, Felix, your hair is a deadly weapon. Now, do something about this baby."

"Like what?" Felix said, and sat on his bed, the baby sniffling and waving its transparent limbs in his lap.

Vimbai reached for the apparition. To her surprise, the baby had some heft—not as heavy as a regular baby would be, but it felt as a being of substance. It cried some more.

"There there," Vimbai said. "You can talk, can't you? Tell us what you want now."

The Psychic Energy Baby (or Peb, as Vimbai mentally abbreviated it) stopped crying. "It was a dark and terrible place," it said in a blur of a voice, barely louder than a sigh.

"What, the phone or his hair?" Maya asked.

The baby pointed at Felix, and its lower lip, itself reminiscent of a bubble of spit, trembled. "Something held me there," it said. "It is not a good place."

"I bet," Vimbai murmured. "Now that you're here, what do you want to do?"

"I don't know yet," Peb said. "But I'm not going back into the dark, neither wires nor him."

"Fine," Vimbai said. "Can you move on your own?" It did look awfully tiny and insubstantial.

Peb could—it turned out, it could walk or float, and walls and floors did not baffle it or contain its movement. It started investigating Felix's room by sinking into the floor halfway, so just the transparent torso moved about, looking under the bed, until it finally crossed through the wall and disappeared from view. Vimbai and Maya sighed simultaneously.

"I don't suppose it will pay rent," Maya said. "It probably has no money."

"It doesn't have any pockets," Vimbai agreed. "We should tell it to keep away from the bathrooms when we're using them."

"Phantom limbs are so much easier," Felix said. "At least they stay put."

"And look creepy," Maya added.

Felix huffed. "And the Psychic Energy Baby that wanders through the walls at all hours is not creepy?"

"Not very," Maya said. "At least, it looks alive."

"It looks like a ghost," Vimbai said. "Only I don't believe in ghosts." It wasn't entirely untrue—Vimbai was never

46

superstitious, and when she examined her belief system, she discovered that it was not sufficiently undermined to admit the possibility of ghosts. Or it was mere inertia, because if psychic energy babies indeed lived in phone wires and god knows what other hidden places, than there was no reason for ghosts not to exist either. And after all, weren't phantom limbs also ghosts of a sort? "Do you mind if I look at your . . . the phantom limbs?" she said out loud.

"Help yourself," Felix said. "Feel free to take any you like—I don't really need them; only it doesn't feel right to throw them away."

Vimbai studied the limbs—smooth like blown glass, with the same sleek appearance, they seemed mannequins, although no mannequin had ever exhibited that many purely human imperfections and malformations. There were deformed nails, ingrown hairs, bones too visible just under the soap skin. There were hammertoes and hitchhiker's thumbs, varicose veins, barely healed razor cuts and an occasional pimple or a scar. She touched one leg, cut off just below the knee, and almost jumped at the sensation of cool smooth and—most importantly—solid form under her fingertips, at the subtle humming of electricity just under the imaginary skin.

She didn't know what she wanted with a phantom limb, but she carefully picked up the half-leg and carried it to her room. It fit nicely by the window, next to the space heater. There was a cold stab of draft coming from the window where the frame didn't quite touch the wall, and Vimbai turned the heater on, letting its pink glow fall on the convex surface of the phantom

calf. She sat at her desk and looked outside, where the leaden
hem of the surf nipped at the frozen shore, and listened to
the quiet rustling of the Psychic Energy Baby exploring the
creaky old house.

SATURDAY CAME, AND VIMBAI DROVE RELUCTANTLY HOME.
The street—so quiet on this cold day, so helplessly suburban—already felt alien. Like in a dream, the sidewalk familiar
down to every crack and pockmark, the leafless peach trees
in the front yard, the woven mat on the steps were just as
she remembered them, seen clearly through the fisheye lens
of separation. This is what coming home feels like, Vimbai
thought, this is how her parents feel when they go to visit relatives in Harare—only even more so, their time and distance
greater hundred-fold, thousand-fold than Vimbai's.

When she came in, she realized that her parents' house
smelled of clean linen and a faint whiff of vanilla and nutmeg—
something she never noticed when she lived here. She was
separate from it now, separate enough to notice its smell.
Separate enough to look at the kitchen table and admire the
gleaming of white bowls in the slanted pale winter sunlight
that poured into the kitchen through a large bay window. The
things she had never noticed before, but now suddenly did.

At dinner, her parents talked the familiar talk—the
department and the hospital, Africana studies and Zimbabwe
politics. So Vimbai kept to her own thoughts and ate, rarely
lifting her gaze off her plate. It was so easy to fall back into
this pattern.

Vimbai's mother still complained about the new head of

Africana Studies. "And he also said just the other day that Mugabe is the worst thing that ever happened to Zimbabwe. I told him that colonialism was really up there among the shitty things."

"But you hate Mugabe," Vimbai's father said mildly. "Why are you defending him?"

"I'm not," mother said. "I'm just sick and tired of hearing about African corruption. Sick and tired."

Vimbai made a small noise of sympathy. One of the things she had learned from her mother was that one did not disparage one's people or culture in front of outsiders. It's different for them, her mother said. They don't know what it's like, they have no sympathy, no kinship. They look and they criticize, they look for cracks, they look for proof of something they are already thinking in their hearts—that we are worse than them, that we should not be allowed to govern ourselves. So you argue and you don't show weakness. And you don't ever, ever agree with them if they speak poorly of your people. What if they are right, Vimbai had asked then. They are never right, her mother answered. They may appear to be right because of the words they use, but their hearts are wrong. To be right, you need to know, to understand, to have a kinship of spirit.

"I do hate what he did to the country though," father said. It wasn't news, and Vimbai nodded along, as one would to a familiar tune. This one was called 'The Land Reform'. Whatever they said, it always betrayed the Africa inside of them.

Vimbai ate her stew, the beef boiled flavorless and the

rice—flavorless to begin with. She had nothing to contribute. Even though she knew the issues, she never felt them deep in her bones, resonating through the drum that was the internal Africa. She cringed at the sudden fear that one day soon her mother would be defending Mugabe and his cabinet from her, from Vimbai—and she thought that really, that was the price of growing up, cutting away the tenuous umbilicus that still attached her to her parents and, by extension, to the Africa within them. And soon she will have to find her own place in the world, somewhere in the dunes and the ocean, among the horseshoe crabs and phantom limbs and psychic energy babies.

Vimbai watched the scar on her mother's forehead—an almost invisible white line, so thin you wouldn't notice it unless you knew it was there. Vimbai knew. She remembered when her mother first showed it to her, along with the similar marks cut into her wrists and her ankles. Vimbai's father had more prominent scars, symmetrically bisecting his cheeks. *Muti*, Vimbai's mother said. When I was a little girl, my mother took me to a *n'anga*, a healer, and he put these marks on me for protection.

Vimbai used to have nightmares for months afterward, dreaming of a man with the razorblades that would cut her up (her own razorblades, much much later, an entirely different matter). That it was for her own good somehow made it worse, and she woke up crying, and her mother had to reassure her that they would never do anything like this to Vimbai. Still, the only time she visited Harare and they had to take her to a healer for her upset stomach, Vimbai had hyperventilated so badly that she almost passed out. Her mother's mother was still alive then.

Her father interrupted the stream of memory that threatened to sweep her along, take her into a different space. "What are you thinking about, *muroora*?"

"Grandma," Vimbai answered.

Her parents traded a look. "You remember her?" mother said.

Vimbai nodded. "Of course. I was what, thirteen?"

"Yes," mother said. "I really wish you'd get to know her better."

Vimbai wanted to say that she didn't, that anyway the old woman barely spoke English, and Vimbai's Shona could, if one was inclined to kindness, be described as lacking. Besides, grandma harbored an alarming number of strange beliefs, and tried to use Vimbai's short time in Harare to transfer the jumble of superstition and ignorance into her young mind. But she didn't say it out loud, of course—one did not speak ill of the dead, and even Vimbai accepted it as right. However, in her heart she had not forgiven the scars on her mother's face and limbs. "Did she really believe in ghosts?" she said, infusing her voice with proper respect.

"Spirits. Most people of her generation do," mother said. "Why?"

Vimbai smiled. "No reason. I was just thinking about ghosts. For that class I'm taking, about pre-Christian beliefs."

Her mother raised her eyebrows and started clearing the table. Vimbai helped, all the while thinking back to when she was little, and her mother embraced her freely and called her *sahwira*—girlfriend, and told her stories she had learned as a girl from her mother. Now, they moved past each other, stacks of dishes and empty bowls in their hands preoccupying their attention on the way to the sink. Vimbai shuddered as she imagined her grandmother, now a *vadzimu*, an ancestral spirit, summoned by a casual mention. Moving between them like a breath of cold air, pushing them away from each other, lacking even the tentative warmth of the Psychic Energy Baby who waited for Vimbai at home, and possibly cried.

Chapter 4

WHEN SHE DROVE HOME, THE IMAGE OF HER GRANDMOTHER solidified, until the tall wrinkled woman with white hair was sitting primly in the passenger seat of Vimbai's car. She had just left the Atlantic City Expressway and headed east, for the dunes. The *vadzimu* shivered a bit in this cold, and Vimbai studied her from the corner of her eye. The house in the dunes was close enough now, and in its sphere Vimbai could cope with ghosts and phantoms and ancestral spirits.

"Hello, grandmother," she said. "Did you come to give me protection?"

She hoped that *vadzimu* did not come because of some great danger—perhaps, it was not a *vadzimu* at all, since such ancestral spirits manifested in dreams. Maybe she was dreaming—the thought was reassuring, even though Vimbai hoped that she did not lose her ability to tell dreams from reality. Or maybe it was a *chipoko*, a simple ghost.

"No," the spirit whispered. " I was sent by the clan spirits, the *mhondoro*, to tell you a story. Listen, and learn well— *ngano* is how children learn."

The house loomed closer now, its windows yellow loving eyes, and under their steady staring Vimbai felt entranced as she parked the car. Her breath escaped in small careful puffs as she unbuckled the seat belt, but the cool and hard hand of the ghost lay on her wrist, transfixing her in her seat. A cold lump formed in her stomach, and Vimbai thought that really, it was shell shock, she simply did not have time to absorb everything that had been happening to her; as she thought that, her breath quickened and beading of sweat started forming on her forehead, until the *vadzimu* spoke.

THERE WAS A TIME ONCE, A LONG TIME AGO, WHEN A HARE decided to take the moon from the sky and put it in his home so that there would always be light. Hares are clever creatures, and our hare (whom we shall call Hare) realized that the sky and the moon were a high way up, and to get to the moon he would have to work at night, and he would have to come up with a clever plan to get there.

Hare waited for nightfall, and climbed the tallest tree in the forest. When he was halfway there, he came across a baboon who was slumbering in the branches. Everyone knows that baboons are dense and quarrelsome creatures, so Hare tried to avoid disturbing the Baboon and hopped over to another branch. He miscalculated his jump in the darkness, and almost fell. As Hare scrambled back onto the branch, he woke up Baboon.

"Hey," Baboon said. "What's all this racket?"

"It's just me, Old Uncle," Hare replied.

Baboon opened one bloodshot eye and gave Hare a mistrustful look. "And what would you be doing in the tree in the middle of the night, Old Grandfather?"

"I'm picking figs to feed my children," Hare lied. "I work in the field all day, and can only go fruit-picking at night."

Baboon went back to sleep, and Hare climbed up up up, all the way to the top of the tallest tree. By the time he got there, the moon rose, and Hare saw that it was just a thin crescent, hanging upside down. "That'll be good enough," Hare said to himself, and reached up. But the moon was still too far—it hung just inches away from Hare's paws, and smiled and laughed at his efforts to reach it (for that, it had to turn right side up.)

Hare shook his fist at the sky and threatened to give the moon such a beating, but the moon just laughed and remained wisely out of his reach. The noise woke Baboon who had been dozing off in the branches below. "Huh," Baboon said to himself. "Looks like Old Grandfather Hare is trying to get the moon, not the figs. I bet I could get it myself and then make him pay me a princely sum in figs."

But the crescent moon remained too far even for Baboon and his long arms, and the next night it did not get any closer. Only when the sickle grew thicker, it started to travel lower in the sky—as everyone knows, the bigger the moon, the heavier it is, and its weight pulls it closer to the ground. Because of that, the full moon is so low in the sky that its round belly can touch the tops of tall trees on a good night.

So on the day the moon was finally full and fat, both Hare and Baboon climbed to the top of the tallest tree. The moon was not laughing anymore, and only looking at them with its white fearful eyes. Baboon's arms were longer, and he grabbed the moon by its pudgy sides, and immediately yelped in pain.

"What's the matter, Old Uncle?" Hare asked and snickered.

Baboon sucked on his burned fingers. "It's hot," he said. "It burns like fire."

Hare, who was quite clever, picked a few leaves off the treetop—they were large and leathery like all fig leaves are, and perfect for carrying coals or other hot burning things. He grabbed the moon with its paws wrapped in leaves, but the moon slipped out like a silvery fish—the leaves were too smooth and slick.

"Let me do it," Baboon said. "You're doing it wrong, Old Grandfather."

"No," Hare argued. "It was my idea, and it is my moon, and my leaves."

Baboon reached for the moon again, burning his fingers the second time (I told you that baboons are none too bright), and Hare maneuvered the leaves this way and that, and he wove a basket in which to carry the moon. Only by the time the basket was finished, the moon had rolled across the sky, away from the treetop.

"I guess we'll never get the moon," Baboon said. "I thought I was quick and strong enough, but I was wrong."

"And I thought I was clever enough," Hare said.

They came down from the tree. In the clearing nearby, they saw a puddle of dark water and a tortoise who came to take a drink of water. Tortoise did not want the moon, he just wanted a drink; but as he drank, the moon reflected in the puddle, and its reflection, cool now, filled Tortoise's mouth and his belly with its milky light. Tortoise smiled and went home, shining like the moon among the trees.

VIMBAI LED THE GHOST INTO THE HOUSE BY THE HAND. MAYA was at work and Felix, judging by the lights in his windows, remained cloistered in his room, doing whatever it was that he did—Vimbai imagined that he played with the phantom limbs as one would with dolls, or with whatever unpleasant things he pulled out of the black hole of his hair.

"There you go, grandma," Vimbai said. "You're welcome to stay here."

The ghost shuffled into the kitchen, looking disapprovingly at the empty coffee cups and saucers stained with syrup piled in the sink.

"It's Felix's turn to do the dishes," Vimbai said, apologetic. "Only he procrastinates."

The *vadzimu* heaved a tremulous sigh and glided up to the sink. Vimbai was about to argue but then realized it was silly to get into a tug of war about dirty dishes with her grandmother's ghost. The dishes clattered and the water poured, and the ghost stopped paying any mind to Vimbai. She hung around the kitchen for a while, unsure whether she should offer help. Then she decided to check on the Psychic Energy Baby, and snuck upstairs cringing at the creaking of the stairs under her socked feet.

Peb was in Felix's room, attaching a pair of phantom hands to itself.

"Should he be doing this?" Vimbai asked Felix.

He rolled his left eye up, and his right one leftward, giving Vimbai an impression of uncertainty. "Let it do what it wants—it stopped crying just now."

"I brought a ghost with me," Vimbai said. "It's my grandmother, so be nice to her."

"Okay," Felix said. "Ghosts sure do like you."

"Me? I thought it was the house."

"The house likes you too," Felix said. "But we sure never had so many ghosts before you moved in."

Vimbai perched on the windowsill, her back against the glass. "Do you mean I'm bringing them in?"

"You just told me you brought one with you." Felix pointed at Peb. "And you found this one in the phone."

Vimbai considered. "I don't know," she said. "I just moved here to be close to the ocean and to the horseshoe crabs."

Felix nodded. "I remember. Maya said you're a student. How's that working out for you?"

"Okay," Vimbai said. "I've been cutting classes a lot lately . . . I don't know what it is about this place, but I keep dreaming that I'm someone else, somewhere else, and nothing seems as important anymore. Is it weird that I'm saying that?"

"Not weird," Felix said. "I found it, you know. And when Maya showed up, things under the porch started shifting."

"What things under the porch?" Vimbai asked, alarmed. "I've been here for a month and never saw any things under the porch."

"Neither have I," Felix said. "But I hear them, and I know they're there and that they're Maya's."

"What are they?"

"Dunno. The point is, the house chooses."

"What for?" Vimbai asked. The house creaked and whispered in her ears, lulling her, convincing her that everything was as it should be, everything was perfectly normal. "Why does it choose and why us?"

"Dunno," Felix repeated, and shot her an irritated look. "Go play with the baby or something, okay? My head hurts."

Of course, Vimbai reasoned, it was easy to believe that they were special somehow, chosen, different, lost and adopted princes and princesses and their true parents would soon reclaim them and reveal their hidden destinies—isn't it what every book we read as children taught us to expect from life? Of course Felix decided that the house chose them for some unknown purpose, but in reality everything was much more banal. It appealed to them for whatever reasons, and they all came with baggage: Felix had his hair and Vimbai her ghosts, and Maya . . . Maya had whatever lived under the porch.

Peb had festooned itself with several hands and feet, and they remained attached to its transparent body through some otherworldly adhesion. Peb resembled an exotic fish decorated with grotesque appendages and outgrowths. Its skin stretched and shimmered with reflected light like a soap bubble, and Vimbai could not help but pick up the unsightly thing. "Come along," she said. "I'll introduce you to my grandma."

Peb babbled in response, talking about ethereal planes and dizzying stars. It seemed to miss other dimensions, too black or too fiery to describe.

"It's okay," Vimbai consoled. "You'll learn to like it here, and my grandmother knows so many stories—*ngano*, the folktales that tell children how to live in the world, and *nyaya*, the myths people make up to pass the time."

The *vadzimu* was done with the dishes and sat on the stool by the counter, her eyes hollow and her wrinkled hands folded in her lap. Such fragile birdlike hands, Vimbai thought, dry like twigs, wrapped in the cured leather of old skin that spent decades in the tropical sun. Vimbai barely remembered this woman, how she was in life—just her own passing embarrassment at the old woman's superstitions, and just as ephemeral a regret that they spoke different languages and thus were unlikely to connect.

Vimbai noticed with a measure of satisfaction that the ghost, at least, was more fluent in English. If it had also grown less superstitious remained to be seen.

"Grandmother," Vimbai said. "Look at this—it's a psychic energy baby."

The old woman looked and reached out, instinctively—as if there was really nothing else to do with babies but to pick them up and hold them, no matter how ethereal and burdened with unnecessary extremities; no matter how dead one was. And even after Vimbai went to bed that night, she heard quiet singing and cooing from the kitchen, along with the thin gurgling voice of the Psychic Energy Baby.

THAT NIGHT THE TIDES HAD GROWN ESPECIALLY, INEXCUSABLY high—through her sleep Vimbai heard the lapping of the waves somewhere very close to the porch of the house, and through her sleep she thought that the sea was pulled so close by the gravity of the moon that sloshed happily in the darkness of Tortoise's belly. She dreamt of Tortoise, his smiling face smeared with moonlight, white and thick as milk, the oceans of the world following on his heels— oceans always followed wherever the moon went, tortoise or no.

Meanwhile, the waves whispered into the yard, their salty tongues singeing the roots of the few arbor vitae planted near the house; they poured under the porch spooking those who lived under it and chasing them up the steps, where they remained, wet and shivering, their backs pressed against the closed door and their fur growing slow icicles. They listened for Maya's sleeping breath in the depths of the house and whimpered softly.

The gentle fingers of the ocean pried the house from its foundation, carefully shaking loose every brick and every cinderblock, never upsetting the balance. The waves lifted the house on their backs arching like those of angry cats, and took it with them, away from the shore. In the darkness, the lighthouses shone like predatory eyes, and everyone in the house slept except for the *vadzimu*, who remained alert and awake, singing to the sleeping Peb, curled up in her lap like a cat, in a language no one but her understood.

THE NIGHT CONTINUED MUCH LONGER THAN USUAL—BEFORE the sun rose, the house had drifted far into the ocean, where water lay smooth as silk, wrinkling occasionally under the sleeping breath of the wind.

Under the several hundred yards of water, down on the bottom, horseshoe crabs burrowed in the sand, their movements sluggish in the cold water, the spikes of their tails pointing uniformly north. They had flat, almost round bodies that glistened pretty shades of dark green and light brown, and their blue blood flowed leisurely through their open circulatory systems. They were spent, depleted—bled almost dry and thrown back by human hands where they lingered in a disconcerting state between life and undeath. They had enough blood not to die—yet not quite enough to keep them living. So is it any wonder that the crabs—ancient, trilobitic—whispered stories of vampires that came in boats and then white medical trucks? Is it surprising that they told each other about people who stole blood from their veins and tossed them back, always back, so they could linger in the cold water never quite recovering?

Above them, the house floated, its inhabitants asleep inside. Vimbai was the first to wake up and come downstairs, where the ghost grandmother was entertaining the baby with some songs and hand-clapping. Peb clapped along, with all eleven of its hands, most of which were far too large for its tiny psychic body.

Vimbai glanced at the window and grabbed the kitchen counter for support—instead of the familiar landscape of dunes and sea, there was just a tapestry of green and pale blue and gray. The dunes had vanished, or so she thought until she looked out of the window and saw nothing but the ocean and the sky stretching as far as she could see, and felt a faint spongy rhythm of the floor below her feet.

"Where are we, grandmother?" she asked.

The ghost stopped singing. "We sail across the sea," she said.

"Where to? Why?"

"Perhaps it's a curse some witch, some *muroyi*, put on you," the ghost said. "Or perhaps it is you who started the journey to get where you need to be."

Vimbai groaned with frustration. Grandmother was just like Vimbai's mother (or the other way around)—both expected her to somehow comprehend her heritage, to become a Zimbabwean like her parents. They wanted her to have a clear purpose in life, even though Vimbai herself rarely thought past applying to graduate schools. And no matter how much they loved Vimbai, she could feel that they lamented the fact that she came out American, as if it were a sad accident, a birth defect of some sort. They wanted her to be like them, to care about the same things they cared about.

"I'm not going on any journeys," Vimbai said. "I have classes, and Maya has work. Where is she?"

"Sleeping," Peb said. "She is sleeping and dreaming of tall spires and the sad creatures on the porch."

"You mean, under the porch," Vimbai said.

"There're only horseshoe crabs under the porch," Peb corrected. "And even they are yards and yards below."

Vimbai faltered then, torn between the conflicting impulses to go check on her housemates, and to stare out of the window, and to see if Peb was lying about the creatures on the porch.

The latter won, and she tiptoed to the front entrance and peeked outside through the transparent window on top of the door. She could only see the edge of the steps, already crusted over with barnacles and wreathed in seaweed, and the tiny waves lapping at the porch. She opened the door and looked out through the screen.

There were three creatures, the size of smallish dogs or largish cats, covered in reddish-brown fur streaked through with yellow highlights. Pointy muzzles and pointy ears swiveled toward the creaking on the door, and the shiny black eyes stared at Vimbai with savage hope instantly supplanted by disappointment. They had narrow tails, bald save for the spiky tufts on their ends, and their needle teeth gleamed like icicles. They were like no animal Vimbai had ever seen, half-foxes, half-possums.

"What are they?" Vimbai whispered, looking at her grandmother's ghost out of the corner of her eye. Funny, at this moment of fear she looked to the ghost as her family, the only kin Vimbai had nearby. Blood always called to blood, no matter how distant.

"They are spirits," grandmother said. "*Mashave*, alien spirits that are following your friend."

"Why?"

"I don't know," the ghost answered, and picked up Peb to give herself something to do. "Everyone has one spirit or another following them, and who knows why?"

"What about Felix?" Vimbai wanted to know. "Is his hair—"

"*Ngozi*," the *vadzimu* interrupted. "It's the maw of an angry spirit that wants to devour him. He must've committed a truly abominable act!"'"

Vimbai decided that it was not the time to investigate this fascinating point. She had to wake up Maya, and together they would decide what to do. The house was working its subtle magic on Vimbai, and she did not consider the possibility of the house sinking—her concern was with finding her way back home, preferably before she missed any more classes.

She ascended the steps and stopped in confusion—the layout of the house had been changed dramatically. The hallway stretched farther than she ever remembered it being, farther even than her idea of the house's size would allow. Moreover, at the end of the hallway where she remembered her room being there was inside a solid wall of fragrant and green vegetation, twining along the walls and cascading from the ceiling like a curtain. Bright flowers bloomed and wilted, their petals falling on the floor as each flower transformed into green and yellow fruit; drops of dew condensed and slid along the midribs of large leathery leaves. Thankfully, the door to Maya's room was still visible.

Vimbai knocked.

Maya's hoarse voice mumbled something, and then rose. "Come in."

Vimbai did. She found Maya sitting up in bed, staring out of the window. "Did that old woman do this?" she asked Vimbai without ever turning.

Vimbai had not considered this possibility, but discounted it. "No," she said. "Of course not. That woman is my grandmother—well, her ghost, in any case. An ancestral spirit."

"Are they good?" Maya asked.

"Usually," Vimbai said and tried to remember what she knew of the relevant folklore. "They are the link between people and the creator, *Mwari*. Sometimes witches command them to do harm, but I don't think this is the case. She said she needed to tell me a story, and then she just stayed. Peb likes her."

"Great," Maya said. "A ghost babysitter for the Psychic Energy Baby."

"There are also animals on the porch," Vimbai said. "Everyone seems to think they are yours."

"Did you see them when you first came?" Maya asked. "I remember you looking under the porch."

"No," Vimbai said. "But I did see them today—they are on the porch now. The water chased them there, I think. They seem cold."

"What happened?" Maya said. "Do you know why we are floating?"

Vimbai shook her head. "The ocean carried us off."

"Or it's a flood," Maya said, grim. "Has it occurred to you? There's another flood and the only ones who survived are us and a few ghosts we have along."

"And your animals," Vimbai added. "What are they?"

Maya shrugged. "They do not like fish, that much I know."

Vimbai looked around the room, not because of any pressing curiosity but to distract herself from the sight of the water and the nagging fear that Maya might be right, that the world had simply disappeared overnight and there was no back to go to, no classes to catch, no parents to reassure. Vimbai rubbed her throat to chase away a large and cold stone that suddenly formed there. She looked at Maya's chairs and the shelf with knickknacks, at the stack of paperbacks, their covers worn into illegibility, and at the beanbag chair that sat in the middle of the bedroom like an imposing toad. It was a simple room, with precious few traces of personality—surprising for a dwelling inhabited by someone as distinct as Maya. In fact, Vimbai thought, the same could be said about

Felix's room as well as Vimbai's own. In this house, there was no need for posters or furnishings or any other mass-manufactured claims to individuality, there was no need of proclaiming to the house that this was a room belonging to any specific person, with formed tastes and idiosyncrasies. The house took care of that—the very fact of them living here was enough to attest who they were.

"Get dressed," Vimbai said and headed for the door. "I'll check on Felix, and you take care of your creatures. Grandma is making breakfast, so we can eat and decide what we should do."

She avoided looking at the wall of greenery hiding the door to her room—instead she headed for Felix's room and knocked. Felix opened almost immediately, dressed and as alert-looking as his bloodshot eyes allowed. Vimbai thought that his hair did look a bit like the open maw of some spectral predator.

"Yes," Felix said. "I saw. And I don't know what's going on."

"Fine," Vimbai said. "Come and eat breakfast with us. And if you want to see the things from under the porch, you can."

In the kitchen, Maya had commandeered a few dishes, and fed the three shivering animals canned tuna. Vimbai was glad that they had just made a shopping trip, and at least there were plenty of cans in the cupboard. Despite being separated from the electrical supply, the refrigerator still hummed and sputtered, and the stove worked as well. Vimbai made a mental note to check the TV and the phone as she settled on her usual stool and poured herself a cup of thick, oily coffee her grandmother had made. She waited for Felix to come downstairs and take a seat, and for Maya to finish fiddling with the pack of half-foxes, half-possums. Even the *chipoko,* the ghost, ceased her shuffling and stood quietly by the stove, the Psychic Energy Baby and all its phantom limbs cradled in the strong crook of her arms.

Satisfied that all the house inhabitants—even the animal, even the immaterial—were present, Vimbai nodded to herself and took her first sip of coffee as a mariner.

Chapter 5

HOUSES FLOATING ON STRANGE AND CALM SEAS UNDER frozen skies that only occasionally work up the energy to scare up a few clouds and sift a few snowflakes are bound to be guarded by different laws than ordinary houses. Dimensions, for example—as soon as the house in the dunes became unmoored from the very dunes that gave it its nickname, it grew larger on the inside, sprouting additional turrets and rooms and crawlspaces, often hidden behind the walls and impossible to get to—but existing nonetheless. And the proximity of the black hole of Felix's hair warped the spaces inside and pulled up additional layers and floors and realities in some phantasmagoric synergy.

At least, this is how it appeared to Vimbai. An act as simple as opening a bathroom door had to be performed with utmost care, because she could not be sure about what she would find on the other side—the best she could hope for was startling one of Maya's needle-toothed critters drinking out of the toilet bowl; they always turned, glowering, their bright eyes looking over their hunched and almost-human shoulders.

"I'm sorry," Vimbai said after the scattering footfalls of clawed and splayed paws. "I have to use the bathroom." Secretly, she was relieved that the bathroom remained as is, for now at least.

Peb lolled in the bathtub, half-filled with cold water. Vimbai regarded him and decided to pee despite his presence—the thing that now had absorbed all available phantom limbs, save for the one in Vimbai's room, always appeared in unexpected and inopportune moments, popping through the walls or the floor or the ceiling.

"And what are you up to?" she asked Peb as she sat thoughtfully on the toilet. "Grandma is probably looking for you."

Peb shrugged its shoulders and several legs. "She treats me as a child."

"You look like one," Vimbai parried. "You told me you were a baby."

"Not in any regular sense," Peb answered. "Do you know what it is like, in other planes?"

"Same as in Felix's hair?" Vimbai guessed and flushed the toilet. Miraculously, it acted as if it was still connected to a septic tank, but Vimbai felt guilty because she suspected that now it was connecting straight to the ocean.

"No," Peb said. "The planes are radiant and singing. Felix's hair is a dark and desolate place."

"But it is a place," Vimbai said. "An actual place, bigger than it appears to be."

"Oh yes." Peb sank underwater and spoke in small exhalations of bubbles. "I think it's a plane of some sort too, but not a very nice one."

"What's there?"

"Find out yourself," Peb said, suddenly petulant. "I am busy."

"You're awfully cranky for a ghost," Vimbai said.

No answer came and she exited the bathroom, ducking just in case there was a tree suddenly growing outside the door. With no classes to go and not much else to do but to explore the house, Vimbai headed for Felix's room.

He let her in. He had changed the least of them all, Vimbai thought, and it was probably a good thing—any more weird-ness added to Felix, and he would be closer in nature to the ghosts and Maya's animals than to Vimbai and Maya. Maya, on the other hand . . . but that was something to consider later.

"Felix," Vimbai said, politely. "May I take a peek inside your hair?"

His eyes rolled wildly, like those of a spooked horse. "Why would you want to do such a thing?"

"Curiosity," Vimbai said. "And considering that we are in a floating house that sprouts new rooms every day, I think there may be some insight gained."

Felix slumped, and shuffled over to his bed, to sit on it in a pose of defeat and remorse. "You're blaming me," he said. "I tried to tell you."

"No one is blaming you," Vimbai said. "What was it that you tried to tell me?"

"That there are forces in the world," Felix answered. "Forces that run along invisible wires—like phone wires of the spirit, and sometimes you get trapped in them like Peb, and sometimes you stumble in the middle and get caught like a fly in a spider web…" He fell silent, shaking his head; the hair undulated along, with a barely noticeable delay—as if air provided too much resistance.

"You're telling me you know what's going on."

Felix shook his head again, with greater vehemence. "I only know that there are forces, and we are crossing their conduits. And we probably shouldn't. Like you shouldn't look in my hair—there's nothing there for you, nothing at all."

"I shouldn't or you won't let me?"

Felix sighed. "I'll let you but I do not think it's a good idea. But go ahead, look, see what I care."

Vimbai felt a cold wave of hesitation rise in her stomach. "I'm not going all the way in," she said to Felix as much as herself. "I'm just going to look, okay?"

"Whatever," Felix said and slumped some more.

Vimbai approached him in small childish steps. The black mass undulated closer to her face, and in it she saw quiet seething, like the surface of a cauldron full of boiling pitch—or at least what Vimbai imagined one would look like. It took an enormous effort for her to stretch her neck until her face—her eyelashes, her nose, her lips—touched its surface. It felt like sinking her face into a basin full of cold water—she was shocked at how cold it was, at how it singed her skin with frost.

She opened her eyes. It was dark at first, but as her pupils dilated and adjusted, she started to make out shapes at a distance—a mountain with a rounded top overgrown with what looked like trees bending in the wind and a faint white sickle (moon?) hanging above it.

Then the mountain shuddered, and two white round windows opened inside it. Vimbai jerked back as she realized that in the dusk she had misjudged the distance badly,

72

and what she thought was a mountain in reality was a human head just inches away from her face, and the white circles were its dead eyes.

"Hello," the head said. "You new?"

"I'm . . . temporary," Vimbai said, and her heart—outside of here, distant—thumped like mad. "I'm just looking in."

"Like all the legs," the head said. "Funny, I see legs and hands and feet and only rarely—other heads."

Vimbai nodded. "I have a body too, only it's outside," she said. "I'm Vimbai."

"Balshazaar," the head said.

Vimbai studied the head—it was quite old and quite dead, and very desiccated; Felix was not lying about that. The sparse hair covering its parchment-yellow scalp did resemble trees— each hair stood alone and separate and rather straight up. Long and deep furrows covered the face, and Vimbai thought that she noticed traces of faint green luminescence hiding inside them. Balshazaar was a landscape in his own right, and Vimbai could not think of a single thing to say to him. "It's nice to meet you," she finally managed. All the other questions rising in her mind were cut off by their overwhelming mundanity—what did it matter who Balshazaar was or where he came from or if he ever owned a body? Now he was just a desiccated head living in the hair of a really weird teenage malcontent. The rest seemed trivial.

"Going already?" Balshazaar said politely.

"Yes," Vimbai answered. "I don't belong here—see, there's a whole other world outside, and—"

"I know," Balshazaar interrupted. "I've seen it."

"You used to live there?"

"No. Felix takes me out sometimes."

"You don't say." Vimbai was angry at Felix now, for not telling her more and certainly for not letting them know that he had dragged a disembodied head out of whatever unknown dimension. It was one thing to amputate phantom limbs, and quite another to show Balshazaar the world. It was just like grandmother said, one did not screw around with things one did not understand.

Grandmother. The woman who used to be so ridiculous was starting to make sense; or at least she lacked Vimbai's streak of rationality, which made her helpful in irrational circumstances. Grandmother lived—or used to, when she was truly alive—in the world where razor cuts protected from misfortune, and cunning *muroyi*, witches, could sic spirits on the living and make them ill. Grandmother would deal with a dead head like she dealt with all such problems—remember a remedy or go to a *n'anga* and have it fixed. Vimbai wished there were a healer nearby, someone who was versed in dealing with the supernatural rather than someone like her, who flailed and hyperventilated and tried to stay calm in the face of it—so far, that was all Vimbai could manage. Even her fear of the Harare healers had receded enough to think of them wistfully.

"I'll be going now," Vimbai said, and straightened. Balshazaar's face diminished as it hurtled away from her, and Vimbai looked into Felix's disturbing eye. She was not ready to tell him anything yet, and so she stalked away without saying a word. Felix was so disconnected from everything anyway that he probably didn't even think her rude.

Vimbai padded to her room along the hallway that had grown a covering of soft, slightly wet moss, and lay down on her bed. A mattress and box spring, really—not a proper bed. She resented her grandmother's arrival and the house's ill-fated journey. Why did it have to happen to her, a perfectly rational person? Were those the superstitions of her ancestors that dragged her along, people long dead but unwilling to let go? It just wasn't fair that someone she was related to by blood alone could do that, as if shared genetic background gave them some sort of power over Vimbai. She wondered if Maya too felt that same pull and resentment.

Maya. Maya who barely talked anymore and instead followed with her feral pack from one room to the next. They roamed like hunters, disappearing into the closets recently converted into thick suffocating forests, they swam in rivers that poured from the downstairs bathroom. Vimbai hated to admit that her worry about Maya was just a pretense designed to mask her envy and disappointment at not being invited. She too would enjoy a pack of furry familiars following her around, she too would like to be unconcerned about their future and the present circumstance.

Peb floated up through her pillow, its smooth skin and several feet and hands brushing cool against Vimbai's cheek. "Don't be sad," Peb said, its former petulance forgotten. "Why are you sad?"

"I miss Maya," Vimbai answered. "I wish I could go with her."

"There are creatures under the porch," Peb said cryptically. "The house found them."

"They were on the porch," Vimbai said. "And now they are gone."

"No," Peb argued. "Still under."

"There are only horseshoe crabs there." Vimbai sat up abruptly. "Is that what you're trying to tell me?"

Peb bobbed over her pillow, floating up then down, until it jetted higher up and disappeared through the ceiling.

Vimbai rubbed her face. "Horseshoe crabs," she murmured. Poor crabs, bled half to death by *wazimamoto* in medical trucks. Vimbai jumped off her bed, reenergized by the possibility of a new discovery. There would be time later for Maya and Felix and Balshazaar; now was the time for horseshoe crabs.

VIMBAI HAD NEVER ANTICIPATED THAT SHE WOULD BE sticking her face into strange and unfamiliar places so much, but there she was—on her hands and knees on the porch, by the very edge of the water. The house had mutated again, developing a coquettish hem of round pebbles and pieces of seaglass, polished and clear. The barnacles hung onto the edge, their quick ghostly feet kicking food in their mouths hidden somewhere inside their chalky shells. If it weren't for horseshoe crabs, Vimbai would've studied barnacles for the sheer weirdness of their anatomy and lifestyle.

Vimbai kneeled on the edge of the porch that currently fancied itself a littoral zone and studied the surface of water— smooth and clear, and so cold. Her breath fogged the air and touched the waves; Vimbai tried to cloud them with her breath like one would a pane of glass, but to no avail. She took a deep breath and thrust her face into the ocean.

The salt and the cold burned her skin, a million needles threading her cheeks. Her teeth ached. She opened her eyes underwater and they burned too, tears not helping the matters at all. The water around her seemed stationary, like a block of green ice. She couldn't see very far, and her breath tried to break out of her chest like a caged and panicked bird.

Vimbai came up for a breath of air, and gasped, still crying from the cold and the salt and the sadness of all this water, always separating her from something she wanted. How could one love something so cruel, something so terrible to her parents? As if answering, a withered ghostly hand lay on her shoulder.

"*Sahwira*," her grandmother said. "Girlfriend, my girl-friend. You look for thing no mortal eyes can see. Let me guide your vision."

Her grandmother's hands lay flat on Vimbai's temples and pushed her gently back toward the water's surface. For a moment, blind fear boiled in Vimbai—what if she were to hold her head down and never let her come up for air, no matter how much her heart thundered and her legs kicked and thrashed? What if she wanted Vimbai to be a ghost, like her, to finally touch the souls of her ancestors?

But it was foolish. The hands on her head were so gentle even without warmth, so kind, that Vimbai succumbed and let them guide her. She opened her eyes, and for a moment there was just familiar transparency without images, the endless wall of thick glass. And then her grandmother's eyes entered her own.

If she were asked to explain how it felt, Vimbai would've

faltered for words, groping for images that best described what she was experiencing. Her grandmother's sight entered her own like a hand enters an empty glove. Vimbai had been hollow and now she had a center, a depth, a density—she felt three-dimensional and alive and aware. She focused her eyes and she could see every grain of sand in the bottom, every rock, every shrimp hiding in the crevices. She saw kelp forests and the silvering of a school of anchovies, the rapid quirk of a shad. On the bottom, hagfishes braided themselves into an incestuous, slithering nest of Gorgon's hair in the empty cavity of a dead shark's head, its gill arches protecting them like the barred windows of a jailhouse.

And beneath and beyond all that, under the sand sifting over the skeleton of a sunken ship, there were horseshoe crabs, pale and unwell. There were hundreds of them, or perhaps thousands, all of their tiny legs moving in unison, burrowing in the sand. As Vimbai looked at them, they stared back with their pinprick eyes. And as if one, they shifted, their legs working in reverse now, digging themselves out rather than in.

Among all the strange occurrences of the past weeks, the fact that the cold-blooded crabs were able to react with such speed and determination bothered Vimbai most of all. She wanted to pull away, to break the surface and to not have to see this, but her grandmother's quiet attention held her, their eyes—Vimbai's and *vadzimu*'s—riveted to the creatures. They varied in size, from the tiny ones as small as a quarter to the adults as big as a dinner plate, and yet all of them moved together, the living carpet of them swarming onto the surface of the sand, their mouth parts open in plea or hunger. As

Vimbai pulled away, the wave of crabs heaved after her; as she moved closer to them, they retreated but never far away.

"Why are they doing it?" Vimbai whispered.

"It's like that story I told you," the *vadzimu* answered. "Weren't you listening?" Her tone was impatient now, stern—just like she used to be in life, the kind of woman who would take her own daughter to be carved up by razorblades—but always for her own good.

Vimbai frowned. "What does the story have to do with horseshoe crabs?"

Grandmother heaved a sigh. "The tortoise," she explained slowly, patiently, as one would to a dim a child, "did not want the moon. But the oceans followed him nonetheless, as they always follow the moon."

"I dreamt about it," Vimbai interjected. "Seas following the tortoise."

"He did not want it, did not ask for it—and yet. He drank the moon, and the moon in his belly was bigger than he, and it commanded the ocean whether the tortoise liked it or not."

Vimbai considered she might have drunk that was so compelling to the crabs, and gave up. It wasn't her first beer in the house and it wasn't the tears she cried in secret, letting them soak into her pillow, her hair, her eyelashes. But there was something inside of her that made her find the house and bring her dead grandmother along, something that made her want to study horseshoe crabs—and now, apparently gave her a power of command over them. They were not as cute as Maya's half-foxes, but they were Vimbai's—at least, they seemed to think so.

When she opened her mouth, the salt water flooded it, numbing her tongue and pounding her teeth with its frozen hammer. Her face did not feel a thing, and she wondered idly how was she able to hold her breath for so long. Nonetheless, she managed to ask, "What do you want with me?"

The crabs answered in a quiet rustling of their legs and mouth parts, in the sad stares of their tiny eyes, *We want you to take care of us, and let us take care of you.* And this is how Vimbai found herself in possession of a horseshoe crab army.

VIMBAI REMEMBERED THE TIME WHEN SHE WAS LITTLE, before the horseshoe crabs and her anxiety about Africana Studies. Back then, she considered New Jersey prosaic and hardly the place where one could hope to grow up while having important experiences. She listened to her parents as they spoke after dinner; when they talked to each other they did it in Shona. Back then, Vimbai did not concern herself with questions why it was so, but now she understood—even though both were taught English from an early age, Shona was a way to set themselves apart, to reaffirm that they were of the same cloth as each other, set against the rest of their surroundings. Later, Vimbai thought it an unnecessary affectation, and forgot most of what little language she knew back then. She did not realize the need to set herself apart—in fact, her childhood was dominated by the opposite impulse, to be one of many.

Her color did not help matters—even though they lived just a few miles away from Atlantic City, their particular town was white; they were the only black family on the block. And no matter how much one tried, there were things that simply could not be hidden.

Afterwards, as an adolescent burdened with an unfair amount of social conscience, Vimbai went through a brief but histrionic stage of embracing her heritage—she reasoned that if one could not blend in, it was better to exaggerate the difference. It brought about a brief resurgence in her interest in Shona and African lit, as well as the love of 'ethnic' fashions. Out of these, the latter lasted the shortest—all it took was one eye roll from Vimbai's mother to plant the seed of doubt. Nonetheless, it was during this time that Vimbai visited Harare and met her extended family on her maternal side.

Harare shocked her by its hasty urbanity—it felt like a city that was created too quickly, without giving a chance to people or the land to adjust to its presence. The tall skyscrapers that wouldn't be out of place in Philadelphia or New York City jutted out of red soil, as if plopped down by some magic tornado. The houses pushed upward among trees; her mother said that they were called jacaranda trees, and that when they all bloomed, Harare was the most beautiful city on earth. They went to African Unity Square, and Vimbai gawped at the flower market that shone with so many colors—several of them not found on the spectrum, Vimbai was pretty sure.

Much later, when Vimbai was eighteen, she watched her mother cry when she read in the newspapers that the flower market was destroyed at Mugabe's orders. She felt like crying too, but was too busy drawing a firm line between herself and Africana Studies and everything they entailed—even the flower markets in her mother's home city. Now she understood the deep hurt of that destruction, the most basic betrayal of one's childhood love. It was not just about the flowers; it was never just about anything. It was always about what one knew to be true about the world when one was a child, and the death of that knowledge.

Chapter 6

———

"We have to get back to New Jersey," Maya said one morning, the ruddy fur carpet stretched by her feet across pale linoleum tiles. "We're almost out of coffee, and the milk is going bad."

Vimbai peered into Maya's cup, the murky coffee in it studded with pellets of milk coagulated in an unpleasant fashion. "Ew." The question of return had been on her mind, even though she tried not to think about her classes and her mother, insane with grief—the moment she did, her stomach felt sick.

"Exactly." Maya made a face and took a cautious sip.

"I suppose I could ask my horseshoe crabs to tow us back," Vimbai said.

Maya smiled. "So they are *your* horseshoe crabs now, huh? Do they have little harnesses?"

"No," Vimbai answered and drank her coffee black. "But I guess we'll need to give them something to grab on. They have to walk on the bottom—they are not great swimmers."

"Why couldn't you befriend dolphins?" Felix said.

Maya laughed, eyeing her half-foxes, half-possums tenderly. "Yeah. Mammals are smarter."

Vimbai shrugged. "I don't care. I like crabs. And they are the ones that can take us home, so be nice."

"Are you sure that they can?" Felix said.

Vimbai wasn't. "Pretty sure," she said out loud.

After breakfast of dry pancakes (they were low on syrup too), Vimbai went to talk to the crabs. Her grandmother came along, quiet and helpful as usual. She helped Vimbai see and helped her talk, and the words that bubbled out of Vimbai's mouth underwater were both of theirs. Moreover, Vimbai had noticed an increased frequency of dreams about Harare—especially the vegetable garden in her grandmother's backyard—to the point where she suspected that the ghost's memories were leaking in and coloring Vimbai's own. Or maybe the proximity of the ancestral spirit reminded her. Oh, jacaranda trees in bloom, Vimbai sighed underwater. Oh, horseshoe crabs. Will you take us home, to the sand bars and beaches of New Jersey, where you come every spring to spawn and dance through the tides on your little segmented legs?

It's not yet spring, they answered. *It is cold and we will die if we leave the safety of our deep sleep.*

Vimbai nodded, her hair floating in front of her face and crosshatching her vision like a mosquito net. Or a fisherman's one—she shuddered when she remembered the quartered corpses of horseshoe crabs sold as bait in every bait shop. They were good to put in eel traps, they said. No wonder they didn't want to go back without great necessity. "Do you know of anyone who can help us?" she said. "If we don't get home, we will die."

The crabs consulted among themselves, their whispers audible only to ghost ears. Finally, they said, *Go back go back home. We will help you—just hang some ropes for us and don't look into the water until you get back home. And promise, promise to protect us from death if we come with you.*

"I'll try," Vimbai said. "But how can I protect you?"

The *vadzimu* pulled her out of the water. "It is simple business, *sahwira*," she said. "Just don't let them die."

VIMBAI HAD SPENT THIS MORNING BRAIDING ROPES THAT would be long enough to reach the bottom—she denuded the closet in her room of its vines, leathery and tough, and she twisted them together into long strands. She found supple branches in the young forest that had sprung where the attic door used to be, and she peeled off their bark. She teased apart the vascular bundles and twined them around the vines to give them enough strength to move the entire house.

She attached the ropes she made to the steel bolts in the porch, and hung them into the water.

It was difficult to avoid the temptation to look, but she resisted. The crabs asked her for a reason, and Vimbai knew enough fairy tales where a violation of explicit prohibition spelled an immediate and cruel disaster—all her sources agreed on that, European and African both. She just had to make do, and simply imagine the solemn crabs grabbing her ropes, clustering on them, their weak legs digging into the wavy sand studded with shells, and pulling, pulling with all their might. Or perhaps they could secretly swim, and no one ever knew about that—perhaps this is why they told her not to look. She imagined them, floating in the thickness of water, suspended like trilobites in amber, graceful as falling leaves.

She thought bitterly that those who featured in those

cautionary fairytales had no graduate schools to apply to—if Vimbai could document such an interesting behavior as swimming, her application would be a snap. Then it occurred to her that the ability to talk was even stranger.

This collision of worldviews—one that allowed for talking horseshoe crabs and one that hinged on graduate school applications—made her breath catch in her throat, bowled her over, brought her to her knees, and she clutched her head in her hands. Ever since she had moved into the house in the dunes (which was now not quite the same house in the ocean), her mind, quite unbeknownst to her, had labored at keeping these two worldviews coexisting but never quite encountering each other. Now, accidentally, the two were brought together by the crabs, and Vimbai rocked back and forth on her knees, her head between her sweaty palms, and struggled to gather her thoughts. What am I doing here, she said to herself. Stupid Felix with his black hole coif and his pet desiccated head, stupid Peb, stupid half-foxes that weren't even all that cute. Stupid Vimbai for playing along with this nonsense rather than packing up and going back home; her mother would've been so happy. She wouldn't even bug Vimbai about staying out late.

Not that Vimbai had much of a social life, but she occasionally stayed late at her study group, and sometimes they went out for a pizza. No matter how sophisticated and urbane, Vimbai's mother had a real hang-up about Vimbai staying out after dark.

She had understood it better in Harare, where her grandmother explained to her that decent girls did not stay out late.

"Why not?" Vimbai had said, in a voice that made her mother frown dangerously. She did not approve of Vimbai mouthing off to her elders.

"Because you know what happens with young men and women after dark," grandmother said.

Vimbai laughed. "What? Sex? It happens during the day too, you know. People might stay out late not having sex, or have sex at 9 A.M."

"That's enough out of you," her mother interrupted, and dragged Vimbai out of grandmother's house by her arm, to go meet the family of her aunt twice removed.

Now she understood what clinging to habit, to tradition, because sometimes tradition was the only thing that kept one sane.

THE HOUSE STARTED MOVING AGAIN THE VERY NEXT NIGHT. They couldn't feel it at first, since for a change they all gathered together downstairs to watch the TV tuned to some foggy ghost channel—it showed nothing but snow-covered mountains and two women talking to each other on their cell phones; Vimbai found the women strange, since, despite the split screen, they appeared to be in the same room. Vimbai shifted in her chair and shot Maya a restless look. Maya smiled lazily back and whistled at the half-possums at her feet.

"Not hunting tonight?" Vimbai asked.

Maya shook her head. "Tired. And what's the matter with you? You hardly ever went . . . well, anywhere!"

"The house has mutated," Vimbai parried. "How do you know it's not dangerous?"

"I don't." Maya shrugged and stared at the TV screen again. "It probably is. But it is certainly more interesting than this."

"Yeah," Felix agreed from the couch, where he lay framed by the ghostly shapes of Vimbai's grandmother and the Psychic Energy Baby. "The TV here sucks. I wish the phone worked instead."

"It's the middle of nowhere," Vimbai said as mildly as she could. "But don't worry, the crabs said they will get us back to New Jersey."

"About time," Maya said. "Are we moving yet?"

Vimbai looked out of the window, and at first she thought that the house remained as it was—there was nothing but water and star-studded sky wherever she looked. But soon she noticed a small wave rising where the porch met the water. She rushed over to the window on the opposite side of the room, and had to clear away a thin, disconcerting layer of fresh meat that had grown over the windowpane just recently. She saw a luminescent wake, and cheered. "We are moving," she said to the questioning gazes of her roommates and ghosts.

And so they were. Vimbai tracked their progress by the rotation of the alien stars overhead, waiting for the familiar clangy shape of the Big Dipper to swim into her view. As the house traversed the waters, Vimbai found herself in little need of sleep, and she stayed up until morning, looking from one window or another, and feeling like a mariner and the discoverer of the world.

Her grandmother sat next to Vimbai, silent, but Vimbai knew that the *vadzimu* did not share her fascination with explorers and pioneers, discoverers and seafarers. They were trouble, they only brought bitterness with them, and they took away and even when they gave back it was not the same. They spoiled everything they touched.

Vimbai's grandmother was not nearly as politically aware as Vimbai's mother, or even Vimbai herself—she had seemed preoccupied with her vegetable garden and her family, and politics and history were dwarfed by these concerns, existing only as distant and vague hurts, a persistent feeling that things were worse than they could've been, and the blame was easy to find. Grandmother grew up in Rhodesia, and she never went to school because the black people were not allowed to. The occasionally heard claims that the English brought education to Zimbabwe sounded hollow to Vimbai because of her.

"Grandmother," Vimbai said, and tore her gaze from the darkened window. "How did you find us? Why did you come with me instead of staying with mom?"

The ghost's eyes clouded for a moment, by memory or regret. "Past speaks to the future," she said. "The present is already crumbling."

Vimbai's heart fluttered in her throat as she pictured her mother—her parents, both of them, still young and beautiful—getting older and smaller and more fragile, birdlike, and finally shrinking away to nothing, falling apart like a handful of ash. She shook her head, no, it cannot be like that.

"And you called me," grandmother said. "Your mother never did, but you called to me, through your anger, through your contempt."

"I never . . . " Vimbai started.

Peb floated up to the window and peered along with Vimbai for a short while; then it went to the *vadzimu* and nestled on her back, like an ugly festooned hump. When Vimbai looked at him and all his absorbed phantom limbs, she thought of the exotic fish that decorated themselves with fins and outgrowths until they resembled a piece of coral or an algal bed.

"Maybe I'll do better with you than I did with your mother," grandmother said.

"You didn't do badly with her," Vimbai said. Really, she didn't—it was not her fault, she did as she was taught, she meant as well as the parents all over the world do.

"She left home."

Vimbai smiled at that. She could not leave home, at least not now—the home was spacious but surrounded by a flat watery expanse that offered little in escape possibilities. Even with the horseshoe crabs in her command, Vimbai would not dare to dream of escaping. Then again, she did not really want to. "I won't leave. Your other daughters did not leave. Why aren't you home, with their children?"

"They have the whole clan. You have no one. No ancestor spirits to protect and guide you, to connect you to the creator."

"I appreciate that," Vimbai said. "And mom would too . . . if she knew, I mean."

Grandmother nodded, consoled or just playing along. "What are you thinking about, *varoora*?"

Vimbai looked around to make sure that neither Felix nor Maya was within earshot. When she was content that there was no chance of being overheard, she moved her head close to the ghost's. "Love," she said. "Being in love, I mean."

BOYS—OR, SHE SUPPOSED, IN HER AGE BRACKET THEY SHOULD be properly called young men or guys—were a minor puzzlement in Vimbai's life, and one more point of tension between her and her mother. Vimbai's mother was downright schizophrenic when it came to Vimbai's dating life—she warned her away from staying out late and spending too much time gawping at men, and yet she worried that Vimbai didn't.

Vimbai remembered going to the prom—just two years ago—and she remembered the dress she wore—a bright yellow silk sheath, golden even, the perfect color of the noon sun. She still kept it, in vain hopes for some occasion to wear it again. She did not remember the boy who took her to the prom. She remembered her parents being happy that she came home early but then whispering in the kitchen.

Vimbai did not know why she wasn't interested in them—like all her contemporaries, she went through the pre-assigned stages of development. When she was in middle school, she read encyclopedias on the sly, hunting for dirty words and hoping for illustrations. She pored in secret over art albums that her parents kept out in the open, but looking at the paintings with them present felt uncomfortable, like a too-tight scratchy woolen collar. And yet, the actual boys with their stained hands and hostile eyes did not appeal to her.

In high school, she wondered if perhaps she was a lesbian—she had a short but intense crush on a classmate named Elizabeth Rosenzweig, a tall British girl with long black hair who looked at everything as if it were too boring to even bother raising her eyelids all the way up for. They had a lot of classes together, and sat next to each during lunch, each thinking desperately of something to say to the other. Vimbai treasured one time they had stayed after school together because Elizabeth needed to copy a part of some assignment Vimbai and she were doing together, and her smooth cool hand touched Vimbai's, chapped and burning.

When Elizabeth went away for the summer, Vimbai missed her with the pointless urgency of first love, and she cut shallow marks into the insides of her arms and thighs—they had healed completely, but if one knew they were there, they could be seen as thin lines slightly paler than the rest of her skin, now just an annoying reminder of past foolishness.

When Vimbai started college, her classes preoccupied her too much to worry about not having a boyfriend or a girlfriend or some sort of significant other. It amused her to think that if she delayed dating long enough, her mother would be relieved if she brought home anyone—even a girl; even a British girl. Perhaps some day she would run into Elizabeth again, maybe at the mall or the coffee shop down the street, when Elizabeth visited home during the break—she went to college out of state. And maybe then they would reminisce and go to the movies, and at least then Vimbai would not have to worry about dating for a while. This passing thought grew into a justification with time—at least, Vimbai used it as an excuse to keep to herself and avoid any possibility of romantic involvement.

She considered it now, and wondered at the relief a part of her felt at being stranded at sea with some ghosts and two roommates—at least, she did not have to explain herself here all the time. And there was no possibility of Elizabeth showing up here, and making Vimbai feel awkward and inarticulate.

"Is there something wrong with me?" she asked the *vadzimu*. "I mean, shouldn't I want to love somebody?"

The ghost shook her head and patted Vimbai's hand. "There's nothing wrong with you or anyone here."

Vimbai smiled and moved closer, as if to cuddle up to the old woman—but then remembered the razorblades. She settled for touching the *chipoko's* hand instead. It felt (and, Vimbai supposed, was) immaterial, just a little warmer than air and light—yet solid enough to hold, just like Peb.

"Peb is falling asleep," Vimbai said. "Why don't you tell him a story?"

Grandmother smiled. "I suppose I could. Which one do you want?"

Vimbai shrugged. "Whatever you like."

"I do know quite a few," grandmother warned. "But I suppose there's no harm."

Her voice soothed Peb and made Vimbai sleepy. She dipped in and out of sleep, like a fisherman's bob on the surface of water, catching brief snatches of serpentine and seemingly endless stories about baboons and rabbits and other animals who all had active social lives and spoke on the phone a lot. Just as the sun rose in front of the window (they were heading east, it seemed), a word her grandmother said jolted her awake.

"Man-fish," grandmother said.

Vimbai sat up. "Is that from Marechera's book? I didn't know you read him."

"It's not just from the book," grandmother said. "It's a *nyaya*, a myth. Everyone knows it's not really true, but we tell it anyway, because it always contains truth, and not the boring part of it."

"Will you tell me?" Vimbai said.

The *vadzimu* nodded. "Sleep, granddaughter, and you will see everything you need."

Vimbai rested her head on the windowsill and dozed off, lulled by the quiet lapping of the waves against the house wall outside and the soft whining of the Psychic Energy Baby.

Her dreams, just like her eyes underwater, seemed an amalgam of her own and her grandmother's notions—a rather disconcerting situation, since the blend of the two had the quality of a comical nightmare about it. She dreamed of a broad river, Limpopo perhaps, or maybe Zambezi. There was rumbling of turbulent water off in a distance, but Vimbai stared at the smooth surface and large shallows by the bank. Her feet sank into the muddy soil, and a few grass stems brushed against her bare ankles. It looked like a good place for a swim, and she jumped into the warm muggy water cannonball-style, releasing a plume of spray and pungent, green smell of the river water.

She opened her eyes underwater, and squinted against swarms of silt particles that swirled before her, carried by the turbulence of her dive. She spotted a hippo with a calf, but remembered that she was just dreaming, and swam past them with nonchalance. A string of bubbles rose from her lips, but she breathed easily underwater, and she swam through the wide flats overgrown with grass, and into the deep channel of the river. There, she noticed that there was no more air escaping her lungs, and that she likely had no lungs left—her feet had fused into a wide lobed tail, and brown patterns covered her skin. A pair of whiskers hung from her lip and registered every disturbance in the flow of water. Vimbai did not need a mirror to figure out that she was now a catfish, and she sank all the way to the bottom and rested in the mud, feeling, listening.

A catfish can grow very large, and they do it by staying close to the bottom, eating anything organic, and growing fast enough to quickly become too large for most predators— crocodiles, perhaps, would still be a threat to a giant catfish, but catfish did not become large by being careless. The mud and the brown color of their skin protected them from view.

Something stirred in the water—catfish's whiskers sensed a wild thrashing, like a panicked impala trying to wrench free of a crocodile's jaws. The catfish headed in the direction of the commotion, staying close to the bottom, stealthy and cunning.

Catfish would eat pretty much anything. If there was a hunt, a death, they would pick up whatever remains fell to the bottom. And if the victim was a person—well, so much the better, so much more to pick up and savor.

It was a stupid boy who had decided to go swimming after a large dinner. He swam too far from the shore when a spasm in his belly twisted him into a knot, and his nose and mouth flooded with the taste of rich river mud. A stronger or a more composed swimmer would not have drowned—he would've calmed himself down and bobbed on the water, breathing, waiting for the spasm to pass. But not a scared boy who thrashed more as water flooded his mouth and his belly grew heavy with the river he swallowed. And everyone knows that a river is simply too large for a human child.

When the boy stopped writhing and sank quietly to the bottom, pulled along by the weight of river in his belly, catfish moved closer. He had no teeth to tear the flesh, and he waited patiently for those who would cut the boy open and let the catfish feed on morsels they dropped in their frenzy—bits of intestine, shreds of skin were welcome; being a catfish, he was not picky. But then he found something he did not expect.

There was fluttering in the water, a movement too small to notice for anyone but a fish with sensitive whiskers. It went past his face, and even though he could not see anything with his nearsighted beady eyes, the catfish opened his mouth and slammed it shut, and felt a small wriggling in his belly. It was the soul of the drowned boy, and the catfish became aware.

Vimbai—her consciousness still distinct within the tiny dull mind of the fish—wondered what the fish would do, and what would happen to the soul of the boy. It bloomed side by side with hers, filling the catfish with a new sense. His small eyes snapped open, and he saw the river for the first time, like he had never seen it before. Even though his eyes were weak, he discerned every undulation of the bottom, every silvery flash of the passing fish. He watched the water turn from green to red as the crocodiles arrived and started their meal; he watched with curiosity as his former body was torn apart by snapping jaws. He ate a few dropped morsels, but the hunger—the forever hunger that propels every catfish forward—had subsided, dulled by curiosity and flood of new sensations as the minds of the boy and the fish circled each other, sizing each other up. Vimbai remained an observer, lodged there in the catfish's mind like a foreign body, a dream splinter.

The catfish—or man-fish as he called himself—grew older and larger by the year, and the boy inside became a part of him. He remembered everything the boy remembered—the faces of his family and how many chickens they had, the name of the prettiest girl in his village, the address of some relatives in Harare. But the memories became mere decorations, baubles suspended in the vast and labyrinthine mind of the fish. He grew more cunning and more clever, but not more compassionate or introspective. He remained a catfish at heart, and he always hoped for another body and another soul.

Chapter 7

THE NEXT MORNING THEY WERE STILL AT SEA; THE WAVES were more restless than ever before—they reared up and flung their foam-topped crests against the walls of the house and expired in salty sprays. Vimbai ran from one window to the next, clearing away either meat or succulent green tendrils that always grew across the panes when she was not watching, anxious for any sign of motion. But the waves masked whatever trail the house had been leaving, and she feared that they had stalled or the ropes had torn or the crabs had died. The memory of her man-fish dream came back, and she imagined the scavenger fish crawling onto the nets, squeezing into the crab and eel traps to devour the gruesome bait left for them by the fishermen.

She imagined her horseshoe crabs now, dead on the cold pebbled bottom of the ocean, devoured by the wily fish—and, she thought, those fish would devour Vimbai's soul as well. If the crabs followed her because they had some connection to her, then, Vimbai reasoned, a fish could potentially get to Vimbai. More and more she relied on her grandmother's way of thinking, and with every passing minute the urge to check on the crabs grew stronger, almost physical, in her chest.

And yet, they had warned her. There were fairytales and forebodings, there was fear. Vimbai felt just like she did when she was little, when her mother left her by the supermarket's entrance and told her to wait. Vimbai waited until the thoughts swarmed: what if mother left without her? What if she forgot about Vimbai? What if she fell and needed help? She knew that she should wait, but anxiety would get the better of her every time and she would go looking, and then they would spend a good half-hour looking for each other along the endless rows of shelves that seemed to house everything except whatever one was looking for at the moment.

Before the memory finished flashing through her mind, Vimbai knew that she would have to check on the horseshoe crabs—whatever fairytale punishment was reserved for her would surely be better than the agony of not knowing and yet driving herself desperate with anxious imaginings, just like her mother's yelling at Vimbai for not staying put was far better than waiting in one spot.

She headed down the hallway but found that the steps leading downstairs had been overgrown by a particularly prickly variety of barberry bushes. She tried to struggle down the stairs, but the thorns left painful scratches on her arms and legs. Vimbai wished she had the machete they kept in the kitchen, behind the stove. She called for Maya or Felix, but no help or even answer came.

She tried to push through the prickly bushes but they pushed right back, gouging deep marks into her shoulders, tearing at her jeans like angry claws. She retreated and the bushes followed, pushing her into her room with unseemly glee. She backed away until her room was overgrown by barberry and a particularly nasty medicinal smell, and her back was pressed against the windowsill and thorny branches studded with bright red berries waved in her face. Only then she realized that the vegetation inside the house was rarely so aggressive, and felt the first prickling of fear and sting of her sweat in the new scratches on her forehead.

Vimbai had no other recourse but to open the window. It was close enough to the surface of water, Vimbai reasoned, and she could easily swim to the porch—despite the cold, she felt confident that the distance was short enough to cover with two or three long strokes. Plus, it would give her an excuse to sneak a look at the crabs, and then she would get the machete and deal with the insolent vegetation. She drew in a deep breath and pushed through the window, dangling ungracefully for a moment and then plunging, head first.

She did not expect the cold to be so cutting—the embrace of steel-cold water tightened around her chest, and Vimbai sucked in a breath and reached for the porch. It bobbed farther away than she expected, and with the resignation of someone in a bad dream she realized that the house was moving away. She tried to swim, but her lungs felt frozen and heavy, and her legs and arms weighed her down with useless bone and cramped muscle.

She called for help then, her voice too small to be heard in the house. Her legs kicked hard as she tried not to let panic set in, and she called for the crabs, for her grandmother, for anyone to come and help her. Her legs leaden, her arms useless, she felt herself slipping, sinking under the surface, and with no grandmother to keep her warm to guide her vision, there was only murky water; it poured into her mouth and filled her stomach, heavy like a brick.

And then, a hand—several hands, several arms, as many as an octopus, lifting her, pulling her head above the water. Several legs kicking by her, various in size, but all strong. Vimbai recognized Peb. She was too muddled and cold to feel real surprise, just extreme gratitude. So there was a reason why the silly thing was attaching every phantom limb it could find to itself.

And then, the porch swam into her field of vision, and she reached out her hand—clawed, unfeeling—to hook it on the edge. Peb helped her up, dragging her out of the water, and held her, protective and sympathetic, as she retched what felt like gallons of seawater. Her teeth would not stop chattering.

Maya and Vimbai's grandmother came out of the kitchen and hustled her inside, to sit close to the stove they turned on for just that purpose, and to be rubbed by large fluffy towels. Vimbai was too muddled to make sense of their exclamations, and only felt vague irritation when they persistently shook her by the shoulder and kept asking if she was okay and if she could feel her feet and fingers.

"Hypothermia," Maya kept repeating. "This ain't good."

The ghost brought blankets and warmed them by the open oven, and Peb hovered nearby. Vimbai closed her eyes—all the movement and noise distracted her from something nagging at the back of her mind, persistently enough to distract her from the fact that she had nearly drowned.

And like a photograph in a vat of developer, the image

appeared in the black background of her eyelids. It was a palimpsest of the image she had seen underwater but was too frightened to absorb at the time. Now, it stood before her with a steady clarity.

She saw the ropes stretched taut and the horseshoe crabs festooned along them all the way from the bottom to the foundation. They did not pull but were carried—and Vimbai cried out and opened her eyes once she discerned the beasts that did all the pulling.

"She's in shock," Maya said to the ghosts, and patted Vimbai's hand. "Hang in there, sweetheart. You'll be fine, you just have to warm up a little."

Vimbai just shivered in response, thinking of the monsters—giant, ancient—pulling the house along. Monsters that left deep gouges in the sand, barnacles on their cracked carapaces, their eyes rotted out, their tails broken. They moved on clawed legs covered in cracked exoskeleton, exposing rotting bits of their flesh. Hagfish followed them, occasionally swimming up and ripping out chunks of putrid flesh, and still they moved—gigantic, undead horseshoe crabs, animated by some ancient and unknown will.

The *vadzimu* took Vimbai's hands into hers. "What have you seen, granddaughter?"

Vimbai shook her head and looked away, afraid that the terrible vision would leak from her eyes into her grandmother's. She did not want to share, not just yet—sometimes one had to be alone with knowledge to absorb the enormity of it. Sure, a burden shared was lighter, but sometimes one needed to appreciate the entire weight so that the future relief would seem all the more precious. So Vimbai swallowed and stared out of the window, feeling blood pulsing in her lips, warming them.

The kettle blew a sharp whistle, and Maya hurried to make her a cup of tea. Vimbai swallowed the scalding fluid, not caring that the skin in her mouth peeled, her stomach filling with warmth—filling with life, and the sensation was enough to chase away the terrible image crowding her mind.

She tried to make sense of it, as she always did—when she was little, she was taught that any problem had a solution, and if one just jiggled the pieces a little and squinted, looked at them sideways, then the general pattern would become apparent and everything would fit, suddenly, in a flash.

When she became older, she learned that some problems resisted such treatment—they were solved not by a flash of inspiration and sudden insight but by tedious, boring work—and too often, one did not truly solve them, just demonstrated enough of the ability to think to earn a passing grade, but the solution of the problem remained unknown.

But neither inspirational nor incremental approaches helped her to deal with the undead crabs. She was willing to accept that the house and the three housemates plus assorted ghosts fit together, that the horseshoe crabs were their allies and the fishes who devoured souls were enemies; she could live with her ability to control the crabs, just like she could forgive Maya her half-foxes and Felix his desiccated heads. But she could not move past the simple acceptance and start finding answers to why and how and who and for what purpose. She could only shiver in front of the stove and drink tea.

The two worldviews were at an impasse again, and there was not much Vimbai could do besides trying to incorporate them both; pinning them against each other so that either one would yield answers seemed far beyond her capabilities.

"Why did you jump into the water?" Maya asked, apparently judging Vimbai to have recovered enough.

"I couldn't take the stairs," Vimbai said. "I was attacked by the shrubs, and didn't have a knife. I called, but no one came. There were prickly shrubs chasing me all the way to my room, and they smelled like a hospital."

Maya arched her eyebrows. "I haven't seen them, but if you say so. It was still a stupid thing to do."

"I know," Vimbai said. "But it's not like there were other options."

"There are always other options," Maya said. "Come on, I'll take you to your room, and I'll show you a workaround for the stairs. And then you'll go to bed and sleep and feel better, okay?"

"Okay," Vimbai agreed and stood up, still shivering, clutching the warm blanket gathered at her neck.

The *chipoko* picked up Vimbai's t-shirt and skirt off the floor. "Don't worry, I'll dry your clothes and bring them to you. Go rest now."

Vimbai followed Maya, sulking a little—how come everyone but herself knew about this workaround? Then she remembered sitting by the window while Maya explored, but didn't feel better for it.

Maya led them into the living room and opened the doors of the cabinet that housed assorted plates, dishes and knickknacks they didn't quite have a place for. The knickknacks were gone now, subsumed by a path carefully marked in white sand, leading into a copse of tall and narrow trees—they lined the path like columns, and their branches twined overhead, creating a filigreed tunnel, black against the pale grey sky.

"Where are we?" Vimbai asked.

"Pantry," Maya said, and shot her a smoldering look. "You really need to get to know the house, you know. It's getting bigger every day."

"But why?" Vimbai whispered, overwhelmed with the weight of accumulated disbelief. "What is happening to us?"

"Who knows?" Maya shrugged. "Who cares? Enjoy it while you can, why don't you? There will be tons of boring shit in your life, okay? I promise."

"Okay," Vimbai sighed and followed along the path, next to a very clear and very fast brook that silvered between the trees. The path turned into a doorway Vimbai did not recognize, past a few skinned couches and a folded ladder dripping fresh white paint. Vimbai decided not to ask, since the questions were likely to yield only additional frustration instead of answers.

Maya grabbed her hand and squeezed hard. "Look, Vimbai," she said. "It doesn't matter why or how, don't you understand? Back home, girls like us, we're nothing. We work hard and make good, and sometimes someone might compliment you for it. But we don't run things; they are run by white guys and rich people. And here, now . . . we make the rules, see? It's ours. Maybe the house will grow bigger, and we'll get some milk from ShopRite and come back here. We can be queens here, queens of all we see, of crabs and ghosts and oceans. We can float like this forever, and no one will ever tell us what to do."

"What about Felix?" Vimbai said.

"What about him?"

"Nothing. Just haven't seen him in a while."

Maya shrugged and let go of Vimbai's hand with one last squeeze. "You can be the queen of Felix if you want, I don't mind."

Vimbai wished Maya would hold her hands just a bit longer. "I don't know," she said. "I mean, it sounds nice. But we're going back, you know? This feels like make-believe. A pretend world that doesn't really matter. Wouldn't you rather matter in the real world?"

"The queen of New Jersey," Maya drawled, and laughed. "Maybe."

They rounded the last outcropping of furniture and rock covered in what looked like fur, and Maya pointed at the mouth of a cave that yawned at them from between two striped signposts. "See? Can't miss it."

"Where does it lead to?" Vimbai asked.

"The hallway by Felix's room," Maya answered. "It's interesting, both Peb and I noticed it—no matter how much this house changes, the paths stay constant. So you can't get lost. Well, you could, but not really, not for long."

"You spoke to Peb," Vimbai said. Not really a question, just a statement of fact heavy with implication.

"Well, yeah. You were either staring out of the window or on the porch with your face in the water and butt in the air. What was I supposed to do?"

Vimbai shrugged, pleased that Maya was so willing to have this argument rather than dismissing Vimbai's words or denying her any demands on Maya's time and attention. "I'm just surprised. Where are your animals?"

"Roaming somewhere." Maya entered the cave, swallowed by the darkness, and only her voice reached Vimbai, strong and clear. "Funny thing how they always come when I call. I wonder now if everyone has a secret animal army."

"Then why doesn't everyone know about it?" Vimbai asked, and followed.

The cave was utterly dark, but just before Vimbai was ready to get scared and start flailing in search of a wall or anything solid, the darkness opened up before her, and she glimpsed the familiar walls with studs incompetently hidden under layers of paint, and the 'Keep Out' sign on Felix's door.

Maya waited for her in the hallway. "You'll be all right?"

Vimbai noticed that she was no longer shivering and nodded. "I'll be fine. I'm just going to go lie down for a bit."

"Okay. My dogs and me, we'll go roaming for a bit, but I'll check on you later."

"Dogs?"

Maya laughed. "I know, but I have to call them something. They act like dogs anyway."

Vimbai headed to her room, pushing aside the familiar curtain of dangling vines, bromeliads, and occasional orchids, their white roots twined like tortured fingers. It was pretty, she had to admit, and the shortcut from downstairs Maya showed her made her mind swell with possibilities. Maybe it was time to let the crabs do what they were doing…. And then she remembered the undead giants again and cringed.

Vimbai lay down on her bed, pulling her blanket over the one her grandmother wrapped her in. She squeezed her eyes shut, chasing away the gruesome images that crowded her retinas as if tattooed there. Funny, Vimbai thought; she was perfectly fine with the spirit of her dead grandmother making coffee in the kitchen and sometimes talking on the phone that was once again full of static and whispers, yet she refused to contemplate undead creatures. Spirits seemed cleaner to her, uncontaminated by rot and flesh. There was purity about the ghost, a creature of mere spirit, with its human flaws falling away, leaving the clean burning fire of the soul. The *vadzimu* was above and beyond her razorblades and her belief that politics was only relevant when it interfered with her vegetable garden.

Warmth came gradually, and Vimbai did not notice the exact moment when she no longer felt cold. She snuggled into the blankets as if they were a nest, and smiled. Tomorrow, she thought, tomorrow she would feel better and she would go roaming with Maya and her dogs, and would not think about the terror that dragged their house along, crawling across the sandy bottom on rotten broken legs. She would forget the aggressive shrubs and the hospital smell that still lingered in her room.

"Wake up, Vimbai, wake up, wake up." The voice droned as if from a great distance, and for a while it was possible for Vimbai to pretend that the voice was a part of her dream.

Then a hand shook her shoulder unceremoniously, and she opened her eyes, annoyed.

Felix's hair had grown restless since she last saw him—it reared up and guttered like flames in the wind, reached out to lap at Vimbai's pillow. One especially long and hungry tongue stretched toward her face but Felix batted it away, his hand disappearing momentarily.

Vimbai pushed herself up on her elbows and yawned widely, too tired to care. "What?" she said. "Why'd you wake me?"

"I am troubled," Felix said. "We are out of beer."

Vimbai sat up, awake now. "Are those separate statements, or are you troubled because we are out of beer?"

"Separate." Felix sighed, miserable. "Although lack of beer doesn't help."

"What's the problem?"

"There are things happening . . . up there." Felix pointed upward to his hair, in a small gesture as if afraid that the hair would notice. "I don't know what to do. There were things . . . crawling out of there, and I didn't know anything could leave there."

"What sorts of things?" Vimbai asked.

Felix shuddered. "Dead things. With legs and long spiky tails, just last night. I woke up and almost died, I swear."

Vimbai swallowed and hugged her knees to her chest to ward off the chill thrumming along her spine. "They are the ones pulling the house now. But what were they doing in your hair?"

"I dunno," Felix sobbed.

"You said your hair separates things," Vimbai said slowly.

The hypothesis was starting to form in her mind but lacked shape, and Vimbai hoped to coax it into proper expression by verbalizing it. "So there were crabs, undead ones, separated from their lives. In your hair. So I assume they crawled in there first, without you noticing."

"I was sleeping," Felix said and glared defensively, his eyes staring in opposite directions, giving him a simultaneously angry and confused look.

"They said it was too cold to go to New Jersey," Vimbai said. "Maybe they decided to become undead to get us there."

"A hell of a sacrifice," Felix said. "But . . . you were in there."

"Partially."

"And yet your soul did not leave you."

"I know," Vimbai said. A thought skimmed at the edge of her consciousness, too fast to grasp properly. "Say, do you know anything about man-fish? *Njuzu*?"

"No," Felix said. "What's that?"

"It's a Zimbabwean urban legend," Vimbai answered. "It's a fish who swallows the souls of the drowned, and then it itself becomes sort of human. Like it can talk and stuff."

"You thinking it might work with crabs?"

"I don't know," Vimbai said. "Only my grandmother was talking about man-fish, and then I dreamed that I was one. And then Maya's pets are afraid of fish."

"And then there's the house that attracts ghosts."

"And your hair."

They sat a while, puzzling, unable to tease any sense from the conglomeration of occurrences and half-baked ideas. That was the trouble with the supernatural, Vimbai thought—you didn't know what laws ruled it, and what was a coincidence and what was a sign and what was weird and what wasn't. It was like a whodunit, only the clues refused to be arranged into any sort of hierarchy or a straight narrative, and most of the time it wasn't even clear if they indeed were clues; a jigsaw puzzle where all the pieces were blank.

Felix's mind was apparently on the same track. "It's like life," he said. "I just don't know what matters and what doesn't and what I should pay attention to. But these crabs, they were just creepy."

"They are victims," Vimbai said, although she was not so sure about the undead variety. "They . . . they are killed and bled half to death, and thrown back in the ocean. And it's not just about them—so many birds feed on their eggs, and without feeding they cannot migrate. They would die without the crabs—these crabs carry so much on their backs."

Felix nodded. "Is this why you're studying them?"

"Uh-huh," Vimbai said. "And because they are so ancient . . . and we can kill something so ancient, so irreplaceable. It's just wrong, you know?"

"I didn't see it as a moral issue."

"All conservation is a moral issue," Vimbai said, and thought of her grandmother downstairs. "Be it animals or people or cultures. Some things are just . . . unique, and if you lose them, you can never get them back."

Felix touched his hair, cautiously. "I think this thing is unique."

"Probably," Vimbai agreed. "God, I hope so."

"You want to look inside again?"

Vimbai shrugged. "Maybe. Why don't you take Balshazaar out and ask him if he saw any crabs or if he knows anything?"

Felix slumped. "I knew he would tell you," he said. "I shouldn't have taken him out, only you have to understand. What, you think it's easy living with this thing?"

"I don't know," Vimbai said. "What is it like, and where did it come from?"

"It was a long time ago, sister," Felix said. "I don't even know what I remember and what I imagined. Does it matter?"

"I don't know. Listen, if you want to talk, maybe we should go for a walk or something. You can show me around."

"I haven't seen much myself," Felix answered. "But there is a place that's sort of nice. I'll wait for you outside."

Vimbai waited for the door to close behind Felix, and got dressed. She really needed to get some laundry done, and she quickly gave up on finding matching socks. One white and one striped, it didn't matter. Thankfully, t-shirts and shorts were abundant.

Felix led her down the hallway and into a closet that abruptly transitioned into a view of a desert, with a lake in the middle of it. The sand surrounding it was red and dry like Kalahari, apparently unaware of the abundance of clear, cold water in its midst. The sun was getting warm, and Felix offered Vimbai a handkerchief to cover her hair; she accepted with a muttered thanks.

A couple of lawn chairs reclined by the bank, surrounded by a sparse growth of dried up grasses and papier-mâché trees, tall enough to reach Vimbai's knee.

"Maya doesn't come here," Felix said. "There's fish in this lake."

"What kind?"

"Take a seat and you'll see."

Vimbai did, and Felix took the other chair. They sat in silence, watching the smooth surface of the lake, gray and reflective like mercury, until there was a loud splash and a fish came bounding out of the water and into the air. It somersaulted and entered the water. Vimbai did not need a second look to confirm what she knew from the moment Felix mentioned Maya—it was a catfish, and a large one at that.

As they watched, the catfish stuck its flat head out of the water and gave them a narrow-eyed, jaundiced look. "You have a tasty soul," it said to Vimbai, and leered.

Chapter 8

BACK IN HER ROOM, VIMBAI COULD NOT CALM DOWN HER heart. She was too disturbed to be really embarrassed about running away from a fish, and only a small measure of her discomfort resulted from her recent show of cowardice. Not that Felix cared—he seemed to have fears of his own, fears of undead things that somehow crawled into his hair and separated their bodies from their mortality. That was enough to make anyone nervous.

They sat on Vimbai's bed, like scared children, and occasionally one or the other would steal a quick look at the door, as if the catfish would somehow follow them here. It was silly, of course, Vimbai told herself, just like it was silly of her to shower with her eyes open for weeks after seeing a horror flick. But some things were just not subject to rational reasoning, and recently that particular mode of relating to the world had been taking one hit after another.

"We have to talk to Balshazaar," Felix said. "I have to know what he'd seen. Only I don't think I should take him out again."

"Why not?" Vimbai breathed a nervous laugh. "He'll fit right in with the psychic energy baby and the undead crabs."

Felix winced. "Don't remind me," he said, and stood up.

Vimbai watched him pace from door to the window, until

he noticed the phantom limb he'd given Vimbai the same day Peb joined them.

He smiled. "You still have this thing."

"What else would I do with it?"

"Give it to Peb."

"I like it," Vimbai said. " And Peb has plenty already. It seems so . . . delicate." The limb indeed resembled a work of art with its translucent veins and milky nerves twisting below the glassy skin like tree branches.

"Take it with you when you go talk to Balshazaar," Felix said. "If you convince him to come out, maybe he can use it to get around."

Vimbai raised her eyebrows. "Somehow you bypassed the point where I agreed to look back there. Besides, you just said that it wasn't a good idea to take him out."

"I don't know." Felix stopped pacing, his eyes simultaneously expressing great consternation in opposite directions. "Maybe you could look inside and see if there are still any crabs left there. I'm afraid . . . afraid to put my hand in there."

"So you want me to risk my face."

"You at least can see."

"What if it takes my soul?"

"It didn't before."

Vimbai thought that after jumping blind into a cold ocean she really ought to know better. Instead she sighed and carefully eased her head inside Felix's hair.

Balshazaar was there, floating vaguely as was his wont. "Hello again," he said.

"Balshazaar," Vimbai said. "Have you seen any horseshoe crabs around?"

"Sure did." Balshazaar bobbed, his chin pointing to his left.

It took Vimbai's eyes a moment to get used to the dusk in Felix's hair, and she saw several small translucent crabs that clung together in a tight cluster. The souls or lives or whatever it was they shed like old carapaces and left behind, just so they could take Vimbai back home. Acute pity made her catch her breath and whisper, "I'm sorry" to the crabs. They remained motionless, devoid of any spark that would indicate that they could hear and understand her.

"Balshazaar," Vimbai continued. "Would you help us? There are things happening we don't quite understand, and since you had a chance to observe the happenings here, perhaps you could explain them to us. Figure out what's going on."

"What's in it for me?"

"A leg," Vimbai said. "A phantom leg, but it is nonetheless functional."

"Interesting," Balshazaar drawled. "Why so nice?"

Vimbai considered telling him that she was usually nice, but instead settled for a reason he was more likely to believe. "We need you."

"I'll help you," Balshazaar said. "Only I'm not sure if I even want to leave here—it's nice. Secure. Bring the leg and then ask your questions. However, know that I promise nothing."

Vimbai extricated herself from the pocket universe, and reported on what she had seen. At the mention of the horseshoe crabs' souls, Felix made a small sound of terror.

"It's all right," Vimbai said. "They are not doing anything. And they are much smaller and a lot less scary than the ones that crawled out."

Felix shook his head and the long tongues of his hair stretched and contracted, reminding Vimbai of the way leeches moved—she had observed them in her invertebrate zoology class, and was endlessly fascinated by how they managed to grow long and thin one moment, and short and stout the next.

"I'll give him the leg," Vimbai decided, "and ask him about what else he saw. And what he knows about fish."

"Not yet," Felix answered. "Let me think about that. I'm not sure I really believe him."

AND SO VIMBAI WAS LEFT ALONE AGAIN, WHILE FELIX RETIRED to his room to do his thinking. He puzzled her—his inability to make up his mind and his frank terror at the things living in his hair surprised and bothered Vimbai. He should've had enough time to come to terms with it, she thought, especially since he had been so nonchalant about extricating the Psychic Energy Baby from the phone wires. It took her a while to realize that he never got around to telling her about how he came to wear a personal-sized black hole around his head. Then again, men were good at avoiding questions.

She remembered how excited her mother had been when they traveled to Harare—especially excited to see her favorite nephew and Vimbai's cousin Roger. Roger seemed to be one of those kids who were so great one could never hope to compare to them—and Vimbai resented Roger before she even met him, even though he was not a kid anymore, but already a grown man, with a wife and intentions of starting his own business. Vimbai's mother talked to him on the phone for hours, making plans, and phone bills be damned.

When they had arrived, Roger was not home—he was not in Harare at all. The relatives said that he was on vacation, but by their sidelong glances and uncomfortable shuffling, Vimbai surmised that the vacation was a polite lie. Roger's wife had stayed home, and nobody seemed to know anything about his destination. Vimbai's mother did not believe the excuses either—she became thin-lipped and taciturn, and did not again mention Roger until they went back home.

It was two years later that Vimbai and Roger finally met. Roger had started his business—something to do with laptops or some other technology Vimbai had only pragmatic interest in, and he traveled to the US under some business pretense or other. In truth, they all knew that he wanted to see Vimbai's mother who was never good about hiding her disappointments—they came through even in long-distance phone calls.

Roger arrived on schedule, and quickly filled the house with his laugh that seemed to be coming directly from his diaphragm and his expansive gestures. He was smaller than Vimbai expected, and sadder—when he thought that no one was watching him. He did not have to apologize—he only hugged Vimbai's mother until she cried and hugged him back. Roger said, "I'm sorry, Auntie," and that was that.

But not as far as Vimbai was concerned. Roger was difficult not to like but she persevered, helped by the eternal teenage sullenness. She watched him across the table, her arms crossed in front of her with disapproval. For all his laughing and joking and telling stories and flashing pictures of his baby son, he noticed.

"What's the matter, Vimbai, cousin?" he asked her one day. Normally, Vimbai would've avoided a direct confrontation, but he caught up with her as she exited the bathroom, and there was simply no missing each other in the narrow hallway. "Did I do something to tick you off?"

"You blew off my mom when we went to Harare," Vimbai said.

He whistled. "That was a long time ago, *muroora*," he said. "You don't forget, do you? Take after your mom."

"Where were you then?" Vimbai said. "Just don't say vacation, or I'll have to slap you."

He laughed unexpectedly. "Why do you care so much?"

"You should've seen her face," Vimbai said. "She really missed you then, and you weren't there. She cried every night."

"That did not necessarily have anything to do with me," Roger said and frowned. It was strange to see him in their suburban wallpapered hallway, blue cornflowers on white background.

"Still." Vimbai leaned against the wall, her shoulder pushing against the familiar solidity of the wall. "Tell me."

"And you'll forgive me."

"Depends."

"No." He shook his finger with emphasis. "You forgive your cousin, okay? And then I'll show you."

She shrugged. "Okay. What did you want to show me?"

He turned his back to her, and Vimbai thought that he was about to head back to his room to bring some evidence—pictures or flowers or whatever to make it all right. Instead, Roger carefully eased the hem of his white shirt from his belt, partially obscured by his nascent love handles, and pulled it up.

Vimbai stared at the very white and very straight scar that slashed diagonally across the left half of his lower back. At first, she thought that it was a particularly vicious *muti* mark, or some other creepy magic her grandmother believed in and that required mutilation. "What is it?" she said.

"A scar." Roger lowered his shirt and turned to face her, blushing. "You're such a curious little cousin, and I just met you and you already asking me questions my wife wouldn't ask me."

"Maybe she should. What is it?"

He sighed. "I needed money to start my business. Twenty thousand dollars—where would I get that?"

"It's a lot of money," Vimbai said. Especially in Africa, she thought. That was a fortune enough to propel one forward in life, not just pay off student loans or credit card bills.

"Yes. So I sold a kidney."

She stared into his face looking for traces of jocularity, but he was serious, and the scar real. She felt herself blush. "I'm sorry I was a bitch to you, Roger," she said.

He waved his hand in the air. "Don't mention it, sister. And don't tell your mom. Believe me, some things only you want to know."

———

VIMBAI HAD TO AGREE AS SHE REMEMBERED THIS conversation. She seemed to have a talent of getting hung up on questions everyone around her circumvented so smoothly—if people were leaves floating on the river surface, Vimbai would be the one that always got stuck against every obstacle, no matter how trivial and easy to bypass.

And now something else was nagging at her. She thought of the man-fish and how he manifested as soon as Vimbai dreamt him; then there was the *vadzimu*, who appeared when Vimbai imagined her as an entity that kept her and her mother so much apart. Now, the memory of Roger worried at her heart in the same way. What did it mean? she asked herself. Why did Felix's reluctance to speak remind her of her cousin?

The scar. That was it, the way Roger hid his scar and its origin. Vimbai jumped to her feet and rushed to Felix's room.

He was there, doing nothing, and only looked vaguely up when Vimbai came busting through the door.

"It's a scar, isn't it?" Vimbai said.

"Yes," he said, paling.

How does a man become a scar, or at any rate end up wearing one around his head? Only Felix knew, what it was like to cut an umbilicus that bound one to the universe that bore him, and to wear the spectral navel that still festered with the remnants of the enclosed space and its dark inhabitants. A dying tiny universe, and poor Felix dangled on the end of it, like a superfluous appendage.

And unlike the Psychic Energy Baby, he could never hope to disentangle himself from the wires that kept him suspended, the appearance of him standing on the ground a mere illusion. Still, he managed a small unconvincing smile. "I didn't know how to tell you or Maya. Or even what to tell you. And I still don't understand how the two of you play into it—you're dragging all those ghosts with you. And her, I don't even know."

"I'm dragging everything with me," Vimbai answered. "Even Africa—only it's not my parents' Africa, it's an imaginary one."

"What is Maya dragging?"

Vimbai shrugged. There were the half-foxes, of course, and there was the wild streak, the talk of being queens of some imaginary kingdom, be it New Jersey or somewhere else. For the first time, Vimbai thought that it might not be a bad idea—perhaps Maya was the expression of their purpose, the reason for them being here, at sea, floating somewhere . . . or perhaps standing still. Or perhaps the house stood still as the world moved under it, offering its watery and glistening curving back as they slid inexplicably toward some destiny, some mystical version of New Jersey.

The house . . . Vimbai gasped a little and sat down on Felix's unmade bed. "All of us," she said. "It's the three of us—your blind universe and my ghosts and Maya's dogs. We did it to the house."

"I assumed as much," Felix agreed. "So what?"

"So maybe we can control it," Vimbai said. "Maybe we can make it into something we want."

"Like what?" Felix asked, perking up.

"I don't know." Vimbai thought of the curdled milk in Maya's coffee and wrinkled her nose. "ShopRite, for starters. Or Farmers' Market, whatever. Something that sells food and milk. I'm really sick of canned ravioli."

"Me too," Felix agreed. He seemed quite eager to divert the conversation to a topic other than himself and his hair. Poor boy, dangled from some impossible hole like a piece of bait on a hook. "How do we make things happen?"

"I have no idea," Vimbai said. "Think of them really hard?"

"Okay," Felix said. "Here, or do you want to go somewhere else?"

"Somewhere else," Vimbai said. "Let's go to the porch."

There, they sat cross-legged, their backs hunched, bracing against the cutting wind that rose from the ice-cold water, slashing their faces like steel cables. Vimbai crossed her arms in front of her chest and stuffed her hands, numb already, into her armpits. She closed her eyes, and for a moment concentrated on feeling Felix next to her, his warm breathing present, so touchingly and surprisingly human.

There was a creaking of the steps and a soft jangle of the screen door.

"What are you doing?" Maya asked. Her foxes sniffed at Vimbai and circumvented Felix in a wide arc. "Can I help?"

"Sure," Felix said. "We're trying to make the house do what we tell it."

"What are you telling it?" Maya sat next to Vimbai, her warm elbow jostling against Vimbai's.

"To make us a ShopRite. We decided that we've changed the house, so might as well try to direct it."

Maya shrugged. "Makes sense."

The three of them sat in silence. Vimbai squeezed her eyes shut and felt her forehead furrow as she imagined the cool aisles of a supermarket, shelves upon shelves, a solid white front of gallon milk jugs and white gleaming egg cartoons. Boxes of butter and cream cheese, bagels stuffed neatly into plastic bags. Thick slabs of meat in their little Styrofoam coffins, yellow cheese, red apples. All of it.

And she pictured her mother, frowning at the row of canned beans. "These are all the same thing," she told Vimbai with irritation. "Same beans. All that's different is a picture on the can."

And Vimbai herself, scowling back, longing to go home. "Come on, mama. These are just brands—you know it."

Her mother rolled her eyes and tossed a few cans into the cart, not even looking at which ones she picked. "Today at the department someone asked me about culture shock, and if I was overwhelmed with choices when I first came here. Americans, they always expect us to be overwhelmed with food."

"I'm an American," Vimbai mumbled and followed the cart and her mother's receding back miserably.

"It's not what I meant. You know that it makes no difference how many different pictures you put on green beans—they are still the same green beans inside. It's an illusion of opulence they expect us to be impressed by and indulge in."

"It doesn't matter," Vimbai had said. "People are just curious, you know? It wouldn't hurt you to be nice once in a while."

"After fifteen years of answering the same questions, my niceness and my patience are almost gone," mother said.

"It's not a big deal," Vimbai said. She wanted to add, "Lighten up," but thought better of it. Nothing brought quicker and more thunderous retribution upon her head than suggestions that her mother should lighten up or relax.

She opened her eyes to the sight of the leaden ocean. It was beginning to snow, and heavy viscous waves swallowed up the snowflakes as soon as they touched water. Why did her mother always have to insinuate herself into Vimbai's daydreams? She did not want a replica of her—*Solaris* had scared her half to death when she first read it, and the thought of an intelligent needy fake with her mother's personality was too terrifying to contemplate for any length of time. She just wanted a gallon of milk and some fresh fruit. And yet, her mother hovered on the inside of her eyelids, insubstantial but persistent, her narrow face wearing its habitual expression of grim readiness to pounce every time a perceived slight occurred.

Vimbai's mother remained in her heart forever, her bitterness as familiar as the smell of coffee in the morning. She wasn't always like this, Vimbai reminded herself—there were times when she was happy and carefree, and laughed easily. There were times when her parents whispered and giggled like guilty children, and no matter how old Vimbai was, these times always made her feel like the rift between her and her parents simply disappeared, leaving no trace, no scar.

But Vimbai had to make an effort to remember the happy times—she often wondered if this was a defect in her, or if it was something common to all people, this reflexive dwelling on the anger and the distance, on all the times where her mother and she squared off and argued in circles, as Vimbai's gentle father sighed and tried to ask them be nice to each other; how desperately he tried to smooth the wrinkles that creased the surface of the life he would like to have, disfiguring it. Vimbai felt guilty for not thinking about him often enough, for focusing so much on her mother and the many ways in which she made Vimbai angry.

"Are you thinking about ShopRite?" Maya asked, jostling Vimbai back to the freezing porch and the cold waves, to the hidden horrors under the deep, deep water.

"Kind of," Vimbai answered, and dutifully imagined the beading of condensation on the sides of milk jugs and the doors of walk-in freezers fogged by breath, hiding stacks of frozen pizza boxes and foil packets of cauliflower and chopped spinach.

"Should we check on how it's going?" Felix said. "I'm cold."

Maya stood and stretched, her dogs following her lead as one. "I suppose, I only wish we knew where to check."

"Huh," Felix said, and stood too, shivering. "This house is very big."

"Can't your dogs sniff it out?" Vimbai said. "They have to be good for something."

Maya ignored the implied insult, and laughed. "A good idea, only they don't know what a supermarket smells like.

I guess we'll just have to go look. Come along, Vimbai." She grabbed Vimbai's arm and pulled her to her feet. "You are just not content with hypothermia, are you? You want to add pneumonia to the list?"

"Or pleurisy," Vimbai mumbled, and followed Maya and Felix inside. "Maybe I like the cold."

They bade the *chipoko* and Peb to hold down the fort in the kitchen, and set out on a search for a supermarket, through the pantry and across a narrow jungle strip. Vimbai contemplated the mountains off in the distance, and did not bother to try and figure out how they fit inside the house.

Chapter 9

VIMBAI HAD TO ADMIT THAT THERE WAS CERTAIN FUN IN discovering a new world and getting to name everything. Thankfully, Felix was content with his stub of a universe, and did not presume to offer names. But Vimbai and Maya, oh how they argued. Martin Luther King Forest was not a problem, and Malcolm X Mountains had a ring to it; Vimbai insisted that the lake with the catfish (which they wisely circumvented, not yet ready to deal with the cunning adversary) had to be named after Marechera, and the thin gurgling brook that flowed from the lake and then roared to magnificence somewhere down at the basement was fit to maintain a literary kick—Achebe River it was, even though it was no Niger. They argued about whether a plain covered in nettles and rusted bed frames was impressive enough to name, and if so—whom would it belong to.

"You can just call it the Bedframe Valley," Felix suggested. "Or think about it later—now, I want to keep going."

"Fine with me," Maya said. "But the next thing will be named after Oprah."

Vimbai snorted. "No way. Wangari Maathai is next. Surely, a Nobel laureate is more important than Oprah?"

"And I want more literary tributes," Maya said. "How about Octavia Butler?"

"All right," Vimbai agreed. "And after that—Tutuola and Fay King Chung."

"Who's that?" Maya asked, and whistled for her dogs to get back as they chased something up a steep pebbled ridge. "I mean, the second one."

"Zimbabwe's former minister of education and culture," Vimbai said. "My mom says, she is Chinese, and in Rhodesia she could get an education and black people couldn't. And she wrote children's books."

"Good enough for me," Maya said.

Vimbai thought how happy would her mother be to visit the house—the only country in the world where not a single pebble was named after a white guy.

"Your mom misses Zimbabwe?" Maya asked.

"Yeah." Vimbai thought a bit about how to put it into words. "It's hard for her. She was a historian back home, she knew all there is to know about Zimbabwe folk traditions, and here she teaches Africana Studies."

"It's important," Maya said.

"And yet it's not the only thing she could do, but it is the only job they had for her. So it's hard, you know? There's tension between the faculty, who are all black, and the department chair who's white."

Maya rolled her eyes. "Figures."

"And Africans and African-Americans." Vimbai heaved a sigh. "The whole voluntary immigration thing."

Maya nodded that she understood and they walked in silence, pebbles and dry leaves crunching underfoot. The whole experience did not quite feel real—Vimbai noticed the especially artificial quality of the landscapes inside the house. Sure, there was a sun and a semblance of sky—at least, if she did not look too closely; if she did, the light fixtures and the whitewash of the ceiling became apparent, as if peeking through the illusion of the natural phenomenon. No, it was something more fundamental, and it took her a while to puzzle out that this quality was due to the absence of smell. She could smell neither water nor knee-high grass, only indeterminate stale and warm odor, like a pillow freshly slept on.

She was about to share her observation with Maya, when Maya pointed to their right.

"Look!" Maya said.

Something gleamed at a distance, just over the spiny ridge made of some unfamiliar rock layered like slate, baby cribs, and a tangle of steel cables, and they hurried up the slope. Vimbai breathed deeply, trying to taste something in the air, anything but the dull stale smell of the old house. The gleaming behind the ridge grew brighter and higher, as if there was a sun hiding behind the jumble of rock and the discarded trash. It spilled over the ridge, casting a hazy halo, and reflecting off the metal guardrails of the broken cribs. Vimbai would've thought that they were in a landfill at sunset, if it weren't for the cursed absence of smell.

Maya hurried ahead and stopped as she crested the ridge. She was cast in silhouette against the golden light, and Vimbai felt her breath catch—there was such beauty in the outline of her roommate, such elegant simplicity in the cast of her shoulders, the set of her chin. Such strength and confidence in her legs and feet planted slightly apart; she was an explorer surveying the new land opening in the water gap, a discoverer of unknown lands and landmarks, the namer of things. Her dogs crowded around her, their black shapes filled with a quiet dignity their usual selves woefully lacked. Vimbai, enchanted, wanted neither to move nor look away.

Maya turned, tossing her hair over her shoulder. "Coming, Vimbai?"

"Yeah," Vimbai said, and reluctantly moved up the slope, into the bright light. "What is it?"

"See for yourself," Maya said.

Vimbai hurried ahead, now that Felix also reached the crest and stood quietly staring down; Vimbai could not see whether he was impressed or awed, or merely waited for Vimbai to catch up to them and share in the view.

She stepped onto the crest, wobbly under her feet, shifting with all the inclusions of broken handles and rolled up spools of cable. She looked down and cried out in surprise and wonder.

The light they'd seen came from the second sun hovering over the rooftops, as if it were about to set, but it never quite dipped below the line of buildings. But it wasn't the houses that drew Vimbai's attention—it was a line of trees covered in blue and purple blooms, blue fire flickering around the branches but never consuming them, the pure ferocity of jacaranda trees in bloom. Even though Vimbai had not seen them for herself, the memory she shared with her grandmother and her mother's stories left no doubt in her mind.

Yet, as she looked at the buildings, she decided that it was not Harare—at least, not the one she remembered.

Town homes from the richer parts of the city mingled with traditional round huts one could still find in the provinces, and suburban New Jerseyan Cape Cods and bungalows. It was Harare of Vimbai's dreams which jumbled things she did not quite remember with those she knew well. These were the streets she sometimes drove in her very first car, a Geo her parents got her, she suspected, as a joke; she drove along them in her dreams, frustrated that she was unable to find home and that all the streets led in random directions, never intersecting in any satisfactory way. The city where she and her mother never fought, and friends and relatives from New Jersey and Zimbabwe dropped by without any rhyme or reason, and dead grandparents were alive and spoke English and told Vimbai they loved her . . . just like the *vadzimu* did.

Vimbai rubbed her face. *Oh, my jacaranda trees,* she thought. *Oh how I missed you and yet I cannot smell your sweet blooms, I cannot feel your breath on my face.* The trees and the flowers and the buildings shifted and multiplied, and rotated and blurred, then swam into focus again like beautiful images in a kaleidoscope. She realized then it was tears that twisted and purified her vision.

Maya touched her shoulder—such a habitual gesture by now, the curve of Vimbai's shoulder felt like it was shaped by Maya's hand to fit into it, just like by her mother's hand before. "What's wrong?"

Vimbai looked up, into Maya's worried face and Felix's eye rotating away and then toward her, like a possessed bloodied apple. "It's nothing," she said. "This city . . . this is Harare, but not really. This is my dream Harare . . . in the Africa of the spirit."

Maya smiled then. "This is it," she said. "This house doesn't become what we ask of it. It's what we dream about—it's our dreams that shape it, not us."

Without saying a further word, Maya started the perilous descent down the crumbling precipitous slope. Felix and Vimbai followed, slipping and trotting awkwardly at times, sliding among the small avalanches of pebbles and refuse. Their feet left deep troughs as they descended, and already Vimbai was worrying about how they would get back up this steep slope.

She forgot all about it when she stood in the street, her heart sinking. From the distance, the place had seemed alive and real enough, but once inside she could not help but feel that she had wandered into a movie set—there were no people, and the houses seemed mere cardboard facades, and a single push would bring the entire street tumbling down. But the trees seemed real enough, and she reached up and touched a knotted branch, leaves like green spearheads, with bright stars of flowers clustered among them. With the slightest of pulls, the branch came off, and Vimbai cringed expecting this violation to dispel the mirage under the forever setting sun.

"It's so pretty," Maya said, and picked a branch too. "To bad I can't smell anything."

"It's not you; it's this place," Vimbai said. "Listen, if this is where our dreams go . . . what's with the dogs?"

"A Freudian nightmare," Felix volunteered.

"Hush, silly boy," Maya said. "I do dream of all sorts of

creatures, you know. About being a queen of animals. I always wanted to work at the Philadelphia Zoo." She said nothing else, but Vimbai could feel the sting in Maya's words all the same—the acute hurt of someone who wanted to work in a zoo and instead served drinks at a casino. Life really had to work on having fewer discrepancies like this, Vimbai thought. And here they all were, surrounded by the ghosts of the dreams they gave up. Maya's foxes-possums howled a bit and wagged their tails, and their beats resonated on the dry ground.

They did not find the supermarket or anything that would provide any variety in their menu. Instead, they collected great armfuls of blue flowers—Vimbai thought that the vadzimu would enjoy them, since she seemed as fond of these trees as Vimbai's mother. And Vimbai herself felt deep gratitude that she was finally able to see them for herself, however distorted they were by her dream-memory, blue-purple, ice-cold. However devoid of scent.

THE *CHIPOKO* WAS PLEASED WITH THE FLOWERS, AND AS Vimbai told her about the dream Harare they had found, the ghost nodded along, her hooded eyes lowered to the opulence of flowers in her arms—so thin, so wrinkled. Vimbai piled the branches higher and the ghost held them like one would a child.

Peb hovered nearby, whispering of supernovas, but seemed drawn to the flowers. The ghost of Vimbai's grandmother noticed too, and gave Peb a branch, which he immediately absorbed. His transparent hide grew suffused with the gentle purplish-blue color, and the twisted twigs of the branch poked out of his back like a grotesque fin. Vimbai did not question his need to incorporate everything that appealed to him, like she never questioned her grandmother's attachment to jacaranda trees and her ability to possess Vimbai's body.

"Maya thinks we're dreaming this house," Vimbai informed the *vadzimu* as soon as the old woman was able to tear her gaze away from the flowers. "Do you think we are dreaming it?"

"Some dreams you leave behind," the *vadzimu* answered, her voice especially old and desiccated today. "Some dreams you discard along your way, like your baby clothes. They litter your past, like small corpses, like shed skins."

Vimbai nodded, thinking, listening to the bubbling of the kettle on the stove—the *vadzimu* did not approve of the whistle, and wrenched it free from the kettle's nozzle, like a pacifier from the lips of a recalcitrant infant. The dead air and the strange apparition, the taste of longing and dust settling over everything, testified to the veracity of the ghost's words, and Vimbai felt like crying as she thought of the expanse the three of them had created and populated with sad little remnants of themselves. And it was so hard to decipher sometimes—was the man-fish Vimbai's or Maya's? Had the cribs comprising the ridge they named after Fay King Chung sifted out of Felix's dead universe, or were they Maya's forgotten memories? It was impossible to tell sometimes.

"Have something warm to drink," grandmother said. "It's getting chilly."

Vimbai poured herself a cup of boiling water, sweetened it with a spoonful of sugar (there was still plenty), added a drop of lemon from a bright yellow squeeze bottle (getting low), and headed to the porch. She had no desire to see the undead horseshoe crabs or their underwater secrets, she just wanted to be away for a while, separate from the crushed hopes that sprawled everywhere and filled the house to near bursting.

She stared into the horizon, gray sky welded to gray ocean, with barely a shadow to separate the two. Vimbai imagined what it would be like, to see a passing ship in the distance; to notice a darkening of the horizon that would then grow into a humped shape, and to yell, "Land ahoy!" To see a bird—an albatross, perhaps, or a seagull—circling above. But the ocean remained as quiet and lifeless as the house, and Vimbai suspected (without verbalizing it, because it would be too painful) that it was not the real ocean but a product of the house, its sick effluvium. And yet, and yet . . . she smelled the salt in the air and the sharp sting of iodine, of crushed seaweed, and she hoped. She hoped that the horizon would split open and finally admit a welcome sight—a sandy beach with humped dunes in the background, boardwalks bleached by wind and salt into a gray weightlessness of driftwood, and a tall figure, her neck craning, her head tilted back to see better. *Come home, baby, come back home. We miss you and we forgive you and we promise that everything will be all right, we promise.*

I'm coming mama, I'm coming back, Vimbai thought but did not dare to whisper. In her mind, the small figure on the beach grew more distant, retreating, until there was nothing but the sky and the heavy sluicing of cold waves.

———

FELIX FINALLY DECIDED TO LET BALSHAZAAR OUT, TO LET him roam around the house—it didn't seem fair, to keep him all alone among the silent souls of the horseshoe crabs; besides, the universe that had been growing and mutating around them did not really seem all that different from the one Balshazaar currently inhabited.

"I think," Felix told Vimbai and Maya at dinner, "it's like letting him from one dream into another. If it were a real world, that would be a different story."

"What is the real world?" Maya said, and gave a cock-eyed look to her fork and the anemic piece of ravioli impaled on it, drizzles of tomato sauce like blood. "But whatever; I don't suppose it would alter things in any way."

"Famous last words," Vimbai mumbled, but did not argue further.

"It's settled then." Felix beamed. "I sort of felt bad about keeping him there after I showed him the world . . . at least if he did not know what was outside, it wouldn't matter."

"Can't miss what you don't know about," the *vadzimu* said.

Vimbai shivered—her mother spoke in these words, her stern intonations bleeding through. "You can't show people the western lifestyle and expect them not to want," she would say. "It's cruel, to show and to lie like this—in a hundred years, people in the rest of the world won't be able to live like we do, but they will want it even more. Greed and jealousy, that's the problem with cultural imperialism."

Another speech Vimbai knew by heart, another one of her daily conundrums where disagreeing would be monstrous but agreeing unbearable.

"Peb," Vimbai said out loud. "Would you mind fetching the phantom leg from my room? Just don't take it—it's for someone else."

Peb rose like fog from the *vadzimu*'s back where it was clinging, blue and smoky like a Picasso painting. For some reason, Vimbai wanted to show him Guernica, and see what he thought of it, if he liked the blind eyes of the little girl who seemed oblivious to the limp hand cradling her. Peb nodded and floated away, like mist, like smoke, like an elusive fish skittering and disappearing in the thick of water.

When Peb returned with the leg, he and the *vadzimu* watched with a mix of curiosity and, Vimbai suspected, a trace of jealousy. Peb had relinquished the phantom leg with a quiet sigh, and now the leg stood on the kitchen counter, perfect and smooth like blown glass. Maya sat back, her arms crossed, her plate bearing an arabesque of tomato sauce forgotten in front of her. She frowned slightly, and her front teeth bit her lower lip.

Felix dug through his hair two-handed. A few times his face twitched into a grimace, and Vimbai guessed that he was touching the horseshoe crabs' little immobile souls. Finally, he gave a small cry of triumph and pulled out the desiccated head.

Balshazaar looked around him, and smiled when his eyes met Vimbai's. "Good seeing you again," he said.

"Hi," Maya interjected, still frowning. "I'm Maya."

Balshazaar was introduced in turn to the *vadzimu* and Peb, and Vimbai thought that he seemed quite unperturbed by the new environment. Perhaps Felix had shown him more than he told Vimbai, or perhaps he could see from the inside of his hair somehow. She chased the thought away as silly—she had seen the inside of Felix's hair, isolated from the rest of the world by inky blackness.

The phantom leg took to Balshazaar, despite the yipping and growling of Maya's dogs—they cowered away from the pruned face perched atop of the transparent leg, which was growing clouded, as if diseased by the contact with alien and dead flesh.

Balshazaar wobbled and made an awkward hop on the kitchen counter, knocking over an empty ravioli can.

"How does it feel?" Vimbai asked him.

"Fine, fine," Balshazaar answered, his thin scarred lips shaping a slow smile. "Will take a bit of getting used to, but I'll manage."

They watched him hop and bounce along the countertop, then jump down to the floor. He traversed the kitchen from the counter to the screen door, and from the screen door to the pantry. He then disappeared inside—presumably, to investigate the rest of the house.

"He'll be back," Felix said, and gave Vimbai a hopeful look from his right eye. "Won't he?"

"I'm sure he will," Maya said. She sounded as though unsure if that was a good thing. "You realize that now real people are in a minority, right?"

"Depends on what you mean by 'minority,'" Vimbai

answered, and shot an apologetic look to the *vadzimu*. "She is my grandmother."

"She's a ghost," Maya corrected.

"Ghosts can be vengeful," Vimbai said.

Maya shrugged. "Should we go look for a supermarket again? Or if you want, there's a new forest by the attic. We could go name it, and see if anything cool lives there."

"In the morning," Vimbai said. "I want to check on the crabs."

"I'll come with you," Maya said.

They sat on the porch for a while. Vimbai looked underwater, her grandmother's sight letting her see the creatures as if they were close by. When she came up for air, she shook the water out of her hair. "I'm not supposed to see them," she said. "And yet I'm supposed to keep them alive somehow."

"While they are undead," Maya said.

"It's temporary, I think," Vimbai said. "They left their souls in Felix's hair."

Maya laughed, the sound resonating far over the ocean. "I can't believe this sentence makes sense to us. That there would be a world in which it's normal shit to say, you know?"

"I know," Vimbai said. "In any case, I suppose they are safe. They will get us home, I have no doubt of that." She did.

"Yeah," Maya said. She sidled up to Vimbai and dangled her feet in the ocean despite the cutting cold and darkness. "Provided we want to go home."

"Sure we do," Vimbai said. "We'll still have the house, you know? If our dreams are changing it, then there's no reason for it to change back once we're in New Jersey."

"Perhaps we cannot dream as well in New Jersey." Maya pulled her feet up and rubbed them with her feet. "The water's freezing. I better go get a pair of socks."

"I'm going to bed," Vimbai said. "I'm tired. And it is hard to look under water, even with my grandmother helping me." She could not quite describe the heartbreak, the dull sickness in her stomach when she saw the creatures covered now with a thick mat of barnacles, hagfishes sliming through the cracks in their carapaces. But their legs kept moving, always moving, like the long restless fingers of a sickly pianist.

"Okay," Maya said and squeezed her arm. "Dream us something nice for tomorrow, will ya?"

Chapter 10

OBEDIENT, VIMBAI DREAMT. HER DREAMS WERE VIVID—
more vivid, it seemed, than the waking landscapes inside the
house. She dreamt of smells and sounds, of saturated solid
planes of color. She dreamt of Africa as she had half-remem-
bered it from her trip, half-imagined from the coloring books
her mother bought her, and then got upset when Vimbai
colored children on the pages pink instead of brown. These
books had lions and vast open plains Vimbai colored rust
orange and brick-red, blue oceans populated by smiling
whales (green polka dot) and their fountains (yellow, like the
champagne her parents drank on special occasions).

Now Vimbai dreamed of a rust-colored savannah, with
green umbrellas of acacias scattered at a distance. Two plush
giraffes grazed among the leaves, their long and unrealisti-
cally pink tongues twining and snaking between black thorns
shining like volcanic glass. A stuffed lion slumped in the
shade, inanimate at the moment, and it did not even stir when
Vimbai passed right by it.

There was a lake on the horizon, a smooth blue mirror, but
Vimbai was weary of fresh water rife with catfish. Instead she
headed for a group of gigantic stones—she guessed them for
the Great Zimbabwe, the ruins that gave her country their
name, even though they seemed grievously misplaced in

the dream. Gray stones towered over Vimbai, their fissures greening with moss and slender grasses, and she thought that if the Great Zimbabwe was to ever fight Stonehenge, the latter would have its ass handed to it.

She passed through the arches and between walls, the remnants of a giants' house, and came to the other side where round grass huts—arranged in a semi-circle, like one would see in a Discovery Channel documentary—teemed with people and dogs.

"Run away," people shouted to Vimbai, and dogs barked. "They are coming, they are coming."

Only then did she notice that they were packing bundles of their belongings and carried children, fleeing from some dream disaster.

At that point, Vimbai was quite aware that she was dreaming, and so she decided to stay behind and see what all the commotion was about. She waited until the huts emptied and the people all climbed into aerial boats moored nearby—long speedy hollowed-out tree trunks, fashioned with bright golden wings where oars would've been, topped by great scarlet sails. The sails filled with sunlight—like a gust of giant breath—and the boats took off through the air, fast as arrows, the wings on their sides beating in unison, the speedboat engines mounted in the rear of the boats strangely helpless and superfluous.

Vimbai watched their departure and disappearance, how they grew into tiny dashes on the horizon and dissolved in the expanse of the molten sky. She smelled dry grass and a whiff of motor oil, and she breathed hastily, lustily, in order to retain and remember them when she woke up.

And then she heard the sound of motors rumbling. It did not come from the boats but from between the stones of the Great Zimbabwe, and she surmised that it signaled the approach of whatever caused the mad flight of the aerial boats.

She heard a siren, and her feet moved against her will—a fear too visceral to overcome, the nightmare given to her by the Kenyan babysitter when she was just a baby, the sound of the medical trucks.

They came from among the stones, emerging from and between them, coming up from the sifting, puckering soil that spat them out like something distasteful. They came like ants fleeing a forest fire, like impala fleeing the drought . . . They swarmed like locusts.

The trucks looked just like Vimbai imagined them—old-fashioned things, reminiscent of army trucks from the twenties, with wheels of solid metal that thumped softly on the dry ground. Brass rails ran along the open cabs and beds of the trucks, one on top and one on the bottom, and several men in blue surgical scrubs stood on the lower rail, hanging onto the top one, giving Vimbai an impression of children peeking over a split-rail fence. Large red crosses were painted on the cab doors.

Vimbai could not see what was in the open beds of the trucks, but she could hear a quiet and terrible slurping that filled her with quiet dread. It's just a dream, she reminded herself. They cannot hurt you. And yet the trucks slurped and sluiced and thumped and moved closer, surrounding her in a ring.

The men in surgical scrubs, their faces hidden behind gauze that only left their tired, kind eyes and sweating white foreheads visible, jumped from the truck closest to her, and Vimbai saw a large flat cistern filled with pale blue blood. Several hoses snaked around its base, and one of the medical men grabbed a hose and motioned for his mates to hold Vimbai. Too late, she thrashed in their arms; too late she tried to will herself to wake up. But the hose got closer to her face, and now she could see a large needle glinting on the end of it. She struggled but the man's gloved hands cradled her face, and the needle jabbed her neck. She felt her life draining away from her, her soul hanging by a thread, as the cistern got fuller. She did not struggle anymore, and the medical men let her arms dangle by her sides, her legs segmenting and treading the dry sand, her gills dry and desperate for the cool embrace of water.

"That's a huge horseshoe crab," one of the medical men said. "Toss it back."

Vimbai wanted to scream and protest, she wanted to ask them to take her to the sea, to the life-giving salt water. But instead, they tossed her into the lake, where a hungry catfish waited for her, wise, smiling with its hard toothless mouth.

In the morning, Maya and Vimbai went for a walk in an aspen grove, which Maya recognized as her own. Her dogs tagged along, their fluffy-tipped tails swaying gracefully and their pointed possum faces grinning, bristling with white conical teeth. Their eyes gleamed brightly.

Vimbai kicked up the leaves littering the path, and they rustled and rose, and then fell back. Maya seemed pensive.

"I had a strange dream," Vimbai informed, and told Maya about the men in medical trucks.

"That is a really messed up dream," Maya said. "Jesus. Bad dreams are a hazard here, aren't they?"

"I don't know," Vimbai said. "I thought the house had our old dreams . . . the ones we have discarded and forgotten about."

"Maybe," Maya answered. "I hope so." She whistled to her dogs and they perked up: their tails wagged, and their tongues hung out. They crowded closer to Maya and stared at her expectantly, as if waiting for her to do something amazing or entertaining.

"They love you." Vimbai sighed. "It's really cool how they follow you."

"Somebody has to," Maya mumbled and bent down to scratch a few dog heads. When she straightened, she shot Vimbai a quick smile. "Don't mind that, I'm just being silly."

"It didn't sound silly," Vimbai said. "It sounded serious, actually."

Maya shook her head. "So I whine a little every now and again. I'm allowed to."

"I'm not saying you're not," Vimbai said. "Only you sounded so sad . . . is there anything I can do?"

"No," Maya said. "There's nothing, really. It's just sometimes I think that all I have is these dogs and Felix and you."

"No family?" Vimbai felt guilty that she had never thought of asking Maya such simple questions. Her own family occupied so much of her internal space that she assumed it was the same for Maya, unable to recognize a sucking emptiness in another's soul.

Maya shook her head. "My grandmother died two years ago, and I never had anyone but her. But I'd rather not talk about it now. Maybe later."

"Okay," Vimbai said. "Fine. You want to go to the lake?"

"No." Maya nodded at her dogs. "They are afraid of lakes—I think it's the fish. The same fish you dreamed about."

"This is what I wanted to see," Vimbai said. "To make sure. Maybe it's not even there anymore, or the lake is gone."

"You're not afraid?"

Vimbai considered her latest shameful flight from the catfish. "A little," she admitted. "But if I don't go in, I can't drown, and it can't take my soul. It can't hurt real live people, can it?"

Maya shrugged. "I'm not about to find out. I don't think you should either."

Vimbai hesitated. It was so tempting, so sensible. But her promise to the horseshoe crabs beat in her heart, like ashes of Klaas. She promised not to let them die, and she had to make sure that the sinister catfish was not hatching any evil plans, like her dream seemed to suggest. "I must," she told Maya.

Maya sighed. "At least, take someone with you. Felix or Peb or your grandmother." There was a hint of struggle as she pronounced the last word, and Vimbai thought that Maya had to feel a little sore, that it was not her grandmother who showed up to look after them and to make them coffee. That the *vadzimu* was Vimbai's, even though Vimbai had a full set of parents and did not really need a ghost. And Maya . . . Vimbai could not be sure, but she suspected that Maya would trade all of her dogs for a glimpse of her dead grandmother.

"The *vadzimu*? She doesn't leave the kitchen—only to go to the porch. I don't think she wants to be anywhere else."

"Why?"

Vimbai shrugged. "No idea. You know how ghosts are always restricted to one room. Or a hallway or whatever."

Maya nodded. "I guess. But you did drive her here."

Vimbai stopped, awkward. It was time for them to part ways—Maya seemed intent to continue down the path covered in yellow leaves, to the bluish grove of firs on top of a hill they named after Oprah. And Vimbai had to head back, past the rich deposits of old mattresses and into the desert, the yellow sand with two chairs on the shore of a silent, smooth lake, where the unspeakable cannibalistic horror of a catfish lurked beneath.

It was silly, Vimbai told herself. Perhaps it was just a fish with no intelligence and no accompanying malice; perhaps she just imagined its words. Perhaps the house was just a canvas onto which she projected her silly fears and believed them to come to life in the shifting, uneven light—much like her own carelessly tossed shirt transformed a peaceful chair in her childhood bedroom into a monster. Perhaps all she needed was a closer look, a light switch, that would let her see her own foolishness.

"I'll see you later," Maya said. "Just be careful."

Vimbai headed for the lake. At first she thought of stopping by the kitchen and talking Peb into coming with her, but it was a bit of a detour. Besides, Peb being the creature of mostly spirit (and soap skin) could be vulnerable to the man-fish—provided the latter was real. It was better to go alone, she decided.

Vimbai waited on the lakeshore, looking for telltale circles in the water. She waited for the flip of a tail, the silvering of a side and the splash of a large slithering fish. She stood among the green cattails and succulent patches of sedges, their green inflorescences tilted like bayonets.

There was no sign of the catfish, and she considered retreating back to the lawn chairs, perhaps sitting down, kicking up her legs and enjoying a nap—for all the weird absence of smell here, inside the house it was much warmer than outside, subtropical even. Vimbai decided not to contemplate the heating bill—and after all, who said anything about a bill? For all she knew, they would never have to encounter anyone from the gas or electric company again. She finally understood what Maya was so jubilant about, imagining a life with no bills and no responsibilities, free to roam the endless plains of this dream Africa, with its forever flowering Harare and plush lions who cuddled and never bit, its mountains and ridges named and explored by them, by Maya and Vimbai, and not some dead unknown people. Their own world, their endless circus that had the good sense to run away with them.

Her feet sank into the soft soil of the bank, and she wiggled her toes, enjoying the sensation of thick ribbons of warm mud squeezing between them. She longed for the rich smell of river, of the green and decay and silt warmed by the sun, and she sighed. Their dream refuge had a serious flaw, no doubt about that.

She lifted one foot, and the mud made a sucking noise, an obscene slow kiss, as it released her. She turned around and froze at the sight of Balshazaar hopping along on his phantom leg, away from the lake. She was not sure if he had seen her, but crouched low just in case he turned around. There was no particular reason for her to hide, it just seemed like a good idea. Balshazaar roamed freely now, and Vimbai saw no harm in keeping a secretive eye on him, even if it meant crouching on the bank and getting mud on the knees of her relatively clean jean overalls.

Balshazaar never turned, and Vimbai watched the back of his shriveled head, parchment skin with a few long wisps of gray hair, disappear behind the straight line of the horizon—she knew that a grove of palms and couches waited just behind it, embraced by a clear gurgling brook with a pebbled bottom, where mayfly larvae built their strange delicate houses from straw and tiny shells cemented with silt.

"What do you want?" a voice came from behind. An unpleasant voice, with a strange suffocated quality to it—it sounded like a person talking without breath, a mouthed voice with no lungs behind it to give it strength.

The man-fish peeked out of water, his fins propping him up not far where Vimbai had previously stood. He was a large fish, beautiful in his way—brown and green patterns covered its wetly glistening sides, like a snakeskin boot. His eyes, small and golden, bulged a little out of his flat head, staring at Vimbai with an empty feline expression.

Vimbai studied him a while. There was no hurry for her to speak, and she hoped that her silence came across as unnerving rather than timid.

The catfish smirked a little, his whiskers hitching up to

expose a wide lipless mouth. "What's the matter? Cat got your tongue?"

She spoke only when she felt certain that her voice would come out without trembling. "Who are you?" she said. "What are you doing here?"

"I live here," the fish replied in the same breathless voice. "As to who I am?" He paused, swallowing air in large gulps, his gill covers falling and rising like bellows. "I think you know that. Or have you lost touch with the stories you learned like you lost touch with your past?"

Vimbai smiled. A few months back these words would've stung. Today, she knew well enough that they were not the truth—at least, not the real truth. Sure, her Shona was lacking and her knowledge of her parents' culture was patchy, to say the least. Yet, Vimbai refused to feel guilty for being the way she was. "I remember," she said. "You're the man-fish."

"That's right," the catfish answered. "And what are you doing in my dream?"

It had not occurred to Vimbai that the house might not be their creation entirely; yet, she dismissed the thought that the catfish was the architect of this place. It seemed too influenced by human things—furniture everywhere, and very little water. Besides, dreams of dreams sounded awfully recursive to her. "It's not your dream," she said. "You're lying."

"Maybe not yet," the man-fish answered. With a single beat of a strong blunt tail, he sent a spray of murky water splashing into Vimbai's face. When she rubbed her eyes dry, he was gone—not even a trace on the surface of the lake, not even a tattoo of concentric circles as if after a fallen stone.

BACK IN THE KITCHEN, VIMBAI'S PENSIVE MOOD WAS dispelled by Peb's frantic cries. He hovered over the stove and wailed and whimpered, inconsolable, despite the *vadzimu*'s and Felix's efforts. Peb cried and cried and fluttered frantically about, like a moth trapped under a lampshade.

"What's the matter with him?" Vimbai asked. She had to raise her voice to be heard over the racket.

"Aaaaaaa!" Peb wailed in response, opening his mouth wide. Only then did Vimbai notice that his tongue was missing—his mouth was an empty cave bordered by two rows of transparent teeth, smooth and devoid of any features, like the inside of a teacup.

Vimbai turned to Felix, who was following Peb around the kitchen, his hands flapping helplessly. "Who did that to him?"

"No idea," Felix said. "He just showed up like this."

"Can you help him?"

Felix shook his head and stopped pacing. "No, of course not. How can I? There are forces, and I don't understand them, and no one ever had a phantom tongue—at least the one I know of."

Cat got your tongue? Vimbai remembered the hissing voice of the man-fish. More like catfish got your tongue, she thought. Perhaps that was the original expression—cat getting someone's tongue just didn't make sense; then again, neither did catfish.

Vimbai's throat constricted, and when a sob squeezed out of it, it startled her, as if it came from an extraneous source.

She had surprised herself; she did not expect to feel such acute grief for the poor Peb and his stolen tongue. The Psychic Energy Baby, birthed in some ethereal realm, had grown to be a part of Vimbai with his festoons of feet and hands, with his relentless desire to absorb colors and parts of people. He became a part of the household, and without Vimbai's ever noticing, they all had learned to love him—even Felix, as unhinged and disconnected as he was most of the time.

Vimbai could think of nothing better to do than to pick Peb up—he struggled in her arms at first and then quieted and felt silent save for an occasional sob. She held him awkwardly, having little experience with babies, psychic or otherwise. As Peb relaxed in her arms, Vimbai thought about what it would be like, to have a baby sibling.

The *vadzimu* touched her elbow, startling Vimbai from her thoughts. "Don't cry, granddaughter."

"But . . . but they took his *tongue*," Vimbai said, and swiped her open palm over her watering eyes. "What will he do now?"

"You can always find what has been misplaced," the ghost said. "You just need to know where to look. Now, who could've taken it?"

"The catfish," Vimbai said. "The man-fish, I mean. Only I don't know how—he was in his lake and I spoke to him."

The *vadzimu* gasped. "Why would you do such a thing?"

"I don't know," Vimbai said. "I wanted to see what he was up to, I guess. And just to make sure he wasn't planning anything . . . I was worried about the crabs because of the dream I had."

"You should be careful with the man-fish," the ghost said. "He is cunning—more cunning than you can imagine."

Felix stopped his pacing. "Maybe," he said, "maybe he took Peb's tongue so that Peb couldn't tell us something."

"Like what?" Vimbai asked, still sniffling. So small, so ethereal. So helpless. Impossible, and yet alive, and yet mutilated. The conglomeration of wrongness was so great that Vimbai felt like crying again.

"I don't know," Felix said. "But Peb, he floats everywhere. He babbles . . . babbled about all sorts of abstract stuff, but he notices things. Right, Peb?"

Peb nodded, his forehead brushing against Vimbai's shoulder, light like sleeping breath of a real infant—or at least, that was how Vimbai imagined it.

She hugged Peb closer to her, and he felt like an air-filled balloon in her arms, smooth and light and real. "What have you seen?" she asked. "Who did this to you?"

Still sobbing, Peb pressed his face into her shoulder.

"Are you afraid to tell us?"

Another brush against her shoulder signified another nod.

"Don't worry," Vimbai said. "We'll protect you. You tell us when you're ready."

Peb wailed a little.

"He can't talk," Felix said.

"I know. He can still point whoever did this out, or answer yes or no questions."

The *vadzimu* patted Vimbai's shoulder reassuringly. "When he's ready," she said. "When we all are ready."

THE HOUSE OF DISCARDED DREAMS

VIMBAI FLED TO THE SMALL TROPICAL GROVE THAT CURRENTLY separated her and Felix's rooms. She left Peb, still distraught but quiet, with her grandmother's ghost, and sought solitude and time to think. She felt exposed and betrayed, as if a dream she was enjoying had taken a sudden and unwarranted turn toward nightmare. She wished Maya was here so that Vimbai could ask her what she thought now, now that Peb's tongue had been stolen, about having their own domain and being wild queens of the dream realm she suspected was Africa of the spirit. What she thought now, when the man-fish was stalking them from its lake and paying no attention to all the great names for rivers and mountain ridges and furniture deposits they had come up with.

She wandered among the thick trunks, flared at the bases like trombones, covered in green ribbons of moss and twisting ropes of vines. She craned her neck to see interweaving branches hundreds of feet above her, right under the painted fiberboard sky. Orchids and bromeliads cascaded from the branches, and Vimbai squinted at the bright red and yellow flowers.

She grabbed onto an especially sturdy vine and yanked it a few times. The vine held, and Vimbai pulled herself up, her toes finding footholds in deep fissures in the bark. She had been a good tree climber when she was younger, and now the skills still remained. The whole thing about tree climbing was not being afraid to fall, and having faith that the next foothold or a branch would be there when one needed it; and

Vimbai had this faith. As she climbed, the bark opened in accommodating cracks and the branches offered themselves to her reaching fingers, until she settled in the intersection of several sturdy branches that offered a perch and a canopy. Her back resting against the trunk and her gaze settling on the idyll of a basket fern housing a white and pink orchid among its feathery leaves, she felt alone and at peace; and most of all, she felt secure from the catfish, so far away in his lake.

Vimbai wished she could stay up in this tree forever, without ever having to go down and to deal with the man-fish or Peb's missing tongue. She wished she could stay here until they safely touched ground in New Jersey, and there she would go home. Her mother must be worrying herself sick about her by now, and her father was probably quiet and reassuring at home, but at work he would spend his breaks phoning morgues and hospitals; he would pull favors with both Camden cops and Camden drug dealers, both of which he had been patching up for years now. He would look for information and come home late after stopping by every morgue and looking at every dead black girl between sixteen and thirty, each body a simultaneous stab in the heart and a sigh of guilty relief.

Vimbai regretted that she had been so focused on her mother and she on Vimbai that they both pushed her father to the sidelines, his relationship with them uncomplicated, reduced to the function of arbitrator and peacemaker. Her father who only lost his cool when either Mugabe or Rhodesia was mentioned. Her father with a secret political past that barred him from ever visiting home, and his vague and undefined fears Vimbai wished she asked about.

It struck her as profound, that she could see her parents' grief with such clarity. It was not an eternal childish they'll-be-sorry-when-I'm-dead mantra but rather her intimate knowledge of how they were, how they functioned in the world, their responses as predetermined and predictable to her as her own. Perhaps even more so. She wished she could go home now, to reassure them and to stay with them so they would never have to worry again.

She wondered about Maya then, about how she managed to survive in the world and to function without such supporting love, invisible and strong, even if it was far away and only imagined. No wonder she clung to her dogs.

As if answering her thoughts, short thin barks reached her from below, and she peered down between the branches. Ruddy backs and fluffy tail tips appeared in the greenery and disappeared again, hidden by the lush vegetation. And there was Maya, her unruly black hair and yellow t-shirt as unmistakable as her half-foxes half-possums.

"Maya," Vimbai called.

Maya stopped and looked around, puzzled.

"Up here." Vimbai waved with both arms when Maya looked up.

"What are you doing in this tree? Have you heard about Peb?"

"Thinking," Vimbai answered. "Yes, I saw him. Terrible, isn't it?"

"Yes," Maya yelled, craning her neck. "Felix thinks it's the catfish in the lake. Did you see him?"

"Come up here, and I'll tell you."

Maya shook her head. "My dogs can't climb, and they'll go nuts if I leave them down here by themselves. You come down."

Vimbai sighed but obeyed. Climbing down was always harder for her. On her way up, she could just keep her gaze on the sky above; coming down, she had to look at the ground, aware how far away it still was. When she finally stood next to Maya, panting, she smiled. "You have to climb with me one day. It's really gorgeous up there. And the flowers!"

"Maybe," Maya said. "What happened with the fish?"

Vimbai recounted her adventure and her conversation with the catfish. When she mentioned Balshazaar, Maya frowned. "You don't think he could be mixed up in it, do you?"

"Why would he be?" Vimbai said.

Maya shrugged and looked around. "I don't know. He just creeps me out, that's all."

"All he knows is Felix."

"Precisely. Maybe he wanted to make some new friends, friends of his own."

Vimbai looked around too, watching for the glistening of parchment skin in the underbrush. A shrunken dome hopping around on its single non-existing leg like it owned the place. "You're a bit quick to jump to the conclusions."

"Who else then?" Maya said. "Not Felix and not the ghost. Not you, not me. Who else is here?"

"The *wazimamoto*," Vimbai said. "The men in medical trucks. In my dream, they were with the man-fish—in cahoots with him, I mean."

"I haven't seen any of them around," Maya said.

"This place is huge," Vimbai said, and felt a chill. "There could be anything hiding in here somewhere and we wouldn't even know it."

Maya seemed worried for a second. "If they came to Peb, they know where we all are."

"Of course. There's always someone in the kitchen. Or the living room, at least."

"We need to find another place to hide out, in case of emergency," Maya said. "I think I know one."

"From your dreams?" Vimbai guessed.

Maya nodded. "Come along. I'll show you my secret, and I'll explain on the way."

Vimbai followed Maya, and the dogs barked and bounded ahead, as if they knew the way very well.

Chapter 11

Vimbai was pleased to have earned enough of Maya's trust for her to talk to Vimbai so openly; yet the story Maya told her left her worried and upset. It just didn't seem either normal or fair, to seek refuge in one's own nightmares. And Maya was a nightmare factory.

When Maya was younger, she used to live in Northern Jersey. Not in the projects as such, she said, but pretty damn close. In Newark there just aren't too many what one would consider 'good' neighborhoods, and she learned early on what gunshots sounded like, and what 'alley apple' meant.

Still, it wasn't all bad, she told Vimbai. As a teenager, Maya carried a switchblade, as a kind of bravado rather than against any real danger. The neighborhood she lived in, while not exactly wealthy, was not unsafe—there were flowerboxes on the windowsills, and geraniums bloomed in them. Late night in August, people sat on their porches, having long and slow conversations, waiting for the heat of the day to let up enough to allow sleep.

Up in her room, Maya used to listen to the drawl of voices outside, as she lay on top of her blue and yellow quilt, her forehead beading with sweat. She listened to the TV in the apartment downstairs, to the sounds of traffic on East Kinney Street. Through the window by her bed, the streetlamps looked like ghostly white globes through the haze rising off the heated pavement, only snatching glimpses of the peeling siding and the wide brick porch of the house across the street. She could not see the porch of her own house, but she knew that her grandmother was there, sitting on the steps with her feet in black shoes planted firmly on the sidewalk, her knitting in the wide hammock of her dress stretched taut between the knobby old knees.

It was too hot to sleep, and Maya tossed from side to side, willing the white curtains to flutter, to bring a breath of fresh wind, any movement of the sticky humid air. Only in retrospect did she realize how happy she had been back then. How sad it was when you left your happiest days behind when you were fourteen.

She was eager to reassure Vimbai that really, it wasn't so bad—so many had it much worse, and Maya was lucky in many ways. She would not call it a hard life; it was just that shit happened with alarming frequency—to everyone, so why not her? She was not too special not to catch some shit every now and again.

Statistically speaking, being raised by one's grandparents put one at a certain disadvantage—life expectancy was a bitch, as Maya's grandmother was fond of saying. Well, maybe not in those very words, but the meaning was the same. This is why she made sure that Maya studied hard and did not slack off at school; this is why when she found the switchblade she chased her down the street, swinging a long leather belt she must've acquired for that very purpose—at least, she never wore trousers, and the belt clearly had no fashion-related application. Even if Maya wanted to grow up ghetto (and she had toyed with the idea), she never had a chance—not while her grandmother was alive, and not after she passed away. Even in death, she threatened Maya's conscience with the leather belt, forever branded into her imagination.

Maya's grandmother threatened to die so frequently that when she actually did, in December of Maya's sixteenth year, Maya felt betrayed and puzzled—she hadn't done anything wrong, and therefore did not warrant this most severe of all punishments, the kind that was supposed to exist only as a threat but never to be carried out. Especially not when Maya was doing so well in school, taking AP lit and biology, and acing her practice SAT tests.

So it was not surprising that Maya's nightmares centered around the simple pine coffin, with a small old lady (and she was small, despite Maya's early memories when her grandmother towered over her, gigantic like God) dressed in black shoes and black dress, a pillbox hat, and a pair of white gloves clutching her knitting needles—she was quite clear on requesting her outfit and her knitting in her last will she dictated to Maya just two weeks before her failing heart had finally given out.

Maya remembered the shining organ pipes in the church and the coffin, but not much else. Maybe this is why her dreams placed the coffin into the building she could never forget, no matter how much she tried.

It was a multistoried monstrosity just a few blocks to the north from Maya's house, and the epicenter of the gunshots that reached their relatively peaceful enclave of the working poor. The building itself seemed the very cause of the violence and other improprieties—at least, this is what Maya's grandmother said. "They stuff people into these egg cartons," she would say, frowning, "and it's so big that no one knows who their neighbors are, and they never have to look them in the face. So they break and steal and put their graffiti on the walls, because only God can see them, and he ain't saying anything. And here, on this street, we know our neighbors, and this is why everyone behaves—shame keeps people decent."

The city authorities were apparently of the same mind, and in their continuing quest for gentrification, they decided to demolish the projects and build a center with shops and coffee bars instead, where people would come to spend money rather than kill each other and sell drugs. Maya's neighbors weren't fond of the projects, but they were even less fond of shopping malls that were designed to drive housing prices even higher, and people who lived there away. Maya and a few of her friends visited the gutted building just before it was razed, to pay their ambivalent respects.

This was the building Maya dreamed about, twisted and distorted by time and sleeping mind, and enough time had passed that she would not be able to say how accurate the dream version was, or even if it bore any semblance to reality. She dreamed of the central staircase ensconced in concrete slabs, spiraling through the center of the hollow, empty building—just the outer walls remained, with all the internal constructions, floors, partitions and doors completely gone. Just a giant echoey brick of space, with a staircase boring through its empty heart, and when Maya looked up it seemed to go on forever.

There were no banisters remaining, and Maya and two other kids, Phil and Janet, climbed the staircase, scared that they would get dizzy on its endless turns and plummet all the way down to the naked foundation, with nothing there to break their fall. And in her dreams, Maya still climbed this staircase, all the way to the top. It ended in a simple wooden platform that held a coffin with a small old lady inside, her gloves and hat and knitting needles just like Maya remembered them—the dead heart of a gutted monster building, useless and unbearably sad.

THE MONSTROUS HIGH-RISE STOOD ON A SHARP CLIFF THAT jutted out of a seemingly endless sea of old shoes and handbags. Vimbai decided not to contemplate the origin of them, but rather concentrate on the cliff itself. It appeared to be made of the same material as the climbing wall in the college gym, and Vimbai felt an acute pang of nostalgia for her classes and the campus and a sky that was not just painted on the ceiling.

There was a path leading to the top, steep but passable, and the dogs bounded ahead—they knew the way.

"Weird," Vimbai said. "You have this place, and I have a Harare. It's like each of us gets our own little fiefdom."

"Or a queendom," Maya said.

"The point is, who decides? Who gives us those things?"

"The house," Maya said. "Our dreams. I don't know; does it matter?"

"We keep saying that it doesn't," Vimbai said. "But we're just saying that because we cannot find out, and it is terrible, living in a place you don't understand. It has some laws we don't know, and there's someone . . . some *thing* that makes everything happen. Doesn't it bother you?"

"A little," Maya admitted. "Maybe it's like one of those stories they tell children, like a morality tale. About kids who ask too many questions, or look when they're not supposed to, and lose everything."

Vimbai thought back to her spying on the horseshoe crabs—involuntary, drowning, and yet she broke an explicit agreement and felt guilty. "I know what you mean," she said. "How much farther?"

The path had been turning and twisting, and Vimbai could not see the house on top of the cliff, only the rough rock face ahead, with the path growing precipitous enough for them to start using their hands. The rock offered convenient handholds, like the ones on the rock wall at the gym, made of metal and plastic. Like everything here, it seemed to hide artifice under the surface appearance of natural things, as if the house tried to disguise itself as a forest or a rock, and still its studs and dry walls and paint showed through the camouflage. She wondered if it was more successful pretending to be a different house.

The apartment building appeared before them as soon as they rounded the side of the hill, as if it decided to meet them halfway—Vimbai was quite certain that they were not yet at the top, and this was not where the building was first visible.

Maya shrugged as Vimbai's puzzled look met hers. "It does that. I never know where it's going to pop up."

Inside was just like Maya had described—an empty shell of a building, so hollow that it was a miracle it did not collapse on itself, supported by nothing but four walls. The staircase, the concrete and iron rods and the steps winding round and round and up, was the only structure inside, and it made the building look even more vulnerable, as if they caught it in a second before the whole thing imploded; the second stretched, liable to end at any time, giving the place an air of simultaneous stillness and the impending catastrophic move-ment, inevitable tumbling down in a cloud of dust and grime and cement slabs.

Maya motioned for Vimbai to follow her, and the two of them ascended the staircase. Vimbai lost track of the floors signified only by turns of the staircase, and she lost all sense of direction, winding and winding around. The empty windows offered no other sights but the blind brick wall on all sides, as if the building was enclosed in another, larger one; Vimbai supposed that it was technically true, but it did not lessen the fear that was rising in her stomach. Round and round they went, as if trapped on some awful merry-go-round. "I don't like it here," Vimbai whispered, addressing herself more than anyone else.

Maya continued her ascent just ahead of Vimbai, her buttocks moving energetically under the jean fabric of her cutoffs. "Neither do I."

"Then maybe we should go back."

"Not yet," Maya said. "Soon. I have to show you something first."

Vimbai's words flooded her mouth yet refused to leave it—but how? She wanted to ask. Is she still here, your dead grandmother, not even a proper ghost but an apparition of her dead body, lifeless? What cruelty was this, when even our dreams and wish fulfillments offered not comfort but relived heartbreak? It seemed shockingly unfair.

They arrived at the top, to the small wooden platform mounted on top of the staircase like a crow's nest. And there was a coffin and garlands of flowers, wreaths and condolences written on ribbons; there was a small dead woman in a coffin, her small face pruned, her black shoes polished to a mirror shine. But worse, so much worse were the traces of life around her—there was a tent built of blankets and couch cushions, a pillow fort children build when they are trapped indoors for too long, some mysterious squiggle in their genes commanding them to convert every blanket and pillow into a den, regressing to the early days of the species' existence. The dogs were there too, stretched comfortably as if they were home—they were home, Vimbai realized with a trickle of cold sweat between her shoulder blades. There were soda cans and candy wrappers, a small pile of clothes, a book, a flashlight. Maya had moved here from her room, this is where she spent every night and most of her days, climbing here away from Vimbai and Felix, to be next to a small woman in a small coffin, to sleep under the funereal wreaths.

"Oh Maya," Vimbai whispered with dry lips. Oh, to be so alone—Vimbai could hardly imagine such a thing, such a separation between self and the world that a pack of mutant foxes and a dead body would be desirable company. And it hurt a little, too—she had to admit, to herself if not out loud—that Maya would prefer this to her bedroom, to the kitchen and to Vimbai and Felix and the poor tongueless Peb.

"It's not that bad," Maya said, answering not so much Vimbai's thoughts, which remained unspoken, but her expression. "It's cozy, even."

"But . . . " Vimbai fell silent, unsure how to say what nagged her. The fact that Maya's grandmother was dead, that she couldn't dream her alive, would sound too much like an accusation. "Do you think it's healthy for you?"

"Why not?" Maya shrugged and sat down, her back defiantly propped against the coffin wall. "And even if it's not, so what? I don't owe it to anyone to do only what's healthy for me. Not even to myself."

Vimbai could not argue with that, and she sat down next to Maya. "I'm sorry. I don't mean to tell you what to do. Do you really think we can hide out here?" She almost kicked herself—her words sounded condescending even to her.

But if Maya noticed, she did not let it show. "Sure," she said. "As good place as any. And no fish or medical truck could get up here—see, safe."

Vimbai nodded. "What about Peb? What do we do about his tongue?"

"I don't know," Maya said with a hint of irritation. "You can go back to that catfish and ask him. Or you can go chasing after the trucks, anyway if they exist at all. Or go talk to your crabs. I'm staying here. You can stay, or you can go for Felix and the rest. Do what you want, but I'm not leaving."

Vimbai sat by Maya for a while, until the silence between them acquired the taut quality of stretched fabric, ready to tear any second. Then she stood up. "Thank you for showing me. I hope you'll be home for dinner."

Maya made a noncommittal sound and jerked her shoulder.

"In any case, I'll see you later."

Maya remained silent, and Vimbai started her lonely descent down the endless stairs and then the rocky hillside, down and away, farther and farther from the dead woman and her coffin and her granddaughter, carrying on the vigil through all the intervening years.

VIMBAI'S FACE GREW NUMB FROM THE COLD, AND THE SMELL of salt and seaweed assaulted her, making her eyes water—she had been spending so much time indoors that the natural smell of the ocean she used to love felt astringent and too strong. She wrinkled her nose and rubbed her eyes with the back of her hand. "Come on, little horseshoe crabs," she muttered. "Let's see how you're doing."

The *chipoko* stood beside her, ready to help and guide and breathe as if one with Vimbai. Her quiet posture and hands, roped with veins, folded in front of her, filled Vimbai's heart with heavy, regretful blood. There she was, her grandmother who moved and talked, and yet she was as dead as Maya's. Just a ghost, a dream of a vague memory from many years ago.

"I'm ready, grandma," Vimbai said, and felt the ghost's hands fill hers, and her grandmother's eyes look through Vimbai's with the wisdom and sadness of too many years. She wanted so bad to be kind to the ghost, even though it was most likely just a product of her imagination; she so wanted to show her kindness—kindness she had been too young and too arrogant to show her in life, her heart hidden away from the old woman by the thin crisscrossing of scars on Vimbai's mother's wrists and ankles.

She submerged her face in the stinging, harsh water, sharp little bites of salt pinching her cheeks. She opened her eyes to look at the crabs. Her mouth opened of its own volition, salt flooding her mouth and nostrils, her eyes disbelieving.

The crabs—undead, terrible—stopped their movement and turned as one, looking back at her. She could not see their eyes, hidden deep in the fissures of their shells, but she could feel the age-old fatigue and stone-cold fear, the disappointment and sadness that seared like a knife across an open palm.

You promised us, they whispered. *You promised.*

"I know," Vimbai said. "I'm sorry—it was an accident. I tried not to peek, honest."

And now you see our disgrace and degradation, our soulless shells, our bodies thrown into death so that they could crawl, crawl forever across the sandy ocean bottom, crawl without fatigue or fear or hunger or thirst or lust. And you promised to protect our souls from diminishment.

"They are safe," Vimbai said. "I saw them—they are safe."

The crabs seemed to heave a sigh, although Vimbai was not quite sure if such a feat was possible without either lungs or air. *Are you sure? We feel uneasy.*

"I'm sure," Vimbai said, the creeping sickness of doubt settling in her stomach. "I'll check again as soon as I have a chance. But meanwhile, I have a question for you—do you know who could've stolen a ghost's tongue?"

Those who don't want anyone to speak, those who keep everyone mute. Those who hate life while they vow to protect it.

Vimbai's lungs felt ready to explode, and she came to the surface with a wracking gasp. Water dripped off her chin, froze in thin icicles in her hair. The vision of the medical trucks and the mute men dressed in surgical scrubs passed before her inner eye. The man-fish splashed in his lake, grinning, his yellow cat eye sly and laughing, cold. The vampires and the stealer of souls, somewhere close. Inside the house, Vimbai almost cried out, inside the house! So close, so ridiculous—like one of those urban legends, she thought, when the victim realizes that the phone calls are coming from inside the house. Ridiculous lies, like the one about a man waking up in a tubful of ice.

She remembered the scar on cousin Roger's back, and cringed. There was no tub of ice, like there was no phone. And yet, the man-fish, the urban legend of a distant place, laughed and frolicked in his lake, and his gravelly voice rubbed the insides of Vimbai's ears raw.

"Where's Felix?" she asked the *chipoko* as soon as the two of them separated and the ghost stood next to Vimbai once again.

"He went for a walk," the ghost said. "Come home with me—the baby needs comfort."

Vimbai felt guilty about forgetting the tongueless Peb's troubles. She only thought of his misfortune as a mystery to solve, to get to those who would harm the rest of them, and did not consider how he felt, alone and mutilated. "What can I do?"

"Tell him a story," the ghost said. "Stories always help."

Chapter 12

VIMBAI TOOK OVER THE PEB-CONSOLING DUTIES AS SOON as she entered the house and found Peb curled up in the oven. Peb whimpered, and the ghost nudged Vimbai—she said she had ran out of stories; not entirely, she was quick to mention, just for the time being. Surely, she would be able to think of something later. Meanwhile, she said, would Vimbai think of a story to tell poor Peb?

Vimbai thought of all the fairytales her African babysitters told her—Ghanian and Kenyan tales mixed with each other in her memory, and she felt ashamed that she had become one of the people who so intensely aggravated her mother—people who could not tell one culture apart from another. But Peb cried, and she sighed. All the fairytales, all the Tutuola she had read would have to do, and her mother was not here to criticize the mishmash. Her mind crowded with images of women turned into beasts and the ghosts calling each others on the phone. Vimbai drew a breath and said, "All right, don't cry and listen. This is a story about a boy named Munashe. His mother turned into a lion one day—or at least, this is what he thought."

OH, HOW SHE WAILED. THE SKY SHUDDERED AND STORM CLOUDS split open at her hoarse, inhuman cries. Munashe cringed at his mother's unarticulated, bare suffering, at her voice rising higher and higher, lunging for heaven. He looked at blood that came out of her mouth and curdled on the earthen floors and rank pallet, black and granular like coffee grounds. He listened to the sound of her fingernails biting into the floor, dragging across it with the jerky movement of the dying.

He sat by her, trying not to be annoyed at her eyes, white with fear, swiveling in her hollow-cheeked face. He made nice, and brushed her long hair out of her face, stroked her cheek with filial attention.

"Let me go," she pleaded in staccato gasps.

He tried to make his voice soothing, reassuring, as if talking to a child. "Where would you go, mother? You're too weak to walk, and no village would take you."

"Munashe."

"I can't, mother. You should be grateful that I am staying here with you."

"Please."

He sighed. "You should've thought about that before you went and turned into a lioness."

She gasped and cried some more, and he could not help but laugh. The woman was deluded enough to think that she was still human. She tried to convince him, thrusting her dark, withered arms into his face. "Look at me. I am not a lion, I am your mother." As if he couldn't see the hungry beast looking out of her eyes, the red glow of its pupils burning hotter than the embers of the cooking fire. He heard from old men that women went wild, turned into beasts, and there was only one way of turning them back into humans.

He took a charred piece of impala meat from the coals, and offered it to his mother. "Will you eat now?"

She cried. "It is too hot, too black. I can't eat this."

He nodded to himself. She wanted raw meat, of course, like any lion would. He tried to do good by her, taming her with cooked meat, but so far she hadn't taken any. And her time was running short. AIDS was killing her, and if she went as a lion, her afterlife would be bleak—if she would even have an afterlife.

He ate alone, in the retreating light of the fire. The darkness reached for him, spreading its hungry fingers like a wrathful spirit, its bottomless mouth opened wide to swallow him whole. His mother made no other sound but her labored breath, and the faint scratching of her fingernails on the floor. Like a beast, she wanted to crawl away, to find a secluded place in the savannah grass, where she would expire alone, lamented by wind, buried by ants, kissed by red dust. Fortunately, she was too weak to do so. He waited for the scratching to stop before he went to sleep, curled on the earthen floor of the grass hut. Far away, hyenas gloated. They knew that a lion would be dead soon.

When Munashe woke up, his mother was dead, her eyes opened wide but blind, her pallet stained with sweat and blood. Munashe grunted his discontent, and hurried toward the doorway of the hut. There, he stopped and clamped his hands over his mouth to hold back a wail of terror that swelled in his chest. Instead of the yellow, undulating expanse of the savannah, punctuated by lopsided umbrellas of acacias, a solid green wall of forest surrounded him. There were no lions or hyenas, but only colobus monkeys chattering up in the trees.

The monkeys saw him, and wrinkled their faces, baring tiny, needle-sharp teeth that curved inward. "Munashe," they sang in nasty childish voices, "Munashe, mother-killer."

Their taunt, as direct as it was cruel, brought him out of the daze. "No," he yelled back. "It was not my fault. AIDS killed her, not I."

One of the bigger monkeys swung on the bough and leapt from branch to branch, until its face was level with Munashe's. The monkey's breath smelled stale, and its inward-curving teeth glistened like small yellow fishhooks. "Really?" it hissed. "Did you take her to the doctor, did you make sure that she ate well? Did you care for her in her comfortable home, or did you drag her away from people, from help?"

"I was trying to help. She turned into a lion—she wouldn't eat anything but raw meat."

The monkey's eyes gleamed; its terrible mouth opened wide, and the monkey cackled, the sound of its laughter like scratching of dead leaves. The monkey leapt and landed on Munashe's shoulders. Before he could toss off the unwelcome rider, the monkey's hind legs and long tail wrapped around his neck, and the sharp claws of its hands dug into tender cartilage of Munashe's ears. "Run now, donkey boy, mother-killer!"

Munashe twisted and struggled to get out of the monkey's hurtful grip, but it only laughed and tightened the chokehold of its tail, and wrenched his ears until they bled. Exhausted and terrified, Munashe ran, as the monkey steered him by the ears, deeper into the forest.

It was dark and stuffy under the canopy of the tall trees, and thorny lianas snagged the sleeves of his shirt and his trouser legs, ripping them, digging into his skin until he bled. His lungs expanded and fell, but sucking in the humid air was like trying to breathe underwater. His vision darkened and he took a faltering half-step, stumbling on the ropy roots, falling, anticipating the touch of soft ferns that lined the forest floor. A sharp tug on his ear made him cry out and right himself, picking up his step.

"You don't get to rest, mother-killer," the monkey screeched in his ear.

He ran until the air turned purple and then black, and strange noises filled the air. Something hooted, something chuckled, something else whined in a plaintive, undulating voice. Before the darkness swallowed him, he saw a single bright light beckoning him from behind the trees. The monkey made no objections as he directed his torn feet toward the light.

He came across a grass hut nestled between two strangler figs. The light he saw came from a small lantern perched atop the flat roof.

The monkey gave him a quick, vicious smack on the back of his head, and Munashe bent low, and hurried through the blanket-covered doorway.

"I brought him as you asked," the monkey said, and leapt off his shoulders, to take place next to a military-style wood-stove that filled the hut with unbearable heat.

In the glow of the embers, he saw a low cot, and an old, fat woman that reclined upon it. Her bare breasts glistened, framing her swollen abdomen, from which a belly button protruded like an upturned thumb. Her bright eyes held Munashe's for a moment. "Well, well," she said. "Looks like Tendai did a good job." She gave the monkey a fond glance, and it hopped and chittered.

"Who are you, lady?" Munashe's cracked and swollen lips moved painfully.

"I am Tapiwa," she said. "You will serve me until your debt is paid."

Munashe was about to protest, to say that it wasn't his fault, but only sighed. The salt of his sweat burned like fire on his cracked lips. He felt certain that no matter what he said, he was already judged and found responsible for his mother's demise. His only hope of returning home was to listen and to obey; perhaps then they would let him go. "How may I serve you?" His gaze wandered involuntarily to her elephantine thighs circled by rims of fat, and to the dark, curly vegetation of her pubic hair.

Tapiwa noticed the direction of his glance, and shook with a booming laugh. "Ah, not that way, boy. I have bad bedsores, and I need someone to take care of them. Tendai and Robert are not strong enough."

"I'll do whatever you need me to, lady. But can I have a drink of water?"

Tapiwa nodded. "You may drink and you may rest. Tomorrow morning, you start."

The morning brought feeble light and the smell of dead embers and sweat, as Munashe started on his task. It took him a few tries to roll Tapiwa's bulk to her side. Waves traveled under her skin with every move, and his fingers slipped on her smooth, damp skin. Two monkeys—Tendai and his brother Robert—watched from the perch atop the woodstove.

Munashe puffed, but finally Tapiwa was stable on her left side, her left breast flopping to the floor. Munashe looked at her back and gagged—where her skin should have been, there was nothing but an open sore, running from her shoulders to her backside. A white mass shimmered and moved inside the wound, filling it, spilling to the pallet with every breath Tapiwa took. Maggots.

"What are you waiting for, boy?" Tapiwa said. "Clean them up."

Munashe extended his shaking hand to the living carpet of vermin, and a few maggots popped under his touch. Still, he gathered a handful, looking for a place to throw them.

"On the floor, on the floor," Tapiwa said, impatient.

He obeyed.

Tendai and Robert left their roost, and gathered the maggots with their long fingers, stuffing them in their mouths.

"You want to help me?" Munashe said.

The monkeys chattered and laughed, and shook their heads, their jaws moving energetically.

And so it went—Munashe scooped out the maggots by the handful, and the monkeys ate them, showing no signs of getting sated. Munashe kept his eyes half-closed, and breathed through his mouth; his mind wandered far away, back to his home village, to the fields worked by women and children, to the smells of manure and upturned soil, to the proud cassava mounds, surrounded by yam and cowpeas.

Munashe missed home every day of his joyless labor. While Tapiwa was not unkind, her wounds grew re-infested every day, and Munashe was starting to suspect that his labor would never be over. And he gave Tapiwa the care he did not give his mother, care he could not give to all the people in his village—hollow-cheeked men that came home from the city one last time, to their patient wives, thin and hard and strong like strips of leather. Tapiwa, the fat spirit—for he was sure that he was in the spirit forest—was all the sick, all those destroyed by the new way of life that he could not heal. Her sores wept for all.

At night, when the woodstove blazed, burning the already hot air of the hut, Munashe crept outside, under the sultry starless canopy of the forest, and prayed to the ancestral spirits to free him. He cried until his eyes ran dry, and rested in a crouch, listening to the night-sounds; there was chittering and chirping, sighing and moaning, wailing and weeping. And grumbling. His muscles tensed as he listened to the approaching roar—could that be a leopard? Twin lights shone through the treetops, and moved closer, like falling stars. Munashe's mouth opened in awe as he realized that the sound and the light issued from a very old, very large Cadillac, painted bubble-gum pink. The Cadillac descended, leaping from branch to branch like a most agile monkey.

The Cadillac gripped a low horizontal branch with its front wheels playfully, swung, and somersaulted, landing in front of Munashe with a flourish.

"Hello, Mr. Cadillac," Munashe said, shaken, but present enough to remember his manners.

"Hoo! What a dim boy!" the voice came from behind the tinted window. The window rolled down, and a smiling skull with red eyes blazing from under an old khaki baseball hat stared at Munashe. "Why would you think that the car was alive, hm?"

"I . . . I don't know, sir."

"It's a spirit car." The car door swung open, letting out a tall skeleton dressed in a tattered tuxedo, with sleeves and trousers that were too short. The skeletal remains of his neck were wrapped in a dirty red tie. "Now tell me what you need. You didn't call me here for nothing, did you?"

Munashe told the skeleton his story, all the while marveling at the ease of spirit summoning in the spirit forest.

The skeleton listened with an inscrutable expression. "So, you want me to rescue you from your servitude?" he said once Munashe had finished.

Munashe nodded. "Please."

"Maybe. But first, tell me—what did you learn from all this?"

Munashe stumbled for words. "I don't know, sir. Maybe that everyone needs to be taken care of?"

The spirit skeleton nodded. "I suppose they do. What will you trade me for my help?"

"I don't have anything," Munashe said.

The skeleton's eyes flashed. "You have flesh, boy. How much flesh will you give me for my help?"

Munashe closed his eyes, and thought about his mother. How emaciated she was. And still she lingered, grasping onto life with her stick hands. "Take as much as my mother had lost," he offered.

The skeleton's grinning mouth moved close to Munashe's face, breathing out the smell of liquor and stale meat. It drew a great breath, and Munashe felt millions of tiny teeth gnawing on him, moving under his skin, shaving off his flesh pound by pound, yet never spilling any blood or damaging his skin.

When he opened his eyes, the skeleton seemed bigger and fatter—as much as a skeleton can be fat. He nodded to Munashe and got into his car. "Tomorrow night wait here for my uncle. He'll help you."

"Wait!" Munashe waved his arms after the Cadillac as it started its graceful ascent. "What's your name?"

"Fungai," the skeleton answered, and he and the Cadillac were gone, swallowed by the weakly glowing branches.

The next day, Munashe felt weak but almost cheerful as went about his task. Tendai and Robert, the monkey brothers, noticed, and each gave him a vicious smack and an ear-boxing. Even that could not dispel Munashe's good mood, and he grinned through the tears.

"Ah, you're learning," Tapiwa said. The living shroud of maggots that simmered on her back did not seem to inconvenience her in the least.

Munashe looked up. "Learning what?"

She shrugged, sending the maggots spilling over the pallet and the floor, where Tendai and Robert made quick work of them. "That there is a point in every pointless task," Tapiwa said.

Munashe was not sure if he agreed. A pang of guilt coursed

through his body—taking care of his mother was a pointless task; she would have died anyway. So instead he chose a task he thought he could accomplish—taming the lion back into human form.

When the night fell, he snuck outside and waited by the giant strangler fig. He wondered if Fungai's uncle also drove a Caddy.

Something tugged on the shreds of his trouser leg, and he looked down. He almost cried out at the sight of a small baby next to him that stood on all fours, its tiny, long-fingered hand clutching the fabric of Munashe's trousers. Worst of all, the baby's face was projected on a large TV screen; instead of a head, the TV perched atop the baby's shoulders, dwarfing his small, withered body.

Munashe swallowed hard a few times. "Are you Fungai's uncle?"

"Yes," flashed the letters on the TV screen. Then, they were supplanted by a large red question mark that took up the entire screen.

"How can I heal Tapiwa's wound?" Munashe said. "How can I go home?"

"One or the other," the screen said.

"Both, please. I can't leave until she's better."

The baby's face reappeared, smiling. "You could. I could help you leave right now," it said. Apparently, the TV had sound too.

Munashe bated his breath. This was better than he dared to hope. Still, he resented abandoning his hopeless task, no matter how pointless. "Help her first, and then help me leave."

"One or the other," the screen said.

"Then help her. I know I can leave after she's better."

A question mark again.

Munashe sighed. "I don't know for sure, but I think this is how it works."

Fungai's uncle shrugged his tiny baby shoulders, and showed his face again for a moment, before displaying a chart. "Find the kobo tree -> Find the Lady-Who-Lives-Inside -> Ask for a wishing thread -> Ask for her price."

"What's a kobo tree?" Munashe asked, but Fungai's uncle was already crawling away, the mahogany casing of his television head striking tree trunks that stood too close to his path.

The next night, Munashe set out looking for a kobo tree. He wasn't exactly sure what he was supposed to be looking for, but reasoned that it would be easy enough to recognize. His expectations were fulfilled once he saw a majestic blood-red trunk, crowned with blue foliage and peppered with small yellow flowers.

"Lady?" he called. "Lady-Who-Lives-Inside?"

The Lady-Who-Lives-Inside stood before him as soon as he uttered her name. She was a tall young woman, the most human-looking creature he had encountered so far. Munashe thought that she was just like any woman in his village, until he noticed her stomach—or rather, that she did not have one. There was a large round hole in her midsection, where her belly should've been, framed by the arches of her ribs and pelvis, and festooned with red fragments of gore that fringed the empty space, as if her organs had been ripped out of her.

"I need a wishing thread," Munashe said. "What is your price?"

The spirit reached inside of the hole and pulled out a thin string of sinew, red and blue and yellow. "For this," she said in a high nasal voice, "I want the same from you."

Munashe nodded and clenched his teeth as the spirit's clawed fingers—ten on each hand—pried apart his skin and muscle, sinew and bone, until a tiny piece of Munashe dangled, dizzying, in front of his face.

"There," the Lady-Who-Lives-Inside said, and gave him her thread. "Touch it to whatever wound you wish to heal, and it will be done."

VIMBAI'S STORY ENDED ABRUPTLY WHEN FELIX WALKED INTO the kitchen. Vimbai momentarily pitied him for his pale translucent skin—she could see a blue vein pumping away on his temple, just where the darkness of his hair started. He looked so vulnerable, so distraught with his eyes pointing in opposite directions. He rummaged through the refrigerator—the habit all of them had developed recently, even though they knew there was little of value there; still, the foolish hope that they had somehow overlooked a soda bottle in their endless searching refused to leave.

"There's nothing there," Vimbai said.

"I know," Felix answered, and commenced rummaging. "Have you seen Balshazaar?"

"Not recently," Vimbai said. "Why?"

"I was looking for him, and he's nowhere to be found."

"This place is big." Vimbai adjusted Peb who was starting

to doze off on her lap. "Say, can I take a look inside your hair?"

"Good idea," Felix agreed. "Maybe he went back in there."

"You would've seen him, wouldn't you?"

"Unless I was sleeping." Felix sighed and slammed the fridge door closed. He stood in front of Vimbai and bent down dutifully, letting her inspect his hair.

She pressed her face forward, cautious of what could be waiting for her inside. It could be a trap within a trap within a trap—she was not convinced that the house was safe, let alone Felix's hair. It took her a while to adjust to the darkness inside, and the sleeping movement and inarticulate mumbling of Peb in her lap were disorienting.

She squinted, looking at the familiar dusty-gray landscape. Balshazaar was not there, and she felt relieved for a moment— until she realized another, more troubling emptiness. The empty spaces were gray like the rest of the contents of Felix's head, and it took her a while to realize what it was she was not seeing, what it was that reminded her of her promises with its nagging absence.

The horseshoe crabs' souls were gone—not a carapace, not an errant leg or a tail spike remained. They had disappeared, and for a moment Vimbai's eyes looked back and forth, searching for what could not be found. The souls her crabs had entrusted her with were gone. She had failed them, and—she suspected—she had failed her own hope of ever returning home, her parents, so sick with worry, and Maya; if they never got home, there would be nothing left for Maya but to play with her dogs and to sleep by the coffin, until she grew weaker and weaker, until the terrible men in the medical trucks came for her—came for all of them, to drain their blood and to toss their weak, not quite alive bodies into the lake, where the man-fish would make short work of their souls, consuming them like he had undoubtedly consumed those of the horseshoe crabs.

Vimbai freed her face from Felix's hair. Her eyes met his, and she frowned. "Oh Felix," she said. "We're in so much trouble right now."

Felix swallowed hard. "I see. What do we do?"

Vimbai drew a breath and petted Peb absent-mindedly, like one would a sleeping cat. "We have to go and find the man-fish and the men in the medical trucks. And we have to get Peb's tongue and horseshoe crabs' souls back."

Chapter 13

"ENOUGH IS ENOUGH," VIMBAI SAID. SHE HAD SENT PEB TO retrieve Maya, and as soon as she and her dogs showed up, she swung into action. As little as it appealed to her, Vimbai decided that now was the time to take serious action. It was her failure that the horseshoe crabs' souls were stolen. It was her job to set it right.

She made everyone assemble in the kitchen, which she thought of as her command post. She also suspected that here they were protected by the benign magic of the stove and the refrigerator, guarded from the eavesdropping of the man-fish and other entities she was not yet sure about. She had decided that Balshazaar was an enemy—after all, who but him knew where the horseshoe crabs kept their souls?—as well as the men in the medical trucks. And she especially did not want the horseshoe crabs to overhear her and to learn about her failure.

She looked at the *chipoko* and Peb in her arms, at the intense, open-mouthed Maya's face, who looked at Vimbai as if she had just met her, and was expecting something profound or interesting. Vimbai noticed Felix standing by the window overgrown with flat hairy leaves, his shoulders hunched over and his hands buried in the black hole surrounding his head with an equal measure of despair and concern—he seemed to be constantly checking for things going in or out, if anything was being stolen away.

"So this is what we're going to do," Vimbai said. "We'll go to the man-fish, and we tell him to give the crabs their souls back. And I bet he would know how to get us home."

"Or how we got here in the first place," Maya interjected.

"Maybe that." Vimbai considered banging her hand on the kitchen counter, but decided against it. "But now we need to take care of business."

"How do we do that?" Felix asked.

"We'll talk to him," Vimbai said. "He's a fish. Maybe we can threaten him or something."

"How do you threaten an eater of souls?" the *vadzimu* asked.

"Surely there's something he needs," Maya said. "Or is afraid of. I'm with you, Vimbai—let's go."

"Felix and Peb should come too," Vimbai said. "We need Peb—he can point out whoever hurt him."

They set out to the lake. Vimbai gritted her teeth and felt altogether grim: she felt her forehead furrowing with long horizontal lines, and her jaws and fists clenching, as if in a movie. She thought that it was the first time in her life she felt such resolve, such simple realization that she had to do something, and there was nothing that could stop her from doing it.

She missed her mother then—her mother who went to work every day with the same clenched fists and jaws, the same stern faith spilling out of her eyes. It had been easy for Vimbai partially because she had a mother like that, a mother who could march into the office of a department chair or school principal, and put forth her demands. She would not be swayed by the appearance of reason, by the soothing voices and sober explanations of why her demands could not be met. She would cross her arms and wait in silence, until they either caved or asked her to leave, thus granting her a moral victory at the very least. Vimbai wished she could be like this.

Then again, her mother had the dubious advantage of having to fight for everything, and most of these fights Vimbai was not privy to. She only caught tail ends of arguments and meaningful exchanges of glances between her parents, or occasional phone conversations with other faculty members in Africana Studies. Of talks over tea, of complaints about white people setting the Africana agenda, and how unfairly colonial it was.

Vimbai felt embarrassed of her ignorant indifference toward these battles, of her dismissal of things that had anything at all to do with Africana Studies or African politics or Africa anything. She was an American, she used to tell herself, and it had nothing to do with her, the only person in her family who spoke English without an accent. It was her parents that carried Africa within them, who could not let it go and kept obsessing over it years and years after it became irrelevant to them—and after they became irrelevant to it, immigrants, deserters, people who left their country and were in turn left behind, as it moved on without them.

"Everything had changed so much," Vimbai's mother kept repeating with quiet wonder as they walked through the streets of Harare, and she insisted that she knew these streets like the back of her hand but kept taking wrong turns and getting lost anyway. At night, she cried about it when she thought Vimbai could not hear her.

But if it was not Vimbai's, this burden, this memory, why did she have an ancestral spirit following her and telling her stories, filling Vimbai's eyes with her sad visions—*jacaranda trees in bloom*—despite everything? Why did she have her own Harare here, in this dune house from South Jersey? Why did the man-fish and the fairy tales, the *wazimamoto* of her Kenyan babysitter, follow her and refuse to let go? She could not shake them like she could not shake her parents and their sins and memories. Tied to them by the tenuous bond of blood, and through them, tied to the continent she neither knew nor particularly liked. She wondered if Maya felt this ancestral bond too, through the intervening generations and the accumulated twin heartbreaks of colonialism and slavery.

THEY APPROACHED THE LAKE THAT STRETCHED, DECEPTIVELY peaceful and smooth, before them. The surface remained undisturbed, like a pane of green glass, and Vimbai decided that it meant that the man-fish was at the very least cautious, and possibly, she hoped, concerned. "You should be concerned, you bastard," she muttered through her teeth. "You better fucking worry."

Maya, who stopped at the lakeshore just ahead of Vimbai, looked over her shoulder. "Whom are you talking to?" she asked Vimbai. "And why are you swearing?"

"The man-fish," Vimbai answered. "And sorry about the swearing."

"I don't care." Maya laughed and turned back to stare at the lake. "In fact, you don't swear nearly enough."

Normally, Vimbai would've felt resentful: she hated it when people told her how she should talk or what she should act like, especially if they accused her of acting white—oh, how it turned her stomach. She suspected that Maya never said things like that because she had had the same words thrown in her face too. "I just never picked it up, I guess."

Felix nudged Vimbai's side. "What if it . . . the catfish. What if it doesn't come out?"

"He always does," Vimbai said. "Let's just wait a little."

The water remained still, and Vimbai picked up Peb who hovered by her elbow, as if having accepted her authority and the hope of help. She cradled him, his grotesque hands and feet brushing against her cheek like soft strands of seaweed. "It'll be all right," she whispered. "Don't be afraid, little Peb. We'll get your tongue back from the bad fish."

Peb moaned and shook his head.

"What? It wasn't him?"

Peb nodded, wailing for emphasis. It tugged Vimbai's hair and pointed with seven or eight of its limbs, at something behind Vimbai.

She whipped around, only to see the quick movement of something disappearing in the low brush behind the stacked couches, just a few dozen yards away from the lake. She was not sure what it was, but it was low to the ground and moved in swift but jerking motion, sending the branches that concealed it into spasmodic trembling. "Balshazaar," Vimbai said.

Felix turned. "Where?"

Vimbai and Peb pointed at the bushes, and Felix took off toward them, with a speed Vimbai had not suspected in him.

Maya looked after him. "Poor Felix," she said. "She chases this stupid thing like it means something."

"Maybe it does mean something to him," Vimbai answered. "I won't pretend that I understand anything about Felix."

Maya nodded her agreement. "He's a strange one, that's for sure. I wonder how it is, to have the remnant of a universe hovering around you?"

"Or rather hanging down from the remnant of a universe," Vimbai said. "Still, do you know what happened to him? Where he was before, and how he came to be here? Can we even comprehend that?"

Maya shook her head. "No way. I don't even think about that—once you start, you can't stop, because then you start asking how come he speaks English and if everyone there does, and how was he able to get a New Jersey driver's license, or even if he did get it—maybe he always had it or found it in his hair, and what is he even doing, existing like that, you know?"

"Yeah," Vimbai said, and cradled Peb closer. "I'm just creeped out by Balshazaar, and Peb seems to imply that it was he who had taken his tongue."

"Could be." Maya walked up to the water's edge and tried it with her toes. "Warm. Anyway, maybe Balshazaar is pissed at Felix and at the rest of us because we're Felix's friends. Maybe he likes the fish for whatever reason."

"And the men in the medical trucks," Vimbai added. At

this, Peb stiffened in her arms but did not utter a sound. Vimbai decided to let him be for now.

"You keep saying that there are these guys in trucks." Maya crouched down and splashed water with her hands. "But I haven't seen them, and no one else did either. How do you know they are even here?"

"Oh, I know," Vimbai said. "Sometimes you just do."

SOMETIMES, YOU JUST DID. VIMBAI DID NOT BELIEVE IN ESP—rather, she trusted that human instincts, having evolved over hundreds of thousands of years, were better at picking up signals indicating danger than her rational mind would ever be. Sometimes, one had to trust the gut feeling, whether it came from quick but persistent observations that had not reached her conscious mind yet or from internalized knowledge, too old and too deep for words. She did not need to hear her mother's voice or see her face to know that she was angry—the anger colored the air in the house, pumped it full of tension that Vimbai could feel as soon as she entered the house.

And just like that, she felt the electric charge in the air, she felt the unseen and unspoken menace—the men and their trucks, the sense of *wazimamoto* crouching nearby. She had developed this fear as a kid, and now it came in handy—or in any case, it felt more constructive than the blind childhood panic that made her dart to the bathroom at night, running so fast that her feet seemed to barely touch the cold hardwood floors. The same panic that forced her to take showers with her eyes open, fearful that the moment she closed them, she would feel the cold hand of *wazimamoto* on the inside of her elbow and feel a long needle go in, so deep, scraping against the bone.

Now, there was still fear and the long sucking sensation in her stomach, and the rising hairs on her arms at the thought of violent needles. She bit her lip and tossed her head back.

Vimbai considered Felix compared to Maya—he did not seem like the same kind of roommate. With Maya, they could bond and argue; with Felix, any illusion of understanding was aborted before it even had a chance to take hold, with just one look at his eyes and his hair—inhuman, inhuman. There was no chance of casual chat, of friendly bickering—as much as she had tried, all she could do now was to try to accept his presence and help him as much as she could; not out of friendship as she would do with Maya, but rather some generalized compassion, the ethical obligation one felt to help other creatures or at least to be reasonably nice to them in order to consider oneself a good person. Even Peb seemed more human: no matter how many phantom limbs it had attached to itself and no matter how many flowering branches it had absorbed, Vimbai could understand its suffering and its pain. She could relate to it. There was nothing to relate to in Felix. So she let him go, chasing after Balshazaar through the low scrub, and let him disappear from her mental landscape as soon as she looked back to the lake. It was not indifference, she decided, just the mind's inability to hold onto something so incomprehensible and smooth like an egg, missing any angles her attention could snag in. Instead, she stood next to Maya, Peb in her arms, and waited for the man-fish.

―――――

THE MAN-FISH FINALLY DECIDED TO SHOW HIMSELF, WHEN
Vimbai was about to give up and suggest that maybe they
should come back tomorrow, although that would certainly
kill the momentum of her accumulated decisiveness and rage.
He popped up among the reeds, his transparent fanned fins
propping him up. He looked bigger now—so huge, big enough
to swallow Peb whole with his thick-lipped fish mouth. He
smiled a little bit, and Vimbai held her breath, as if afraid that
the fish would suck her soul out with the next exhalation. It
also gave her time to look over the fish.

The lips and the whiskers, she thought, were just like
Vimbai remembered them—undoubtedly catfish, and yet
suffused with very human sarcasm as the fish thrust out
his lower lip and eyed Vimbai. The eyes, golden and cat-
like, seemed to smirk and wink, a difficult feat without any
eyebrows or eyelids. His flat head, mottled gray and brown
like a stone, seemed too heavy for his weak fins—it wobbled,
and the massive long body had to follow suit, tilting slightly
from side to side, compensating for the head's appearance of
feebleness.

"Did you take Peb's tongue?" Vimbai asked as sternly as
she could.

Maya did not say anything, but her right fist gave a short,
resonant punch to the open palm of her left hand. A simple
but highly suggestive gesture, Vimbai thought, and smiled.

"No," the man-fish said, studying Maya with some curiosity. "Don't have any tongues, I really don't. But I do wonder

why are you threatening me—I've done nothing to either you or your despicable half-breed rats."

"I'm not threatening," Maya said. "But since you've mentioned doing things . . . you wouldn't happen to have a few dozen horseshoe crab souls, would you?"

"Don't be silly," the man-fish said. "Crabs don't have souls—even fish don't, unless we swallow some drowned ones."

"Is it true?" Maya whispered into Vimbai's ear.

"Don't know," Vimbai whispered back. "But makes sense, sort of. Only those things I've seen in Felix's head—what were they?"

"Apparitions," said the man-fish, whose hearing turned out far superior to what one would expect from two holes on the sides of his head. "Accretions. Come closer, and I will show you."

"Vimbai, don't." Maya's hand wrapped around Vimbai's forearm, the strong protective warmth of her fingers encircling like a sigil guarding from evil.

Vimbai gently freed her arm and handed Peb to Maya. "I'm just going to listen. Nothing will happen to me while you are watching over, right?"

"I'll see what I can do," Maya mumbled, and showed her fist to the man-fish. "Don't make me cave your skull in, fish-stick. And don't you think this lake will protect you—my dogs will drink it dry if need be."

The man-fish rolled his eyes. "I do not mean you harm—not at this very moment, at least. But perhaps once you understand what it is you're defending you would be more inclined to leave me alone."

"I won't leave you alone until Peb has his tongue back, and the horseshoe crabs are whole again," Vimbai said, and regretted it immediately—perhaps, this was not a good time for threats she could not really fulfill, especially not so close to the man-fish's hypnotic gaze—he floated in the shallows now and she stood knee-deep in warm water, fat mud oozing between her toes, and wondered how she got here. Before she could verbalize her question, the man-fish bobbed up and down on the waves, and swam closer. "Do you even know what horseshoe crabs are?"

ARTHROPOD AND OTHER ASSORTED INVERTEBRATE classifications turned out to be irrelevant, and Vimbai almost regretted memorizing their mouthparts, tiny, numerous, and confusingly named. Mouthparts did not make the horseshoe crab—or at least this is what the man-fish said.

When something is as ancient as these crabs, when it lives on the bottom, scavenging, for so long, it is only a matter of time before spiritual accumulation becomes as significant as the chitinous growth of the shell. Tail spikes and fragile little legs, eyes hidden behind the spiked bumps of their armor—all this was just surface. But there were other shells, other eyes, built from things less tangible than chitin.

The ocean is awash in the souls of drowned sailors, or rather in their remnants—time passes, years wear on, and the souls are rent apart by the constant action of the waves, their endless back and forth over the seesaws of coral reefs and jagged cliffs. The souls become small fragments of memories and preferences, of vague longings and dreams one could not forget no matter how hard one tried. These soul fragments, small as grains of sand and just as inconspicuous, permeated everything on the ocean floor. And they became accumulated and accreted in the shells of the horseshow crabs—forming a similar but spiritual structure that gave them not only consciousness but also fortitude and memory, persistence in the face of being quartered and stuffed into eel traps and bled half to death for profit.

And listen, listen, here's the best part: even if you end up in the sea a few minutes after your death, your soul would still be liable to become a part of it. And the Atlantic coast—there are so many bodies there, there are so many people thrown overboard because they were dead or dying. Yes, yes, little girl—I mean the slave ships.

The *wazimamoto* are real, and they are not fools. Even if your soul is in shreds and a thousand miles away, a part of a horseshoe crab with a spiked shell and a long tail, even then they will find you, even then they will steal your blood. It is their nature, see, and it doesn't matter to them if you're a man or a crab—as long as you are helpless and alone and vulnerable; as long as there is blood (red or blue, doesn't matter) for them to steal.

"So you see," his gravelly voice tinted with hidden laughter said. "Your precious crabs are just people in different guises, and what you thought were their souls are just simple carapaces, same as their regular shells. They have no meaning or importance, they are not at all like human souls."

"And yet, you took them." Vimbai opened her eyes—she did not remember closing them—and stared into the man-fish's, yellow and bright, so close to her face. She swam in the golden ocean, weightless, bathed and suspended in pure sunlight, just slightly blurred by the film of tears. "What did you do with the souls . . . shells you took?"

"I didn't take anything," the man-fish replied. "If you don't believe me, come to my lair with me, I'll show you."

"Vimbai, don't!" Maya's voice reached her from the shore distorted by water as she sank, slowly and obediently, following the whipping tailfin, the serpentine twists of the mottled green and brown scaleless body. The water turned muddy around her, and soon she could see nothing but the clay-colored murk and the undulating tailfin before her.

It had occurred to her then in a lazy, sleepy way reminiscent of a sluggish dream, that she was not being wise, following the catfish like that. Perhaps she should turn back or swim for the surface, where she could breathe air instead of water slowly filling her lungs . . . that was not good and she started, as if jolted awake.

The *vadzimu* was not here to guide her senses and vision, she was not here to help her breathe—and the water was not the cold, singeing salt of the ocean, but tepid bland mud. How could she be so stupid, forgetting not to inhale? There was no time for it now, and Vimbai swam for the surface, already struggling against a pressing cough rising in her chest. If she coughed now she would swallow even more water, and that she could not allow—already her lungs strained under the weight of water as well as the overwhelming sense of suffocation, of absence of oxygen.

She kicked her feet and propelled herself upward, and she

saw the sun through a thick layer of dung-colored water and thought herself saved, the motes of silt playing in the amber light, the surface so near now. But then there was a shadow darting over head, a large shadow—as long as Vimbai, or perhaps even longer. A shadow with two fanned fins and a blunt, flat head.

Vimbai kicked faster, almost reaching the surface, but the shadow returned now, and its flat face, momentarily close and clear, blotted out the sun and Vimbai felt a strong nudge as the fish butted its head against Vimbai's, forcing her underwater. She tried again, pushing the fish away with her hands and feet, kicking it away, reaching for the surface, but the fish was too strong and too slippery, too old and too large. The impact of its massive head felt like a hit by a basketball, rubbery and yet heavy, disorienting.

Soon enough, Vimbai was not sure which way was up, and the silt particles in the water swarmed like myriads of tiny flies, blotting out the light and sense of direction, even the sight of the man-fish. Vimbai only wished she could breathe, and covered her face with her crossed arms.

She felt him approach again and waited for him to get close, within striking distance. As soon as his face touched hers, her hands shot out and grabbed at the sensitive whiskers, the only part of him she could hope to grasp and to hurt. She pulled and punched, aiming for the eyes, and the catfish thrashed, one of its whiskers held firmly in Vimbai's hand, wound for security across and around her palm.

Vimbai's fingers clawed blindly until they felt a glassy slippery fish eye underneath; then they tore. The catfish thrashed more, the paddle of its tail whipping Vimbai across her chest and face. Every second stretched and went on forever, and even their fractions dragged like funeral hearses—at least, this is how it felt to Vimbai's flooded and exhausted lungs.

Another slap of the tail, and Vimbai closed her eyes; but even through closed eyelids the flood of sunlight was unmistakable and welcome. She gasped, sputtered, and spat out half a gallon of tepid water just as her lungs expanded, drinking in tasteless but welcome air. She thought at first that she had managed to struggle to the surface, but then she realized that her feet were planted firmly on the bottom of the lake.

Her gaze cast about, to see the man-fish, his whisker still in her left fist and his face under her right, flapping in the shallow water—the level of the lake was no higher than two feet now, and falling. Vimbai saw the Psychic Energy Baby kneeling on the lakeshore, his face in the water, his chest and back rising and falling with great measured gulps, and only then did she realize that he had saved her once again—he had drunk the water of the lake, saving Vimbai and trapping the man-fish. As if sensing her looking at him, Peb raised his face and gave Vimbai his new and terrible tongueless smile. Then he resumed his drinking.

Chapter 14

MAYA HELPED VIMBAI OUT OF THE MUD IN THE LAKEBED, AND sat with her on the grass by the lawn chairs, rubbing her shoulders with her large, warm palms. Her touch was comforting to Vimbai, and she struggled with an overwhelming desire to rest her head on Maya's shoulder, to let her hold Vimbai and make her feel at peace and at home.

The Psychic Energy Baby swelled up with all the water he had swallowed—an entire lake's worth!—and sat back on the bank, great quantities of lake water sloshing inside him, as if he were a giant distended wine-bag, half-sunken into the soft mud by the shore. The cattails and sedges nodded in the breeze, sleek and green in the subdued glow from the sky-ceiling. It seemed so peaceful here, so calm—if one were to ignore a gigantic catfish flailing and thrashing in the wet mud where barely two inches of water offered it some comfort.

"I'll die like this!" the man-fish rasped. "I swear to you, I won't harm you again."

"And you'll give back his tongue and the horseshoe crabs' spirit shells," Vimbai said. "Right?"

"I promise!" the man-fish pleaded. "I'll do what I can, but I don't have those spirit things . . . they are of no use to me."

"The *wazimamoto*," Vimbai said. "Where are they? Do they have what we want?"

202

"Yes," the man-fish said. "I'll help you, I swear. And I'll tell you now, that bald head on one leg is also helping them. See? I am on your side."

Vimbai nodded to Peb and he leaned forth, a thin stream of water dribbling through his slightly parted lips. He let out just enough water to let the man-fish lie on his side, gills submerged, but the other side still exposed to harsh drying air.

"Tell us more," Vimbai said. "Tell us about the *wazi-mamoto*, and where they are." She did not ask about their purpose—after all, it was their nature.

The man-fish remained silent for a while, greedily pumping the tepid muddy water through his gills. "All right," he said. "I'll tell you how to find them."

What he told them did not surprise Vimbai—as the man-fish spoke, Vimbai realized that she had known it already, but was too embarrassed to admit that it was her part of the communal creation within the house that gave the vampires shelter. It was too painful to think that the blooming jacaranda trees, their branches heavy with purple and blue flowers, sheltered and blessed those who sought to harm Vimbai and Maya, and had already harmed Peb and the crabs.

The man-fish hemmed and hawed, but finally told them that the vampires did have a truck and all sorts of medical equipment. They asked the man-fish about things, and they promised him favors—he hinted at it obliquely but Vimbai felt a cold hand constrict her throat when she realized that the man-fish was looking forward to swallowing her and Maya's souls, after their blood had been drained away.

He only shrugged at her terror and disgust. "We all do what we have to. This lake here, there aren't many drownings, as you can imagine. Very little to feed on. And if you find someone who can help you—hey, why not?"

"You understand why we would be unsympathetic," Maya said. Her arm wrapped around Vimbai's shoulders in a protective gesture, and Vimbai felt gratitude flood her eyes, making them suddenly warm. Being held like that . . . it felt like being home from school, back when she was still a kid and getting out of school was precious because it was rare, and it was made even better by her mother's cool hand smoothing Vimbai's burning forehead. She was also reminded of the touch of Elizabeth Rosenzweig's smooth hand, and thought that she rather liked Maya holding her—almost as much as she would if it were Elizabeth.

"My dogs wouldn't even come near you," Maya said. "Although right now I do have half a mind to call them and let them have their way with you."

The man-fish thrashed, and Peb let out a bit more water— just enough to let the man-fish flip onto his belly and remain submerged save for his dorsal fin and its sharp spikes. Vimbai rubbed her forearm, which bore four long protective gouges, and winced. "So they are in the city. Is there any special weapon and tool we could use to defeat them?"

"Always looking for shortcuts," the man-fish admonished. "Always wanting the easy way. Think about it—if there was a vulnerability, would they tell me? Would you?"

"No," Vimbai said. "I see your point."

"But I can explain their nature to you," the man-fish

continued. "I don't know if it would help, but please accept it as a show of good faith—I do expose myself as much as the others when I talk about such things."

"Of course," Maya said. "Go ahead, talk."

That's the thing about injustice, the man-fish said. Those who are affected by it naturally wish for vengeance, for a manifestation of their rage and pain; and manifestation comes, although rarely in the form it is expected. When Lilith was banished from Eden, they say that she was the mother of giants, but really, the giants were just a sign of the injustice done to her. They roamed and rumbled and shook the earth.

Monsters followed Cain to the land of Nod, and monsters bred and lived in the shadows, on the underside of history— like thin fabric grown transparent in the sunlight, it showed them briefly and in shadowed outline inhabiting human- ity's dreams. They bared their teeth and claws, and their eyes watched people from every fold of darkness, waiting for them just beyond the edge of sleep.

So were the *wazimamoto*, the vampires, born out of injus- tice, as its manifestation and burden. They took residence in Harare built by Vimbai's imperfect recollection, the closest they could get to the Africa of dark dreams and cruel- ties not talked about, and did what they were imagined to do, embodying the terror and the despair of those who had birthed them.

"I think I get it," Vimbai said. "I just don't understand why you . . . and them, I guess—why all of you are here? Are you just my nightmares?"

"It's never that simple," the man-fish said. "Now, give me

my lake back and go—I mean, if you care at all about your friend."

Maya and Vimbai stared at each other.

"Shit," Maya said. "Where's Felix?"

"I hope to God you're not lying," Vimbai said to the man-fish, and turned to Peb. "Come on, sweetie. Spit out the water so I can carry you."

Peb obeyed, and Vimbai marveled at the stream of water spewing endlessly from his mouth, as Peb himself deflated gradually. The man-fish bounded and swam to the bottom.

"Don't you worry," Maya told Vimbai, "we can always get to him if we need to. Do you think they really got Felix?"

"I haven't seen him after he went chasing after that freaky dried up head," Vimbai said. "Then again, I wasn't paying attention with all the drowning."

Maya laughed and patted her shoulder. "You really have to cut it out," she said. "It's the second time this has happened, and the second time Peb saved you."

Vimbai nodded, and Maya pulled her to her feet. "Come on, let's go. It's over the Malcolm X ridge, right?"

Vimbai smiled. "We've named everything there. I wish I'd written it all down."

"I remember," Maya said.

Vimbai nodded. "I do too."

The two of them almost ran now, through the kitchen where Maya's half-foxes joined them, and into the closet. They crossed the plain of discarded sisal rugs and mattress boxes, past the mound of gumboots and handkerchiefs. They passed through the valley of Five Percenters (named on Maya's insistence, since Vimbai's understanding of the doctrine consisted of the vaguely remembered class on African-American History, where it shared a lecture or two with hoodoo and other not-quite-religions for which the lecturer seemed almost apologetic. Even back then, Vimbai could not understand why the professor thought that these religions were less legitimate than the big three, or even the African religions and voodoo and *muti* magic.)

THEY REACHED THE HARARE OF VIMBAI'S DREAMS LATE AT night, when the sun was already setting. They looked from the ridge at the long shadows falling over the city, starting at the no man's land surrounding it and reaching deeper into the streets, serpentine, both familiar and strange—as, Vimbai supposed, a dream city ought to be.

"Perhaps it is not wise to go there in the dark," Maya said. "For all we know, they can see in the dark."

"They can," Vimbai said. "And it is a real problem for Felix right now."

"That's right." Maya frowned. "Felix. How do we find him here?"

"We let them find us." Vimbai sighed. "I just don't see any other way."

"Unless my dogs can sniff them out." Maya turned to her animals, smiling. "Go search," she told her pack. "Search for Felix."

"Wait," Vimbai said, and dug through her pockets. "This is the handkerchief he gave me—maybe it still smells like him."

"And don't forget Peb," Maya added. "He must retain some

smell of Felix—after all, he and all his limbs came from his hair."

They made sure that the dogs got a good and thorough sniff of the handkerchief and Peb both, and Maya sent them into the streets below. Maya and Vimbai followed the silent pack as they sniffed the air, no doubt stumped by its lifeless quality.

"It's win-win," Vimbai told Maya and Peb. "Either we find them, or they find us. In any case, I hope we get to Felix in time."

"Wait," Maya said. "Should we take Peb with us?"

"Good point." Vimbai propped Peb in the branches of the nearest jacaranda tree, blue and languid like the night itself. "Stay here, little Peb, and if something bad happens, go get my grandma, okay?"

Peb nodded that he understood, and smiled a little. In the dusky gloom, he seemed transparent, but happier than he had been ever since his tongue was gone. He was either aware that his tongue was nearby, Vimbai thought, or the ability to help them in their search had distracted him from his troubles. Vimbai kept turning to look at him, glowing like a ghost of the moon in the low blue branches.

As they wandered through the streets, following the meandering track of Maya's dogs, Vimbai looked for landmarks, for any signs that signaled that this city came from her dreams. She recognized the painted stone, the stone friezes, stiff and intricate like frozen lace. She looked into the windows, dark on the inside, and saw stone carvings everywhere—birthed from her memory of the small coop stores that sold such carvings by the artisans. Stone green and black, simple flowing lines hinting at the outline of a face with a single sweeping turn. There were flowers inside, heaps upon heaps of them, as if every house Vimbai peered into was a stall at the flower market. There were people—or rather, signifiers of them, little more than dark faces in the dark corners, hovering above moth-white crucifixes of t-shirts. She remembered how much of a shock it was to her, walking down the street with her mother, and the two of them not being the only black people around—in fact, almost everyone was black in Harare. She expected that, of course, but her heart could not be prepared for the exhilaration she felt then; the sheer intensity, the reality of it could not be anticipated.

Then there were houses that seemed to belong more to South Jersey suburbs than Harare, but Vimbai's careless dreams plucked them from her memory anyway and dropped them among the trees and houses they did not belong with. In those, vinyl siding reflected the moonlight in fuzzy, opaque pools, and the floor lamps inside lighted the endless repetition of Vimbai's parents' dining room—the sturdy formal cherry table and the straight-backed chairs that surrounded it, haughtily expecting guests whose bottoms they would soon cradle. The tables were covered in the same white cloths with red trim—unusual, some sort of a heirloom, Vimbai suspected, but never cared enough to actually ask. The TVs glowered from the corner, with blue artificial static of their fisheye screens.

There were houses with tricycles on the lawns and plastic toys, large and bright and terrible in their garish inno-

cence, strewn across driveways. There was asphalt and red
dirt, and the signs for streets one would find in Zimbabwe
mixed together with the ones from New Jersey. There were
underpasses too steely and desperately industrial to be properly connected to a place, steel and concrete and humming
of wires—the same in Zimbabwe as they were in northern
Jersey and everywhere else in the world. Vimbai thought that
humanity always managed to dream these not-quite-places
everywhere—structures and interiors that remained the same
from one continent to the next, airports and highways and
hospitals, the dining rooms of franchise restaurants, prison
cells. Even if the small details differed (and they rarely did),
the overall sense of alienation remained the same, marking
them as similar to each other and separate from the rest of the
world, from the vibrant life that flowed and smelled differently in different cities, that made them all unique and recog-
nizable—even in dreams.

Vimbai stopped as soon as she saw the sign. It winked at
her from afar, its sideway neon grin fractured by the dark
outlines of tree branches. "HOSPITAL" the sign read. Of
course, Vimbai thought, and pointed out the sign to Maya.
"This is where they are."

"You're taking the medical truck literally, huh," Maya
observed, but moved closer to Vimbai, ever so casually.

Vimbai smiled—she did not begrudge others their fear.
"Yeah. Plus, if they collect blood, they would have to keep it
somewhere, right?"

"If it's a dream, they can keep it in an old hat," Maya said.
"But I do see your point."

The two of them walked toward the hospital, the slash of its sign disfiguring the night like a scar. The hospital seemed familiar, and with a squeezing of her heart Vimbai recognized it as Cooper, the University hospital where her father worked—the same tower of glass and steel and painted concrete, the looping driveway and the parking lot, and the parking garage—a towering structure alongside with the hospital proper, the path inside it winding endlessly, corkscrewing into the sky.

Vimbai motioned for Maya to be careful, and the two of them bent low, holding hands, moving in short dashes between the wrought iron gates and a small copse of trees and shrubs surrounding a couple of bird baths and benches—a handkerchief-sized piece of nature, wedged mercilessly among all the death and artifice of the towering stone.

Maya's dogs waited for them by the bird baths, and only signaled their joy at Maya's appearance by drumming their tails on the ground.

"Good dogs," Maya whispered.

"I think we better go through the garage," Vimbai said. "I've been at this hospital before."

"You know where the blood bank is?"

Vimbai shook her head. "No, but I know how we can get to the offices and the patients' rooms and the nurses' stations without disturbing anyone."

"Okay," Maya whispered. "Lead the way."

Sneaking by the turnstile that dispensed tickets and let the cars through was not a problem, and they tiptoed under the white dead light of halogen lamps that lit rows upon rows of rusted cars on cinderblocks, cars that would never drive anywhere—not even in this dream made substance. The pavement between the rows of cars had cracked, letting through thin, anemic stems of grass. Large chunks of asphalt had been cleaved off, as if by the stomping feet of giants, but Vimbai knew that it was grass and the young saplings that pushed upward among the cars that did it. Young trees, jacaranda and cherries, apple trees and maples reaching eagerly toward the fluorescent lights. They did not know any better, and mistook their artifice for the real sun.

They walked to the floor marked 'D', and Vimbai judged that they were sufficiently high above the ground. Maya's dogs stayed subdued and pensive, and clustered around Maya's ankles like a rust-colored, clumped and very scared rug. Vimbai calculated that they were somewhere on the fourth floor, and it suited her—she figured that if the *wazimamoto* expected them, they would watch the ground floor and the security checkpoints with vigilance. A quiet entry through the service corridor linking the parking garage to the hospital was a stroke of brilliance, Vimbai thought.

The emergency exit linking the parking garage with the main building was closed, and Maya heaved a sigh. "I suppose we have to go back down now, and risk the main entrance."

"Not yet," Vimbai said. "Let me try something." She patted her pockets and smiled when she found her wallet—habit was stronger than reason in her, and even though she had not anticipated a need for an ID when she left the house this morning, she still stuck her wallet into the back pocket of her jeans.

"You'll set off the alarm."

Vimbai shook her head. "My dad works here. I mean, in the real Cooper. He showed me how to do this."

"You think it will work here?"

"It should. It is my Cooper, I think." Vimbai pressed the edge of the credit card between the doorjamb and the dented edge of the door, where the underlying blue-gray aluminum showed under the chipping yellow paint. She wriggled the card until it clattered and caught something—a sense of solid metal transmitted to Vimbai's fingers as she felt the tapered edge of the lock and pressed, pushing the door smoothly open.

"Wow," Maya said. "You're good." She and her dogs followed Vimbai inside, into a short and blind corridor ending in a set of swinging double doors. Vimbai remembered those doors—they led through storage closets and sometimes surgery recovery rooms, the utility spaces filled with rolled up cables and wire to the actual corridors, wide and well-lit, which would take them to the patients' rooms, and various doctor offices and the nurses' stations.

Oh how little Vimbai loved them, those small islands of order and clean-smelling paper, tables and desks where the ragged doctors and interns could sit down to catch their breath or eat a meal or catch up on paperwork. So clean, so sane—and among this order in chaos, these islands in the stormy sea, was her father, like a king of his atolls and the captain of the ship, always calm and composed even when people hemorrhaged on the gurney while he fitted the IV bag, even when there were so few free beds they had to park the gurneys by the nurses' station. He moved among them, elegant and dignified, like royalty in charge of morphine pumps and gauze packs, the lord of disposable syringes and enameled bedpans. With the same smooth motion, he slid a needle into a collapsed, pale vein and handed Vimbai a cup of hospital Jell-O, the taste of which was still one of her favorite things in the world. She was proud of him, and unlike her mother he never felt compelled to say more than was necessary, and thus largely avoided being embarrassing to her.

Now, she poked her head through the double doors, to survey empty corridors—not even the memories of patients' shadows graced them, and even the nurses' station—this forever source of light and comfort—remained silent and dimly lit.

"Where to now?" Maya whispered.

It was a good question, Vimbai thought, and the one she had no answer to, except peering into every room on this floor and then going to the next. How many floors? Ten? Fourteen? How long would it take them? "Can your dogs sniff him out?" she said.

Maya crouched down next to her dogs. "Come on," she told them. "Go search. Search, okay?"

The dogs pummeled their tails on the ground and smiled, their open mouths and bright tongues colored scarlet-red. Finally, they stood as one, and walked tentatively toward the stairs on the other end of the hallway.

The dogs yelped a little until Maya hushed them, and started up the stairs. One floor, two, three—Vimbai was starting to lose count, and followed mechanically, barely noticing the turns of the stairs, reminded of the hollowed out building that had become Maya's grandmother's shrine—just as cold the stone, just as endless the stairs. Vimbai shivered and wished the morning would come.

The dogs led them to the top floor, and then into the hallway. Vimbai saw a sign for some medical department—a Bone Clinic? She did not remember one being there. She followed the dogs and Maya, her legs tense as if ready to take flight at the slightest provocation, into the reception area of the Bone Clinic and then into the office.

At first, she thought that she was looking at a row of chairs, and half a second later she realized that these were backs of the medical men, clad in green scrubs, all the same height and size as they crowded together, side by side, around a narrow surgical table. There were tubes conducting some black and foul liquid, and there was a pale body, translucent even—and Felix's disjointed eyes looked at them (one at Maya, one at Vimbai) with raw suffering.

The *wazimamoto* turned to follow his gaze, and as they parted, Vimbai wanted to scream—Felix's hair, his little cursed universe was gone, taken apart and slurping down the tubes. Then she heard Maya gasp and clutch her hand, and as she looked at the *wazimamoto*, she felt like gasping too. Their faces were concealed by gauze surgical masks and caps pushed low over their white brows beaded with sweat. But even these contrivances could not disguise the fact that the *wazimamoto* had neither noses nor eyebrows, neither lips nor chins; even their eyes were the barest hints, slight depressions in faces otherwise smooth as eggs. Vimbai only made a sound when she realized that, despite these limitations, the *wazi-mamoto* managed to smile at her somehow, with the invisible predatory smiles of nightmares.

Chapter 6

_____

VIMBAI'S FEAR BLINDED HER TO EVERYTHING BUT HER faceless opponents—her field of vision narrowed into a tiny spotlight over the bloodless, featureless faces that managed to leer at her. On the edges of her vision, a black vortex swirled, blotting out Maya's pleading mouth and the incredible paleness of Felix's face, the rusty-colored dogs. She only saw the green cloth masks moving slowly in and out, like an air sac on a frog's neck, with a terrible mockery of breath.

The words she had carefully prepared and rehearsed in her mind were nowhere to be found, and Vimbai wished that her mouth wouldn't be so dry and so sour, and the _wazimamoto_ didn't advance on her so slowly and menacingly. She took a step back, and felt the smooth surface of the door with her back.

Her vision slowly returned, and she could take in the buckets filled with sloshing fluid, viscous and black like tar—the sad remains of Felix's universe, she guessed. The buckets were so many, the tar in them so unlike the air and the vibrant movement of Felix's coif . . . it made her want to cry.

"Why?" she whispered, addressing no one on particular. "Why did you do that to him?"

The answer came in a crowding of words and images thrust forcibly into her mind, without any gentle mediation if words—this felt like an assault, like any true telepathy would, thought Vimbai. This flood of images, this relentless and redundant droning that penetrated even into the secret places behind closed eyelids. The words insisted that Felix's universe had to be destroyed—must be destroyed, they said, it must be destroyed because with too many conduits there were too many drafts blowing the ethereal dimensions through and through. It had to be destroyed because Balshazaar made it a condition—he did not want to go back in, or even risk having to go, and he promised to deliver the delicate soul shells of the crabs in exchange for their promise to get rid of the stupid remnant, an appendix of a universe. They did so, they kept their promise, and that was a good thing, wasn't it?—they got rid of it in the same way they went about accomplishing anything: draining. They drained Felix, and now his face was as white as the sheets underneath him, and his skull, fragile like an egg, traced with a web of veins like cracks, shone in the dusk of the Bone Clinic, unprotected and pitiful.

And then there were the crabs—the soul-shells, the crab-ghosts—scattered about as at a market. Vimbai though back to the time where she was driving home from college, along one of the many quaint little roads linking the behemoths of the Atlantic City Expressway and Black Horse Pike, and she saw a small shop by the road, with a hand-painted "Fresh Crabs!" sign. She pulled over, figuring that a quick dinner of local crabs would be both delicious and socially responsible, and walked into the store. The crabs were indeed there—stuffed by dozens into buckets, they struggled and churned, a seething mass of captive bodies, too dumb to understand that the ocean was too far away to escape to, and Vimbai ran from the store, gripped by sudden disgust and despair. It seemed too cruel, too indifferent somehow—and now she wished that instead of running she should've bought as many as she could and driven them to the shore and released them into the ocean.

That would've been a noble thing to do, she thought as she watched hundreds of ghost crabs strewn about the ward. Some were cracked open, with long needles stuck in their gills and carapaces, the needles that pumped the blood (life force, the intrusive voices corrected) out of these soul shells and into the plastic bags, like the ones hospitals used for IVs. They drained everything, Vimbai thought, and remembered the words of the man-fish—it was their nature, to drain. They wanted to get to the horseshoe crab bodies, trudging restlessly along the bottom, getting them closer and closer to home, but meanwhile they were not going to pass up the opportunity to drain their life essence instead of blue, material blood. It mattered not a whit—like all colonial creatures, the *wazimamoto* were vampires, concerned only with taking and not so much with putting anything back in, or even giving any thought to the results of their actions. Even now, they told Vimbai about what they did without a trace of deceit or embarrassment— they could be ashamed about stealing blood no more than a bee could be ashamed about collecting nectar, or a beaver could be embarrassed about building a dam.

This, Vimbai thought, this was the trouble with evil—it was rarely malicious, usually born out of single-mindedness and narrow views. She wanted to share this insight with Maya, and Vimbai forced her eyes to find Maya, and to absorb the sight of the *wazimamoto* fitting a long rubber cord around Maya's well-muscled upper arm, encircling her narrow but heavy biceps, and waiting for the vein in her arm to swell to the surface like a deep purple river upwelling with rain, to puff up under the skin like a tense wire.

Maya kicked at her captors, and her dogs growled and tore at their legs—but there was nothing for them to either kick or grab with toothed narrow jaws, nothing but the billowing green scrubs with an outline of shadow underneath. It was something neither of them had considered, and the man-fish of course did not warn them—the *wazimamoto* had no flesh and could not be hurt, they had no conscience and could not be deterred.

They grabbed the dogs and tied them together, lashed their paws and jaws with rubber hose and ropes, and tossed them in the corners, like they had done with the crab souls.

"Leave her alone," Vimbai pleaded. This was neither a game nor an adventure anymore. "Please, let her be."

The *wazimamoto* did not answer, absorbed as they were in their gruesome business. Their movements, spare and terrifying in their calm efficiency, seemed matched together, as if they had been working side by side for an eternity—and Vimbai guessed that they had been.

Before she could move, they surrounded her, moving swift and silent and smooth like water, and their hands found her arms and her neck, her eyes, her face—she looked and looked, in unrelenting terror, once she realized that each one of their hands bore ten fingers, long, sinuous and multi-jointed. They wriggled in a complex, spiderlike manner, as if following an internal rhythm.

They held Vimbai fast, just as they held Maya and her dogs—just like they held Felix on his narrow stainless steel table. Not a surgical one, Vimbai realized—at least, it was not intended for human surgery, it was too short and too narrow, a stainless steel table more suited for Maya's half-foxes than full-sized humans—a vet's table, just like the one Vimbai's childhood cat was put to sleep on, meowing and distraught under the harsh lights and foreign hands that held it down.

She felt the stainless steel under her own back—quick and cold like water—as well as the tightening of rubber cords around her wrists and upper arms, the wrenching sense of bones being pulled against the coiling of muscles as she tried to bend her elbows, to keep her arms close to her sides.

The fingers on her skin felt cold and slippery, slightly trembling as if in fear, as they lashed her wrists to the restraints built in the side of the table. She waited for the inevitable kiss of the rubber hose around her arm, for the sting of a needle and the slow, lightheaded descent into unconsciousness. She half-welcomed it, as one welcomes relief from fear—so exhausting that one had to smile a little at the prospect of finally surrendering and not having to be afraid anymore, not having to tiptoe under the glare of white fluorescent lights awaiting a scare or betrayal at every step. Giving in and letting go was easier, and a moment of pain would be worth it.

She closed her eyes, but the prick of the needle did not come—instead, there were voices. The *wazimamoto* were speaking to each other, and although Vimbai did not understand the words, she recognized the intonations, wobbly with doubt and abrupt with panic.

She opened her eyes, almost regretful, to see that Maya had been left alone. Her hand swelled and turned a disconcerting shade of dusky purple, but her blood was not being drained, and her dogs, restrained but unharmed, did not dare to bark at the *wazimamoto*.

Vimbai was about to ask their captors what was going on, when the scars on the insides of her arms started to itch. She wished her hands were not tied to the table and that she could scratch the maddening burning. Oh, Elizabeth Rosenzweig, she thought, why did you have to be so insidious, why did I have to be stupid enough to think that cutting these sigils into my skin would make you love me, or at least protect me from heartbreak?

She forced her head to her shoulder (it felt heavy now, disobedient and dumb with fatigue), and her eyes snapped wide open and her breath caught in her chest at the sight of the scars. They had changed from the barely visible, slightly raised traces of connective tissue into bright red, burning rivers shooting small flames and exhaling pungent sulfurous smoke. They twisted into fiery dragons and straightened into moats spewing fire, they coiled and flowed into complex patterns, and otherwise behaved in a manner no scars had any reason to.

She had reached a state of fatigue and surprise that made everything appear as a dream, and she accepted the dragons and the flames, as she accepted the thought that the *wazimamoto* were deterred and terrified by her scars, as if they were magic somehow, a charm against them.

"Hey," she called to the assembled faceless surgeons. "Untie me, or else." She did not know what to threaten them with and was afraid to bluff and make a bad mistake that would make it obvious to everyone that she had no understanding or control over her sudden power.

The medical men consulted among themselves, their surgical masks rising and falling, rising and falling, and one of them approached her cautiously, to untie the restraints on her right hand, and then quickly jumped back to join the others.

Vimbai used her free hand to free the other one, and sat up, rubbing her wrists. The scars on her arms flared, glorious tattoos of fire that burned but did not consume, and Vimbai jumped off the table, protected by their halo. She untied Maya, and smiled at her. "Are you okay?"

"Yeah." Maya looked at her with a new expression, of deep respect and surprise. "Boy, did I ever underestimate you."

"Get the dogs," Vimbai said. "I'll tend to Felix. And the crabs." She turned to briefly glare at the *wazimamoto* and to show them her fist, just in case they forgot that they were afraid of her. No one had ever been afraid of her, and Vimbai found the new experience not altogether unpleasant—she suspected she would've enjoyed it more if she were not so shell-shocked by the experience, if indifference did not seem like the best coping mechanism available to her.

Felix remained on his slab, his head a defenseless egg, so unfamiliar and strange that Vimbai felt like weeping every time she looked at it. Her eyes met Felix's tormented gaze—for once, his eyes seemed to be pointing on the same direction. "Felix," she whispered. "Can this be fixed?"

He shook his head and cringed as the newly exposed skin touched the cold steel. "No," he whispered back. "I think this is it—I hope there wasn't anything valuable in there." The loss of his private tiny universe had not seemed to reach him yet.

Vimbai unfastened the archaic leather belts that affixed his wrists and ankles to the table. "Come on," she said. "Let's get going."

Felix made no attempt to move, listless and disoriented like a cat without whiskers.

Vimbai grabbed his hands and pulled him off the table. He let her, inert, and stood, swaying slightly, making no attempt to walk or even flinch away from the medical men who clumped tightly together, watching them with the blind eyeless depressions on their featureless faces.

"I think we'll have to lead him," Vimbai said to Maya, who had finished freeing her foxes. "Help me to pick up the crabs."

Maya nodded and motioned to her dogs—they seemed the least affected, and growled at the apparitions in green scrubs as they scuttled about the Bone Clinic, picking up the ghosts of the horseshoe crabs in their red mouths.

Vimbai and Maya stuffed the remaining crabs in their pockets and down their t-shirts, and Vimbai linked her arm with Felix's. The glowing sigil on hers crossed over to his skin, and he shuddered a little, as if waking up. "Come on," Vimbai urged. "Come quick."

She felt uneasy now—the medical men seemed to have come to some decision, and even though they made no attempt to stop Vimbai and her roommates from leaving, there was a new sense of purposefulness about them, as if they just waited for them to leave the room to spring into action. Vimbai was also uneasy about the man-fish and Balshazaar, free and roaming the depths of the house somewhere.

Vimbai took a deep breath and pushed open the door, Felix hanging limply on the crook of her arm, and took a step into the silent and bright corridor of Cooper Hospital, inexplicably thrust into the center of her dream Harare.

THEY FOUND PEB WHERE THEY HAD LEFT HIM—HE BOBBED up and down in the tree branches, seemingly content. Vimbai wondered if he experienced time in the same way they did, if he ever worried or became bored or counted to sixty to gauge how long did a minute take.

"Come with us," Vimbai told him. "I can't carry you now."

Peb sulked but bobbed along, silent and obedient. Vimbai felt her stomach churn—she had forgotten all about his tongue. "I don't have it," she said out loud. "But we know where the *wazimamoto* are, and I can probably make them give your tongue back to me, but I need to talk to my grandmother first."

It wasn't exactly a lie—Vimbai did hope that the *vadzimu* would be able to shed some light on the mystery of the sudden burning signs appearing on her skin. Even though she probably didn't know anything about the *wazimamoto*, she probably knew more about magic than Vimbai. Vimbai wished her mother was here too, because she was the one who wrote papers comparing voodoo with hoodoo, and correcting the many misconceptions she believed white Americans to have—it always puzzled Vimbai that those articles always seemed to be written for white people; possibly the ones who read those articles and became qualified to run Africana Studies departments. However, they still managed to focus primarily on the aspects of *muti* that used human organs cut out of living people, which annoyed Vimbai's mother to no end. "It's as if they only want to see the folk magic practitioners as savage mutilators," she would say. Vimbai would then think of cousin Roger and nod in agreement; economics simply didn't make for as compelling a monster as a dark-skinned medicine man in traditional garb. And mutilation certainly held a kind of grim fascination that always made the headlines.

They made it home when the sun was rising among the slanted ceiling beams of the main hallway, and they made it to the kitchen by midmorning. Vimbai's dead grandmother had a coffee pot waiting for them, and apologized for the lack of sugar, even though it was certainly not her fault—the ghosts did not eat or drink a thing, and only cleaned excessively.

When the *vadzimu* saw the marks on Vimbai's arms, she gasped and looked closer—even though the flames had died down somewhat, the patterns still glowed the angry red of molten iron. "These are *muti* marks," she proclaimed. "And they protected you from danger—did your mother have them done?"

There was an intensity of hope on the grandmother's voice that made Vimbai cringe. The ghost still waited for forgiveness, and seeing her daughter follow in her magical footsteps would be a certain sign that Vimbai's mother was not angry with hers anymore. "No, grandma," Vimbai said. "I made them myself—only I didn't know then what they were." (*Protect me from a broken heart.*)

The *vadzimu* shook her head. "One needs to be a *n'anga* to make those; one needs to practice *Un'anga*, the folk medicine. Or voodoo, like witches do."

Vimbai wished she paid closer attention to her mother's articles—she only remembered that *Un'anga* used both medicinal herbs and spiritual cures, and that most people frowned upon it nowadays. People had no use for spirits anymore, the ghost grandmother said, shaking her head from side to side. They even called the creator by a different name, just like they called their country by a wrong name. It was always the British missionaries, renaming things and demanding respect for their god, the same respect they were so unwilling to offer anyone else.

According to the *vadzimu*, the protection marks that glowed so brightly on the inside of her arms could not be made willy-nilly, by just anyone. One had to go to a *n'anga* for things like that, or to *muroyi*, the witches shrouded in mystery of such a malignant and disreputable nature that only the truly wicked and desperate dared to inquire into it. Of course, Vimbai had spent enough time with her mother to interpret it to mean that the witches were mostly unpopular with the white Christian missionaries and thoroughly vilified by same. Just another form of control, but right now it seemed of little use to her. She was more curious about the roots of the magic, the source of *muti* power.

On the other hand, she wondered at her ability to perform such magic—was it that the *vadzimu* was wrong and *muti* marks could be drawn by anyone with enough conviction? And really, how often did they get tested anyway, in the outside world so devoid of magic, be it in Harare or Atlantic City?

Or—and this is what gave Vimbai such a headache—could it be that she was special somehow, that in her genes there were little coils of African nucleotides that knew somehow about the *muti* and the scars, about protective and injurious magic alike? "This is such a stereotype," she heard her mother's voice in her mind, and smiled at the ridiculousness of it all. "Like being of African ancestry means that you automatically know voodoo—it's such offensive nonsense." Still, the thought lingered, even though she knew full well that revealing herself to be a conjure woman would be a political disaster in her mother's eyes.

Maya and Vimbai had put Felix to bed, to let him recover from the awful draining he had just undergone and quite unsure of what else they could do for him. They convened in the kitchen by the coffee pot to survey their progress and plot further plans of action.

"It doesn't look great," Maya said and made a face at her black and bitter coffee. "Not terrible, but not great. Pluses: we got the crabs back, and Felix too. We know where they are. We know that your marks repel the medical men but not the fish."

"And we still need to get Peb's tongue back," Vimbai said and sighed. "And I feel so bad about Felix—we should've protected him."

"I'm not the queen of Felix," Maya said, scoffing. "He took off all by himself, and we had other things to deal with, remember? Like you jumping straight into the catfish's mouth."

"I did not," Vimbai objected weakly and without much conviction. "In any case, we did not protect him. But the crab souls are back, and maybe we should hide them somewhere where neither the *wazimamoto* nor the man-fish would find them."

"Good idea," Maya said. "Where?"

Before the word left her lips, they both knew the answer. The safest place there was—a tall hollow tower, glass and concrete, the lone platform on top where there was a coffin with an old woman, and blankets and empty candy wrappers betrayed Maya's secret nest. "Will you take them there?" Vimbai asked. "The dogs can carry them, and no one will get to them there."

Maya nodded. "It's okay, I suppose, as long as it's temporary." She breathed a short laugh. "That's a silly thing to say. I guess everything is temporary, especially here, right?"

"Right," Vimbai said. "Just make sure you keep an eye out for Balshazaar."

"I don't think he would ever bother us again," Maya said. "I mean, he got what he wanted, right? Felix's universe is destroyed and he would never have to be locked up in there."

"Maybe." Vimbai thought about Balshazaar's parchment skin and sunken eyes, the grotesque phantom limb fused to the withered remnant of his neck, and sighed. "I just don't think we can trust him."

"Of course we can't." Maya smiled. "We just have enough shit to worry about without him, so I'm saying don't worry about him unless he pops up."

"Sounds good." Vimbai momentarily envied Maya this clarity, this ability to separate the essential from the secondary. Vimbai lacked that skill, doomed to forever swim in the soup of relative values and conjectures, where everything was conditional and everything seemed to have equal importance, always competing for her attention. It was good to have Maya around.

"Okay then," Maya said. "I'll go take care of the crabs. What about you?"

"I'll try to figure out what the deal with my scars is," Vimbai said. "I'll check on Felix, and then I'll figure out how to get Peb's tongue back."

Chapter 16

VIMBAI SAT BY FELIX'S BED, WITH PEB BOBBING NEARBY LIKE an obedient and grotesque fishing float. Felix slept, or possibly descended into a deeper and more disturbed state—his eyes flickered back and forth under the closed eyelids, like quick little mice in the grass.

Vimbai put her hand onto his forehead—smooth and cool, not a sign of fever —and considered whether she should keep it there for a while longer, to offer comfort, until he moaned and thrashed, twisting from under her hand as if it were too heavy or burned his skin.

Vimbai sighed and withdrew, under Peb's silent and, she imagined, accusing stare. To avoid it, she studied the bare walls of Felix's room, just slightly covered with lacy lichen and peppered moths camouflaged between the lichen patches, only their black eyes and long, twitchy antennae betraying that they were still alive. She leaned closer to one of the moths, to take a closer look at its small furry body and the delicately powdered white and gray wings. The moth fluttered, and Vimbai could hear the high-pitched squeal of the scales rubbing together and the soft whispering of the body hairs brushing against each other.

The *chipoko* stood on the threshold—Vimbai only noticed her when she looked up from the trembling velvety moth, and her gaze stumbled over her grandmother's. She seemed as troubled and as silently accusing as Peb. *I didn't do anything wrong*, Vimbai wanted to say, but the burning on the insides of her arms belied her innocence. Somehow, she had managed to do it to herself, Elizabeth Rosenzweig or no.

Oh, Vimbai remembered her face so well, the curve of the soft cheek fuzzed with tiny hairs only visible under direct sunlight, light and dear like the crosshatching of a peach. Same color, and, Vimbai imagined, same taste—would it be that a girl with such a sweet blush, such soft creamy cheeks was not so different from a piece of fruit, not animal but plantlike in her innocence and sugary sweetness? Bees should be following her around, attracted by the invisible dripping of soul nectar; birds should be building nests in the dark thickets of these eyelashes, long and tangled like the branches of sagebrush.

The memory ached, and the ache resonated in the curves of her inner arms, doubled and tripled and twined around her elbows as the scars puckered and reopened, rivers of gray ash shot through with some residual sparks, playing and skittering across the surface. Now it seemed that just a memory of Elizabeth was enough to bring these formerly dormant charms to life; so Vimbai decided to remember.

She was not particularly good at love—never had been, too awkward and easily discouraged, too self-conscious and ungainly. It had always been easier to back away and cry quietly after dark, so that her parents would not hear, so that her hot tears soaked into her hair and the cool cotton of the pillowcase, so that they burned her eyes like coals. It was easier to treat love as something imaginary, as something one indulged in in one's head, guiltily yet zestily, like daydreaming. Loving Elizabeth Rosenzweig from a distance was a snap—it was even easier when they went to different colleges and never even talked anymore, since Vimbai was too preoccupied with love to have bothered to develop a friendship or even a casual bond.

The scars, she realized now, were just like those daydreams—not action but a symbol, a substitute for doing. Neither cutting nor daydreaming accomplished anything but they offered a refuge, an escape from otherwise painful thoughts—painful enough, she realized, to have possibly pushed her into action as long as she didn't let herself become distracted. And yet, her longing was potent enough—*important* enough, she told herself—to imbue her scars with some protective magic. She made them to protect herself from having to go out there and declare her affection, and probably being rejected—to protect her from a broken heart. Who could have imagined that they actually worked?

"Enough staring, grandma," Vimbai said. "I'm not a witch, and you know that. You should be grateful—you should be happy I have this magic, or I would've been dead otherwise."

"I realize, granddaughter," the *vadzimu* answered. "Would you like to see the crabs?"

"Yes, please." Vimbai smiled—she missed the sight of her silent underwater army working so hard—their legs so brittle and segmented!—to get them home, despite the cold and the season and the cruelty of the man-fish. They were entirely too good, Vimbai thought, and she promised to herself to dedicate her life to making sure that horseshoe crabs were no longer chopped up for eel bait or bled into near-oblivion by the faceless monstrosities that holed up in the Cooper Hospital of the Harare of her dreams.

THE WEATHER HAD GROWN MILDER—THE WIND OUTSIDE died down, and the smell of the ocean did not seem as sharp. It had grown almost spicy, heated by the tremulous and pale sun that reminded Vimbai of spring rather than fall. Could it be? No, she chased the thought away as ridiculous. No, just a slightly warmer-than-usual day, common enough at any time of the year. She waited for the *vadzimu* to enter her, to occupy the same Vimbai-shaped amount of space as she herself occupied, and pressed her face underwater.

"You are safe," Vimbai reassured them. "Your souls are safe, waiting for you in the tallest tower where neither fish nor truck can get to them."

The horseshoe crabs mumbled and whispered their thanks, reassured, and their legs worked faster—Vimbai watched the shadow of the house, a square small outline that did not at all match the bounty of space and landscape within, crawl and flicker over the long narrow sandbars, glide like a manta ray over the deeper trenches where small fish played in silver schools. The horseshoe crabs picked up the pace—they almost flew now, their cracking undead legs working so fast that Vimbai feared that they would suffer a final break and fall apart, splinter and disintegrate like termite-infested wood.

Vimbai was no longer terrified of the crabs' unnatural undead state but rather felt profound pity and anxiety, now that the crabs' souls were back and protected by the death magic of Maya's grandmother. Vimbai did not know whether the *wazimamoto* had any ways of finding out information except for what Balshazaar and the man-fish told them. What if they had some hidden sense, the way villains always know everything in horror movies? What if even now they and their medical truck were on their way to intercept Maya and her dogs, to steal the crab souls back, to be drained and dissected, and quartered afterwards to be stuffed into eel traps, fish bait, useless in death as they were in life?

She chased these thoughts away as she watched the bubbles of her breath rising to the surface. They stretched and danced, their surface radiant, as they multiplied and shimmered and burst as soon as they reached the surface. There were none coming out of the crabs, which wasn't surprising, but Vimbai wished she did not know that the gills—delicate feathers she had studied under the microscope so many times—remained unmoving and useless inside their chitinous shells.

"It's okay, little crabs," she said. "We're going to make it home soon, and it'll be warm and nice, and you will all come ashore and lay your eggs—there will be plenty for the birds and still there will be thousands of new crabs hatching and playing in the waves. And I'll keep your souls safe for you."

The crabs chittered back, excited. *Soon*, they agreed. *We know that we are close—we recognize the signs, the sandbars. We feel the scent of the familiar water, we recognize the manky stench of river silt flowing into the ocean. We know these salt marshes, we know the screeching of terns and gulls overhead. We are close, so close.*

Vimbai smiled and moved to straighten—her face had grown numb under water, and the *vadzimu*'s eyes felt indistinguishable from hers, a sure sign that she had spent too much time with her grandmother's ghost inside her, and that the two of them were at risk of confusing self with other. But before Vimbai's face had breached the surface, she felt a blinding pain in her side and stomach, as if from a kick strong enough to knock the wind out of her, and her arms and knees buckled under her, sending her toppling sideways into the cold, cold water, where nothing but the undead crabs waited for her.

THE *VADZIMU*'S PRESENCE SAVED VIMBAI—BECAUSE OF THE ghost, she had grown more impervious to cold, and her breathing underwater, while labored, was still reasonably comfortable. She grasped the rope that linked the house above to the crabs beneath, and hovered in the thickness of water, next to the clusters of dormant crabs. Her chest and stomach still hurt, and she could feel an ugly bruise spreading under her shirt, tracking its progress with a sensation of intense heat. That would be not even a bruise but a hematoma, Vimbai thought. Of course, there was also a question of who it was that kicked her under.

Balshazaar, her own and her grandmother's voices whispered in unison. Who else but that conniving, shriveled old man? What other appendage was capable of such a swift and decisive kick if not a phantom limb they had voluntarily given him?

She considered getting out of the water, but decided against it—surely, Balshazaar was waiting for her on the porch, waiting for her to surface and to betray that she was still alive, still presented a danger or, at the very least, an obstacle. In the water, she would be vulnerable to him—apparently, her scars did not protect from any desiccated heads (or, as far as she could tell, from anything but the *wazimamoto*, which made some twisted sense—African magic deterred African phenomena.) He could drown her or hurt her while she trod water, helpless. It would be better to wait him out, to let him think that she was gone and drowned, so that he could tell the man-fish and they both could regret that her soul fell to the horseshoe crabs instead of the wily catfish. Then, it would be safe for her to come out.

Even though she had not seen her assailant, she felt sure that it was not the *wazimamoto*—they could not come into the house. Her Kenyan babysitter was quite clear on that—she insisted that they left people in their houses alone, and only drained blood of those who were destitute enough to sleep in the streets. Poor people, migrant workers, prostitutes, homeless children—they were the preferred *wazimamoto* targets.

And then there were her scars, her protection. She wondered if the *wazimamoto* were so scared of them because they did not expect *muti* but if they would find a way to work around them. She found thinking easier in this thick green water, bobbing halfway between the bottom and the surface, a perfectly balanced float, her hand holding the rope that dragged the house home. Maybe she could stay here for all time, she thought—it wasn't bad, and she would be perfectly positioned to study her favorite crabs, with her mind and her grandmother's special vision and the ghostly ability to breathe underwater.

Then she worried that she would spend too much time with the ancestral spirit inside her, and that their souls would get entangled somehow, would become one. Vimbai certainly did not want to become her grandmother: even though she liked her better now than before, she still did not want the old woman's superstition or the conviction that *muti*, the mutilation magic, was somehow good for her children. She did not want her laments of the old days and the insistence that things used to be better when the British were in charge, just like she did not want her death, her endless stories that went nowhere, her narrow-minded ways.

A memory niggled at the edges of her mind, a half-forgotten fact from a botany lecture. She remembered the delicate, steady crosshatching of her drawings, the smiley faces of monocot vascular bundles and the perforated plates of the sieve tubes. The branching of the leaf's veins, and the delicate internal structures of the anthers and pistils. And then there was something, something else—she remembered tracing the thin fibers snaking in-between the tissues of a vine's stem, almost invisible filaments that penetrated the plant's food and moisture supply, coiled into every cell and narrow space between vessels.

The parasitic plant, Vimbai remembered, the thing that hid inside another plant and only became apparent when it bloomed with its horrible febrile flowers—gigantic, three feet across, red and warty white. A gruesome flower that looked like slabs of meat and stank of rotting flesh; *Rafflesia* it was called, she remembered. Still, it took her a while of silent bobbing and being dragged through the numbing cold water to realize what the flower reminded her of—she recognized in its quiet creeping the same deceiving calm and even tenderness that she had felt as the *vadzimu*'s memories blended with hers, seamlessly twining between the threads of Vimbai's life. She recognized the imperceptible shifts and subtle rearrangements of what made Vimbai the girl that she was, she felt the memories of her first love (Elizabeth, Elizabeth, her memories and dreams sang in unison) being pushed to the side to give just a hair's breadth more space to the memories of red soil and dry summer months, of the red dust that hung relentless in the vegetable garden, the squash and the yams ailing in the heat. Her mother's face shifted and flowed in her memory—from a stern woman with sharp cheekbones to a soft-faced girl and back again, the marks on her face changing from fresh cuts to almost invisible scars.

Vimbai resented herself for thinking of her dead grandmother as a parasite—everything else aside, the *vadzimu* was the reason Vimbai was still alive in the freezing ocean, breathing underwater. Her memories offered Vimbai a glimpse of a life so different from her own that really, she should be grateful for the opportunity. Her mother always told Vimbai that she was too sheltered, too ignorant of how the rest of the world lived—and yet, Vimbai thought, she was the one doing all the sheltering. Just think about what it took for Vimbai to move out of her protective fierce embrace—it took a house that was filled with landscapes and contained the entirety of Vimbai's idea of Africa, and two very strange roommates.

Vimbai thought of the jacaranda trees and the horseshoe crabs, their fine delicate claws combing the white sand of the bottom with the speedy mechanical motion of a small windmill; her memories of her children intertwined with her memories of her parents, and for a few dizzying moments she could not tell which was which. Her eyes filled with tears of either childhood helplessness or sadness of old age, useless underwater and superfluous in the ocean already filled with salt, and unknown hard words filled her mouth—Shona words she had neither used nor remembered since she was little, too little for kindergarten; it was kindergarten where she stopped talking Shona, she remembered now. Before, Shona and English were inseparable and the same, one become the other in her mouth as easily as in the mouths of her parents— they did not discriminate, and the languages switched in a joyful leapfrog of words not bound by rules. When Vimbai was little, she found the words that best filled the void, be they Shona or English; she had lost this ability on the first day of kindergarten, when she answered her teacher's question in Shona and everyone in the class laughed. Her parents still spoke a mix of languages at home, and how she envied them! She wished she could forget the laughter of the kids and just speak the way she had been doing before.

And now Shona forced its way back into her throat, just like the memories of Harare forced themselves back into her mind, and Vimbai closed her eyes, her warm tears flowing into the cold ocean and disappearing there without a trace, leaving no imprint. She had to go back now, she thought, back to the surface, into the warm embrace of the house and its smells of dank domesticity and over-boiling coffee, where she could disentangle herself from her dead grandmother and be herself; she just wanted to catch her breath and examine what was and wasn't her anymore.

But the feat of returning proved more difficult than she had hoped; it always was, after all, the impossibility of the act implied in so many language clichés and morality tales. She kicked her way to the surface only to discover that the surface as such had disappeared—instead, there was a thin layer of oily and impenetrable darkness, as if some mythological version of Exxon Valdez had suffered an accident and spilled whatever mysterious substance it carried and that could poison an imaginary ocean.

Not Exxon Valdez, Vimbai realized when her face touched the murky substance and entered it as one enters a summer night, clammy and humid and warm, from the crisp chill of an air-conditioned house—the too-warm, too-humid air wrapped around her skin and beaded it with sweat. There was darkness and nothing at all to see, and there was neither sky nor the house anywhere in view.

Shocked, Vimbai sank again, back into the comforting and familiar chill of the ocean. Her thoughts raced and her heart thumped harder against the delicate cage of her ribs—she could feel every contraction, every pump resonate through every bone in her body with a hollow echo. She looked around her, at the newly vivid green of the water and the white of sand, studded with black and blue bivalves, twined in the yellow and brown and green of seaweed. She could not comprehend what had happened to the surface, but there was no doubt in her mind that it was the work of Balshazaar and the *wazimamoto*.

And then it came to her, the memory—thick, viscous fluid, the extraneous membranes of space in Felix's universe. It was the remnants of space from his denuded head, she realized, it was what had been drained from him—a layer of foreign dimensions floating atop of the ocean like oil, cutting her off from the house as effectively as any barrier. There was no crossing this pocket universe, even as it spread in an infinitely thin layer—she could only stick her face inside and squint at the impenetrable darkness and the faint taste of rain-beaten dust in the thick, immobile air.

The urgency of Vimbai's situation caught up with her occasionally and then she would bound for the surface, crazed and weightless like an air bubble (and those had ceased leaving her lips a long time ago), only to find again and again that the barrier persisted, and she still did not know how to breach it. Then she sank back, to the crabs, and floated by them as they dragged the house and Vimbai clinging to the rope along with them. There, she thought that maybe it would be okay, maybe she could stay there until someone—either Maya or Felix or Peb—found her. Or perhaps she would be okay all the way to New Jersey—didn't the crabs say that they were close?

But she knew that these were idle fancies, and that she did not have time to be found or rescued. With every passing second, the wrinkles on her grandmother's face grew more and more familiar, with the same inevitability as one's face is recognized in the mirror. Soon, the *vadzimu* and Vimbai would not be able to tell where one ended and the other began.

"I'm so sorry, grandmother," Vimbai whispered, and immediately answered herself, "I'm so sorry, granddaughter."

It had occurred to Vimbai that lately she had been spending quite a bit of time drowning or otherwise under water; she wondered if there was some significance to it.

"What say you, crabs?" she said out loud.

The crabs chittered and whispered among themselves, such disconcertingly high-pitched and birdlike sounds. "What pierces the darkness?" they finally asked.

Vimbai sighed. Stupid riddles, she wanted to say, sthe ame riddles that surfaced in fairy tales—just feeble-minded guises for simplistic morality lessons, not at all challenging or enlightening. "Light," she said out loud, struggling not to let her irritation show. "Light pierces the darkness. Thank you, this is very helpful. Only I have no sources of light here, and neither do you."

This is not true, the *vadzimu* in her mind answered. *Remember the story I told you, remember the story you told Peb. Both are* ngano—*and* ngano *is how children learn. Your task may be hopeless or you might not even know that you have a task in the first place, but there are things within you that you can reach.*

Vimbai only sighed in response. It seemed silly, the same psychobabbly message of hope she'd been hearing from school counselors and the books that were supposed to instill 'values' (no one ever told her what those values were supposed to be) into her. It didn't change, she thought. There was always someone offering a simple solution, there was always this belief that only if you try hard enough, want something bad enough, there would be a wellspring of miracles and you would always get whatever it was you wanted. One could always triumph—but she knew, she had learned through a long and disappointing string of letdowns that sometimes there were circumstances beyond one's control. Sometimes one was too short for basketball or too stocky and thick-boned to seriously consider gymnastics. Sometimes one did not have the complexion to play Snow White, no matter how much enamored one was of this role at the age of five. Sometimes one had to throw away the dreams, no matter how dear or powerful, after first experiencing a bitter sting of reality. But then again, this is what this house was for, wasn't it? The old dreams that everyone had forgotten about, so she really had no right to get angry at them.

She thought of the tortoise in her grandmother's story, and hated the smug beast who got everything everyone else wanted without even trying. Humility indeed. And yet, and yet . . . there were dreams in this house, she thought, and what were dreams if not irrational wish fulfillment? What was the point of ever dreaming if one could not be a ballerina anyway? And didn't the sea follow her? It followed her in her dreams as if it was her, Vimbai who was the moon, round and heavy like an old silver coin—a coin tossed by a careless hand, heads or tails, and now stuck in the middle of the sky. The coin that attracted all the seas in the world, heavy and smooth, grave and yet pouring out bucket after bucket of pure light, reflected though it might be—it didn't matter in the slightest.

Vimbai closed her eyes and imagined pure white light, white as milk, as the tortoise's beak slurped it up as if it was candy. She pictured all this cold, pure whiteness sloshing inside her belly, heavy and round like the moon, with enough gravitational pull to attract all the oceans in the world, and then she thought of her slender fingers reaching inside, into all this light, asking for a wishing thread—and receiving a white burst of light instead, the kind of light that burned bright as a carbide lamp, and before which no darkness could resist.

Chapter 17

THERE WAS ONE MEMORY VIMBAI RARELY THOUGHT about—not because she had forgotten and not because the memory was in any way unpleasant. Rather, Vimbai felt that some things were too precious to tarnish with frequent reminiscences, and thought around it, obliquely, while always retaining the warm feeling the memory gave her.

But now she felt it was a good time to remember it—she chose this memory from among all the others for its golden light and the overwhelming sense of joy that radiated from it. It all happened when both Vimbai and Elizabeth Rosenzweig were in eighth grade, when Vimbai was still too clueless to realize what was happening to her.

She remembered that day with such clarity—it was May, and their class was mercifully sent on a fieldtrip to one of the dinky little museums that peppered the shore towns like lighthouses and souvenir shops. Vimbai did not remember which town it was, and she did not remember much of what she had seen at the museum—there were vague memories of old fishing nets and handmade fishing floats, rusted antique anchors, and the musty smell, the same as every tiny and ill-conceived maritime museum she had visited over the course of her life in South Jersey. There were stuffed blue marlins mounted on the walls and insipid paintings with white-sailed ships frozen on the brink of white-capped waves, and things rescued from shipwrecks of dubious authenticity mixed in with preserved specimens of octopi and other strange-looking invertebrates; if Vimbai was so inclined, she could've traced her fascination with marine biology to these dusty jars with discolored eyes and tentacles in them.

What made this museum different, though, was Elizabeth's presence—she had just transferred in from whatever glamorous life she had previously lived, and Vimbai tried really hard not to follow the new girl too much but found such restraint difficult, due to Elizabeth's interesting way of speaking. At the museum, Vimbai spent little time looking at the exhibits and a lot trying to maneuver herself next to the new girl so that it looked like an accident, in case anyone actually paid attention to Vimbai.

She had finally managed to stand next to Elizabeth, who yawned and looked at an old, sepia-toned photograph of one fishing vessel of the bygone days or another.

"Hi," Vimbai said, staring at the photograph with a greater intensity than it warranted and keeping her tone casual.

"Hi," Elizabeth answered and smiled at the photograph. "Vimbai, right?"

Vimbai felt a happy little flutter in her stomach that the glorious new girl remembered her name, and even pronounced it correctly. "Yes," she said. "And you're Elizabeth?"

The girl nodded and finally tore her gaze away from the photograph and gave Vimbai a slow, half-lidded look, which gave Vimbai goosebumps on the back of her neck and head. "I don't like any of the diminutives of my name," she said. "And I'm bored. Is there anything else to do around here?"

"Well, sure," Vimbai stuttered and looked for the teacher who was just ahead of them, pointing something out on some stupid diorama. "There's the beach, and the shore towns always have a boardwalk. But we're supposed to be here . . . I think."

Elizabeth shrugged one shoulder, took Vimbai's hand—so confidently and thoughtlessly, as if it was her right to grab Vimbai's digits like they belonged to her doll or stuffed bear—and dragged her along, to the diorama. "Excuse me, Ms. Burns," she said to the teacher. "My allergies are acting up because of the dust, and I don't have my medication with me. Vimbai will take me outside, and we will meet the group by the bus later."

Maybe it was that snooty accent, Vimbai thought. Maybe it was the way Elizabeth carried herself—she didn't even ask, she told the teacher what she was going to do, and Mrs. Burns just nodded and told them to stay out of the sun. Or maybe, Vimbai realized much much later, maybe their overworked teacher, who was looking back to the summer recess more than her students did, had a small moment of mercy and just decided to let them go and enjoy themselves on the board-walk. Such a small kindness that seemed such an enormous stroke of luck back then—such incredible escape from the dark and dusty and boring sepia-colored museum and its stench of formalin, into the blinding sun and the smell of salt in the air.

The boardwalk was not crowded, since it was only May and

a work day, too early for the tourists to swarm in earnest. But there was salt taffy and small shops that sold cheesy t-shirts and painted shells and hermit crabs that allegedly made excellent pets.

Elizabeth dragged Vimbai along, laughing, stopping at every store that caught her attention. She bought Indian lapis-lazuli jewelry and canvas bags that said nonsense like "Visit Ocean City." Vimbai passed on the jewelry, but made up for it in cotton candy and funnel cake—the latter invention Elizabeth had been woefully unfamiliar with, and Vimbai did her best to remedy the situation. They quickly got covered with powdered sugar and Elizabeth complained that her hands dripped with oil and she couldn't possibly clean it off with napkins. All in all, it was the best day of Vimbai's life, even though she was too inexperienced to realize that it was due to the fact that she held hands with Elizabeth, rather than the boardwalk and the funnel cake.

The memory of that golden, sun-drenched day was her most precious one, and as she recalled the sun and the red and white stripes of the shops' awnings, the smell of salt from the ocean and the fried dough on the boardwalk, the overwhelming sense of freedom and happiness at being allowed to break out of the museum—just the two of them, marked as special enough for such privilege by the teacher—and to roam the town instead of doing dull and educational things. Oh, how she missed Elizabeth now, how she missed her magic.

The magic was never far from Vimbai's skin's surface—the scars, the sigils glowed again. Not with a red hot protective fire, not with the hidden lava of painful love magic Vimbai

had not realized she knew so well—but instead they burst
open, split like the seams of a pea pod and released not some
prosaic seeds but sunbeams, the light Vimbai had drunk in
years ago, like the tortoise who did not know what he was
doing—he thought that he was just slaking his thirst, just like
Vimbai used to think that she was just cutting school and
eating funnel cake. The acts of great personal replenishment
went unnoticed and unrecognized, and their significance
could only become apparent in retrospect.

Vimbai's skin split and narrow sunbeams shot out. The
horseshoe crabs, the undead ones running below and the little
ones encrusting the ropes as if they were Christmas orna-
ments stood out in bright relief, in their true color—emerald
green concentrated into dark khaki by the water. The beams
crossed the thickness of water and sliced into the oily darkness floating on the surface, and Vimbai let go of the rope
and swam after them, trying to keep inside the narrow road
of light that seemed to lead—somewhere.

To HER SURPRISE, SHE DID NOT REACH THE HOUSE OR THE
surface. To make the matters worse, the *vadzimu*'s mind
inside her grew stronger and louder, jamming her memories, chasing away the perfect recollection of a perfect day
in adolescent love. The light pouring out of her opened cuts
grew dimmer and the skin, held open and taut by the sheer
intensity of the light stream, sagged and wilted, closing the
open scars and diminishing the light further. Oh, this was not
good, and Vimbai scrambled for more.

The only trouble was, there was not enough in her love for

Elizabeth to sustain a long examination or contemplation—surely, there was plenty of material for navel-gazing if she was so inclined (and she had been in the past). But the simple truth of the matter was that Vimbai's first love was an exercise in cowardice, where she never dared to say anything first, and expressing her feelings remained entirely out of the question. She had failed by clinging to this one infatuation well into her college career, as the means of letting herself escape any other kinds of entanglements—she was even too afraid to find out whether she only liked girls, or if boys were an option as well. *I lied to you, grandmother*, she whispered, mournful and dimming, almost lost in the darkness that approached from all sides, engulfing her once more. *I'm sorry for lying—I don't really worry about boys, I worry that I would never be able to love anyone for real, and this is what I'm afraid of.*

Don't worry, granddaughter, the *vadzimu* replied. *We all have fears, and none of us knows a perfect way of dealing with them. But maybe you just need to take a look at the person you love now, and learn bravery there.*

Vimbai felt neither outrage nor shock, just weary acceptance, and she had no strength to deny. There was no point—from the first day she sat in the (now unrecognizable) living room of the house, from the moment she watched Maya sling her long legs over the armrest of the worn chair, she knew that she wanted to stay. Yes, the house pulled her in—but so did Maya's voice and face, so did the prospect of having a roommate such as her, seeing someone as breathtaking every day. And she thought of Maya's lonely tower, where she slept like a fairytale princess, among the crumpled candy wrappers and empty soda cans, her sleep guarded by an unmoving and dead grandmother. She had nothing left but to coax this reluctant love (those who had lost, she remembered now, those who were honest were the most delusional) into its real form, and she tried to coax herself into admitting what it was and why it mattered.

Vimbai's grandmother did her best to help as well—she pushed on Vimbai's eyes from inside, forcing forth the visions of her daughters, of them growing up. She lamented the deaths of her friends with the same quiet clarity as she lamented the passing of the country she once knew—she did not miss the British, but she found a total collapse frightening. She pushed forth the memory of independence and the jubilation in the streets when the Land Reform was first announced. She grieved about the failure of the 'willing seller, willing buyer' paradigm. Then she thought about all the strength and all the love she had seen in her life, and it filled Vimbai's heart with hope, and her scars with light. The light pulsed and pushed them open, forcing Vimbai's own confessions out of them.

Maya poured out of Vimbai's scars and her eyes, and there was darkness parting before her. The little eddies and layers of darkness floated and separated, and tore like stormy clouds in the November sky. Through the holes she could see snatches of the real sky above and the shingles of the house's roof. With one final thrust and a kick of her tired legs Vimbai pushed herself through one of the openings and came to the surface, just a few feet away from the porch.

Balshazaar was nowhere in sight, and Vimbai swam up to the porch in quick strokes. Her vision doubled, and she feared that the *vadzimu* would become too entrenched to ever be separated from Vimbai. Her own hands already looked strange to her—pruned from being in the water for so long but young, too young, with pinkish full moons of fingernails and the skin that was lighter than what it was supposed to be—and it took her a while to remember that she was neither eighty nor dead. She clambered onto the porch, simultaneously panicking at her grandmother's insidious presence and addressing herself as *sahwira*, trying to talk herself down and thinking that young people spooked entirely too easily nowadays. Despite her confusion, she felt the cold in the air, and the sticking of heavy wet clothes, and she crouched on her hands and knees, shivering violently and vomiting gallons of salt water—now that there was air to breathe, the water in her lungs become heavy and unwelcome, and Vimbai remembered that it was unnatural for human beings to breathe underwater like that, even though spirits could.

Somewhere along with all this salt water and an occasional tiny fish, Vimbai managed to expel the spirit too—or perhaps the *vadzimu* had extricated herself without Vimbai's help, and now she stood by her, patting her back solicitously, as if burping a baby. Vimbai spat out a couple more mouthfuls and stood up, her legs trembling under her, and queasiness filling her stomach.

"It's all right, *sahwira*," the ghost said, seemingly unperturbed. "Go change your clothes, I'll make you some tea. And then, then you better go and set things right—poor baby still doesn't have his tongue."

MAYA HAD RETURNED FROM HER EXPEDITION, AND REPORTED on the successful stashing of the horseshoe crabs' souls. Vimbai felt almost relieved that Balshazaar had chosen to turn his questionable attention to Vimbai and away from Maya—the fact that the crabs were safe and undiscovered by him made it almost worth the blind, panicked flailing under-water, with nowhere to go but the oily dying space off Felix's head.

"Oh, poor Felix," Vimbai said out loud. "Should we check on him before we go looking for Peb's tongue?"

"This is an awful way to pose a question," Maya said, her voice teasingly scolding. "I can't say either 'yes' or 'no' without agreeing to go look for Peb's tongue. And I have to say, I don't like these weird quests. What's with the body parts, anyway? Can't we go looking for some Book of the Dead or Amulet of Awesome Power?"

"No," Vimbai said. "Looks like for us it's all about Felix's Hair and Phantom Limbs and Peb's Tongue. Speaking of which . . . "

Maya heaved a sigh. "I know. Don't nag, please. We'll go as soon as I get a chance to take a nap, okay? I've been climbing stairs all day long. And you've been drowning, so maybe you should do the same. Then we check on Felix and go looking for the tongue."

Vimbai nodded. "I'll check on him first. See you in an hour or two."

She tiptoed past the forest of what looked like coat hangers and fishing poles and hat racks, and across a brand new meadow, sprinkled with white and pink flowers, that hadn't been there this morning, on her way to Felix's room. Thankfully, he remained unmolested, and asleep. Vimbai thought of waking him but decided against it—there seemed no point in exposing him again to the shock of his transformation, to the realization that his parent universe was gone forever, his umbilicus to his home world, however tentative, severed with unnecessary brutality and machine-like efficiency, and that the effluvia of the dead universe were dumped onto the ocean surface. Vimbai wondered if it would affect marine life at all, or if they would be able to surface through the ghastly space remnants with no problems. Maybe waves would disperse it, she thought; maybe it was the sort of thing only people noticed, like time. No, it was better to let him sleep—perhaps his dreams would help him when he woke up.

Vimbai reached her room and curled under the blankets. She thought idly that she probably should hang up her wet clothes from earlier today so that they could dry properly, but dismissed the thought as something best left for later. Now, she had to concentrate on the strategic dreaming—she had to dream of something that would help them to retrieve Peb's tongue. Vimbai closed her eyes and, before uneasy and fitful sleep claimed her, pictured the grotesque body of Peb, with many arms and hands and feet bristling from it in every direction, and the empty hole of its black crying mouth.

VIMBAI'S DREAM FELT STRANGELY SEDATE, EVEN ORDINARY —she dreamt of being a petulant twelve-year-old, shopping for shoes with her tight-lipped mother. It was important for some reason to get new shoes right before the school started again, and Vimbai's mother was determined to make this experience as stressful as possible—even worse than the rest of obligatory back-to-school nonsense.

First, there was the issue of the overall effect malls had on Vimbai's mother—there was something about the sheer volume of the superfluous consumption that put her in a foul mood as soon as she parked her car. Wherever they went afterwards, there were more and more irritating things, and the stream of muttered commentary never ceased; it eventually grew in volume, causing the shoppers nearby to look at them. Vimbai felt embarrassed and hissed at her mother, and she snapped back. And it went downhill from there.

Second, there were the shoes themselves. Vimbai, being twelve, liked them square-nosed and funky, with chunky heels and bright colors; her mother tended toward more demure and practical styles, preferably of the Mary-Janes variety; lime green and three inch wedges or platforms were out of the question.

Third, there was the political side—it took them forever to find shoes that were not made in a sweatshop, and made by those who were either the US unionized workers or at the very least fair wage workers in China or elsewhere in the world. That took forever, and it drove Vimbai insane—nothing she liked could possibly meet her mother's approval, and if by some miracle it did, there was almost no chance that it would pass the fair labor test. Vimbai thought that it wasn't fair that her shoes had to be a political statement by her mother, but there didn't seem to be a way around it.

In the dream, Vimbai saw herself as if looking on from the outside, hovering disembodied and invisible, and looking with her adult eyes at the sulky and young version of herself—was she really that chubby as a kid? Young Vimbai scowled at the brown shoe that enclosed her foot like an ugly polyp. Her mother kneeled before her, tying the laces with uncalled-for vigor, as if she were trying to strangle Vimbai's foot.

"It's ugly," Vimbai said. "I hate it."

Her mother looked up—one of the very few moments in Vimbai's life when her mother was looking up at her. "Vimbai, *sahwira*, please. These are the only ones in your size."

"Mom, this is ridiculous. There are tons of shoes here. And some of them are not even ugly."

"You know why we can't get these," her mother said, exasperated, her pupils narrowed into needle points, her voice so taut it was ready to tear into a scream at any second. Dangerous, dangerous, not the woman to toy with or to piss off just now.

Vimbai rolled her eyes. "Mom, buying a pair of shoes is not a political decision. It's just shoes. It's not fair to put it on me, you know? There are countries and governments and all these people in the world who could make sure that there are no sweatshops or child labor, so I can just get a pair of fucking shoes without drama and without you telling me how everything is my fault."

To her surprise, her mother's lips relaxed and her shoulders sagged, as if the tension wire had just been pulled out of her, leaving her without the ringing terrible support she relied on all these years. "It's not your fault," she said. "I never said anything was your fault—why would you even think that?"

Vimbai shrugged and nodded at the ugly hoof on her foot.

Her mother laughed, unexpectedly. "I suppose it feels like punishment, doesn't it?"

"Yes." Vimbai kicked off the shoe, now that she realized that argument and screaming had been miraculously averted.

Her mom sighed and stood. She took Vimbai's hand and pulled her along, away from the imitation leather benches and the low mirrors on the floor, away from the shelves crawling with mismatched shoes, away from the smooth hardwood floors and the restless children and annoyed mothers. "We'll find you something," Vimbai's mother said. "Just understand one thing for me, all right? It's not your fault, but sometimes we have to do what we can to correct wrongs done by other people. Sometimes those who committed them are dead or they don't care or they don't see it as a wrong. But this is what makes us human, this—the fact that we are able to fix other people's mess. Even when it's not fair."

Vimbai nodded that she understood. "You can just get me canvas sneakers," she said. "Now let's go get a pretzel."

Her mother smiled, nodding, and her firm warm hand squeezed Vimbai's in unsaid gratitude. When Vimbai woke up, it was dark outside, and she felt like crying.

MAYA WOKE UP BEFORE VIMBAI. SHE SAT IN THE KITCHEN, darker than a storm cloud. "We're out of coffee," she announced as soon as Vimbai came downstairs.

"Bummer," Vimbai mumbled, unwilling to meet Maya's eyes. "Any tea?"

"Just loose green tea that's been sitting in the cupboard since the previous tenants," Maya said. "Whoever they were."

Vimbai sniffed at the yellow paper package with green lettering, and laughed. "That's not tea, that's *mate*."

"What's the difference?"

"It has a better kick than coffee," Vimbai said. "Only you have to drink it through special straws, otherwise the leaf debris would get into your mouth."

"I don't care," Maya said with a suddenly renewed enthusiasm for life. "How do you make this thing?"

Vimbai put the kettle on and poured boiling water over what she judged to be sufficient quantities of a substance that resembled dried grass in appearance and smell.

Maya drank greedily. "Yuck," she said. "Then again, it does have a kick." She looked at Vimbai and stopped smiling.

"What's the matter?" she said. "You look bummed out."

Vimbai heaved a tremulous sigh and sniffed, all the while aware that it wasn't really fair to Maya who did not have any family left. "I miss my parents," she said. "Especially my mom."

"I thought you fought a lot."

"We did. We do. But it doesn't matter; I still miss her."

Maya nodded. "I suppose families are like that. Anything you want to talk about?"

Vimbai considered the offer—it was tempting, to tell Maya about her mother's obsessive social consciousness and the liability it brought to her teenage daughter, amplifying the usual embarrassment every offspring had suffered while interacting with their peers in their parents' presence. Vimbai suspected that her social status suffered doubly—for her mother's insistence on responsible consumption and her accent. Even though she was a college professor, her accent and her color marked her as an immigrant, a first-generation, and Vimbai preferred to downplay her mother whenever possible—which was not often. Yet, all these complaints seemed petty now, especially in Maya's presence. Maya, who did not have any parents, did not deserve to listen to Vimbai's unsubstantiated bitching. Instead, she said, "I just regret that I never invited my mom over to this house. I think she would like it, and she would love you."

Maya laughed, took a hasty sip of her mate, and coughed, her face turning dark purple.

Vimbai patted Maya's back, trying to dislodge whatever renegade *maté* leaves had lodged in her throat. "No, really, she would. She would try and adopt you, of course. And then she would drive me nuts telling me how I should be more like you."

"Why would she say that?"

Vimbai shrugged and sucked in a mouthful of *maté* through her teeth, trying to filter out the debris in the manner of whales. "She wants me to have more positive role models. See, I'm not African enough, and then I'm not American enough, and I'm not really anything proper. And my mom . . . she means well and she tries hard, but I know that she secretly wishes that I had grown up in Zimbabwe so that she wouldn't have to deal with a spoiled American kid. Or she wishes that I would know more about the Diaspora, at the very least. She wants me to understand why it matters to everyone but me that my parents came over here voluntarily."

Maya nodded. "We all have our problems, I guess."

"I guess. And I know that mine are not important; they are just the ones I know."

Maya finished her *mate*. "I understand. Well, I have a job and a roof over my head, so I have no reason to complain either; still it doesn't matter if I do. Meanwhile, let's take care of those who can't complain even when they want to."

Vimbai finished her drink and stood. "Oh, grand. We'll go find the *wazimamoto* and ask them for Peb's tongue."

"That's right," Maya said. "What are you afraid of? You seem to have power over them."

Vimbai sighed. "I hope it still works."

Chapter 18

VIMBAI AND MAYA DECIDED TO LOOK FOR THE TRUCK—IT was day, and the *wazimamoto* were more likely to be roaming around. Maya's dogs trotted ahead, sniffing the ground, barking in short bursts and occasionally peeing on the ground, excited.

Vimbai thought guiltily that she wouldn't really mind walking like this, through the plains overgrown by skeletal umbrellas and yellowing sedges, with rare clusters of what looked like forks piled high with calamari salad off in the distance—just walking and talking to Maya, about anything they wanted to talk about.

"Your mom sounds really cool," Maya said. "And smart, too. I think it is awesome that your parents came from overseas and managed to make a good life here."

"I guess it is good," Vimbai said. "Only my mom complains so much, you never would guess that she is happy."

"Maybe she complains because she sees how things could be better."

Vimbai nodded, all the while imagining bringing Maya over to visit her parents. They would hit it off, Vimbai thought, her mother and Maya; they would really like each other. They would probably understand each other better too—they would sift through their collected experience, looking for similarities in stories of privation, shutting out Vimbai who really never missed anything. Maybe this is why her mother got so angry—maybe it was because they were too good as parents, they provided too well, spoiled her too much. They made it too easy for her, and thus failed to raise a child they could relate to. Vimbai could not decide whether it was truly sad, or if it was a ridiculous thing to feel bad about.

She was distracted from her thought by the appearance of something tall, stone, and domineering on the horizon—even if she hadn't seen it in her dreams, she would've recognized it anyway. The Great Zimbabwe, this version made of concrete slabs and wrought iron. When they traveled closer, Vimbai saw that there were occasional Legos and plastic building blocks sprinkled in the great seams where one slab joined the next.

Maya's dogs dispersed over the grassy area between the giant structures—houses of giants, Vimbai thought, temples of dragons. The sort of thing that made one want to believe in ancestral spirits and their ability to bring messages from the creator. Vimbai smiled and looked around her, a vague pride filling her heart with joy.

She wanted to look for people's houses, for the round houses she remembered from her dreams as well as her travels to the outskirts of Harare, so perfect and almost fairytale-like, with their smooth walls and grassy roofs. She wanted to find people from her dreams and their winged boats, the delicate contrivances that allowed flight from the terrible draining of the *wazimamoto*. She wanted to hear the powerful whooshing of these wings, displacing the air with great beats, and the shouts of people in the boats, not looking back but intensely staring ahead of them, already forgetting what they had escaped, intent only on finding out what waited for them in whatever new place their boats carried them to.

But there were neither houses nor boats, and Vimbai sighed with disappointment. Maya wandered between the great stone contraptions, her mouth alternatively hanging open and shaping a delighted smile. "This is yours, isn't it?" she asked Vimbai as if it was something she had made herself. "You have such wonderful dreams."

"Thank you," Vimbai said, and felt a bit silly at being complimented on the quality of her subconscious. "This is something I've really seen—it's The Great Zimbabwe." She explained to Maya what it was, all the while keeping her gaze on the openings between the stones, where the green canopy of the surrounding forest, punctuated here and there by tall gray spires of unknown origin, met the grass of the clearing. Vimbai could not see any roads, and yet it offered no comfort.

She was not surprised when she heard the sound of engines, getting closer and closer. She thought then that the *wazi-mamoto* were like European ghosts, unable to do anything but revisit the places that had mattered to them when they were still alive. Like clockwork, their truck went in circles, regardless whether there were victims to be had.

"Quiet," Vimbai whispered and took Maya's hand. A normal protective gesture, she told herself, no reason for Maya to think anything was up and to reject Vimbai on the spot and outright. She pulled her along, to hide in the tall grass between the jutting cliffs and leaning slabs of the construction, parts of it resembling not so much the Great Zimbabwe but radioactive spill sites—those were always covered with concrete slabs, in indifference or foolish optimism, it was so difficult to decide. All Vimbai knew that every single one she had ever seen had cracked concrete with thin tree saplings pushing through the cracks, nothing contained, and thoughts about where the radioactive spill went were best left unthought and unanswered.

Maya followed her, and the two of them lay on their stomachs, behind a piece of concrete that jutted partway out of the ground, forming an inclined smooth surface that was so easy to hide behind. The noise of the engine came closer, and Maya barely had enough time to whistle to her dogs, who came to her call and lay behind the slab too, a rusty river of fur and pricked up ears, of bright black eyes and long pink tongues separating Vimbai from Maya like a legendary sword.

Vimbai waited for the sound of the car engine to get closer—so close, it seemed to be shuddering in her heart now, the ashes of Klaas, the thunderous choking beats that made her want to jump up, her hands over her ears, screaming, *enough, enough, please stop!*

Instead, she clung closer to ground, trying to disappear in the narrow space between the concrete slab and grass, her eyes squeezed shut. Maya's elbow pressed against hers, and only this warm touch offered a measure of comfort. The scars on her inner arms glowed with a pale yellow light, as if they felt the approach of this specific danger. Or perhaps something different—just as the engine fell silent, Vimbai felt a gentle tap on the shoulder, and turned around to come face to face with the man-fish.

He did not seem much inconvenienced by being out of the water, and perched among the small saplings sprouting through the cracks in the stone. The man-fish managed to maintain a semi-upright position; his fins must've gotten stronger since the last time, Vimbai thought. Or maybe he found more souls to swallow, and this is what sustained him.

"Hello," the man-fish said in his gravelly voice. Vimbai thought that if he only twirled his whiskers, he could've passed for an operetta villain. "What are you doing here?"

"What are you doing out of your lake?" Vimbai countered. "Don't you need water to breathe?"

"Eventually, O girl who would not drown," he said. "But now I am here to help those who help me—they cannot deal with you, apparently."

Maya moved closer to Vimbai, crouching by her side, her knee touching the side of Vimbai's thigh. "Neither could you."

The man-fish ignored her, and turned his slightly glassy eye to the dogs, who whimpered but stayed close to Maya—out of loyalty, or possibly out of fear of something else hidden within this dream replica of a great monument. His mouth gulped air in quick, convulsive breaths, and his gill covers rose and fell like miniature beating wings. "What have we here?" he said. "Little fox-creatures, little girl's imaginary friends—all little pieces of her soul, all tasty morsels."

"What is he talking about?" Vimbai whispered to Maya.

Maya only paled in response and gathered her pets in a protective embrace.

"That's right," the man-fish said, leering. "You know I can suck them all in as if they were candy, slimy gummi worms. You know that these misshapen mutts are just little free-wheeling bits of you, and if I swallow them, what will become of you, hm?"

Vimbai drew herself up, straightening between the man-fish and Maya and her whimpering creatures. "You won't be swallowing anyone today," she said. "You better tell us where Peb's tongue is, and then we'll be on our way."

The man-fish seemed taken aback—he deflated somewhat, shrank away from Vimbai and looked smaller than he ever had. "And you think you can command me: why?"

Vimbai thrust her carved-up forearms that glowed brighter and spilled their pale yellow light in narrow beams, like the weak spring sun, into the man-fish's face.

He backed off a bit. "Where did you get this magic?" he asked, with curiosity rather than fear.

"I made it myself," Vimbai answered, deciding that going into great detail would be counterproductive.

The man-fish nodded with respect. "Very nice," he said. "With magic like this . . . it's very impressive, really. If one had such magic, one wouldn't need to beg for soul scraps from others."

"You mean—" Vimbai started.

The man-fish nodded again. "I mean that with such magic, I wouldn't have to go to *wazimamoto* or even help them drain your blood and your soul—and I could, I'll have you know, I totally could. Child's play. I'll even strike a bargain with you—you carve me a spell like this, you *muroyi*, you. You little witch. You carve me a spell and I tell you how you can get the psychic tongue back."

"So you lied to us the first time," Vimbai said. "It wasn't in the hospital."

"Oh, it was. Only not where you'd think. The *wazimamoto*, see, they are just nightmares, blind and dumb. They are nothing—they need psychic energy to even exist, let alone talk. The tongue you're looking for was there with them the whole time."

Maya gasped. "So Peb's tongue is what's keeping them talking."

"It's what keeping them existing," the man-fish said. "Which is a good thing for me, because this place is not exactly rich in life, and therefore in souls. They had drained what they could off your friend, and then off that funny head on a single leg. They give me what they don't use. But if you offer me something better . . . "

"I'm not going to let you steal more souls," Vimbai said. "Or help you to do so."

"You don't have to," the man-fish said. "If you make me a spell that would let me live without souls, that would let me collect the energy I need from the air and the water around me, then I would be content."

Maya nudged Vimbai. "You sure he's not lying?"

Vimbai shook her head. "Of course not. I mean, he probably is. About some of these things, at least."

"Can you put a spell on him?"

"Yes." Vimbai's fingertips stroked the scars on the insides of her arms, left hand to the right arm and the other way around, crossed, entwined. "I'm not sure I understand how it works or why I even can do that, but I think I could. But only after we get back Peb's tongue."

"That's rather inconvenient," the man-fish said. "If you banish the creatures that sustain me and then your spell fails, what will happen to me then?"

"We'll release you into the wild," Vimbai promised. "There are plenty of lakes in New Jersey, and there are dead people's souls you can swallow to your heart's content—if the spell fails, that is. As soon as the crabs get us there."

The man-fish appeared to scowl, even though Vimbai was not quite sure how he managed that without any eyebrows. "And I should trust you: why?"

"Because we cannot trust you," Vimbai said. "You tricked us twice already—it would be stupid to believe you again, you have to agree."

The man-fish muttered but conceded the point.

"So you see, you'll have to trust us, or we'll be at an impasse," Maya said. And added, in a flash of brilliance, "Besides, how long do you think before they decide to drain your blood?"

"That's a very good point," Vimbai said. "Can you really trust any creatures who do nothing but rob everything alive of its blood?"

The man-fish considered, his small eyes slowly moving from one girl to the other. "You won't trick me?" he finally asked.

Vimbai rounded her eyes at him. "How could we? You are quite smart, we wouldn't dare to."

"Yeah," Maya said. "And we give you our word—it actually is worth something."

The man-fish sighed, his gill covers fluttering. "All right," he said. "Now, get closer."

Vimbai and Maya approached the man-fish on their hands and knees, cautiously, as Maya's dogs hung back, whimpering with their fluffy tails lodged between their hind legs.

"Now," the man-fish said. "The tongue you're looking for is shared between all of them, split into many fine energy strands, psychic energy fibers, if you will. And to draw it out of them, you will need something inert, something that would accept this energy and hold it. It's like osmosis, see? Spirits would move into a greater spiritual vacuum—so you just need to find something that is a greater spirit vacuum than the *wazimamoto*."

"Is there such a thing?" Vimbai asked. "Is there anything more devoid of soul than colonial vampires?"

"Undead crabs?" Maya suggested.

"Their souls are too close," the man-fish argued. "But something close, something dead . . . "

"Oh no," Maya interrupted. "You're not touching my grandma."

The man-fish chuckled softly. "Even if it's just a memory of her death? Even though it would let you fix your little psychic energy friend?" His flat head and beady eyes thrust forth, his slimy skin almost touching Maya's face, his wet cold lips almost on hers. "Even though you could make her alive again, even for just a little while?"

THE *WAZIMAMOTO*'S TRUCK HAD FALLEN SILENT AND THE man-fish crawled away, muttering dark obscenities and vague promises; he begged them to come and visit him at the lake as soon as Maya made up her mind. Her dogs had grown bored and dispersed, hunting crickets and whatever other small and timid life crawled between the great concrete imitations of real boulders—real somewhere in the outside world, the world beyond these walls, the world that seemed a dream sometimes.

Vimbai had run out of comforting words, and could only sit next to Maya, her legs folded under her cold and numb, with only occasional prickling of phantom pins and needles suggesting that they were still alive; Vimbai's arms, goosebumped and heavy with fatigue, wrapped around Maya's unresponsive shoulders. How long had they been sitting like this?

Forever, Vimbai thought. Her head grew heavy with thwarted sleep, leaning against her will on Maya's indifferent shoulder, merciless gravity pulling her eyelids close. Galaxies were born and fell to dust, constellations swirled and traversed the skies millions of times, changing their position slowly, imperceptibly—and still, the two girls sat in the ruins of a great civilization, quiet and uncertain about the fate of a dead grandmother.

"Come on," Vimbai coaxed gently. "Let's go home—you don't have to decide anything here."

Maya shook her head, and Vimbai was unsure what she was objecting to. Finally, Maya shook her head one last time and stretched, breaking open the protective ring of Vimbai's arms. "I don't suppose I have a choice now, do I? Let it be, then. How do we get her to the *wazimamoto*?"

"We can wait here," Vimbai said. "We can wait for them to

show up. I will ask the horseshoe crabs to bring her to us—on their little backs, on their slender legs. They have no souls that would leak into her."

Maya nodded. "Ask your crabs to bring her then, I don't mind." She heaved a shuddering sigh. "I wish my grandmother was more like yours."

Vimbai understood what she meant—a bare spirit was better than a lifeless body. The separation of flesh from soul was a terrible thing—all death was terrible. But the ghosts, the *vadzimu* and other spirits, were pure and comforting, offering protection and advice, telling stories and doing dishes, really alive rather than dead. After separation of flesh and spirit, it were the spirits that remained alive. Vimbai shuddered at the memory of Maya's grandmother—nothing but a flesh suit, grotesque and unwieldy in its white gloves and floral hat, especially meaningless because the corpse did not need protection from the cold or embarrassment. It was inert and still, its trappings betraying the anxieties of the living.

And this is how she was when the horseshoe crabs, summoned by Vimbai's insistent call, aided by the *vadzimu* (who Vimbai could not see but easily imagined as she stood on the porch, peering into the water and gathering the undead arthropods for their mission), marched to the concrete tower somewhere on the edges of the house, as far as Maya's consciousness could reach, and picked her up on their backs. They moved like a lumpy river of olive-slick carapaces and gray infested meat and pale broken legs, dragging through the dust and the linoleum of the house, a small dead woman on their backs—her face peaceful, as if she were lying in state with her hands crossed on her chest and her starched white slip barely peeking from under the edge of her black skirt. Dead—certainly dead enough to suck away whatever psychic energy the *wazimamoto* had squirreled away, inside of their faceless, soulless bodies—if the man-fish was to be believed, at least.

Chapter 19

WHEN THE PROCESSION OF CRABS APPEARED, SO SOLEMN, SO grotesque, carrying the small dead woman, Maya suppressed a quick sob and covered her face with her hands. Vimbai could not help but hug her again, a mute comfort of companionship and implied understanding the only offering she had to give. And after the crabs had settled in a patient unmoving (undead) circle, surrounding the dead woman and her hat.

"You better leave," Vimbai told the crabs. "Please. If you stay, Peb's tongue . . . the psychic energy we're after might jump into you. I mean, you're not wearing your souls now, are you?"

No, the crabs whispered, mournful. *Our brethren have their souls, but ours were drained and stolen, damaged forever—why didn't you tell us that you couldn't keep them safe?*

"I'm so sorry," Vimbai answered, a deep blush blooming forth under her skin, ready to reach the surface as soon as she finished speaking. "I thought I found them in time." And then, the blush; the memories of the horseshoe crab souls came forth, unbidden—their spirit shells impaled on long needles, the ghastly *wazimamoto* contraptions penetrating their gills and their eyes, their shells, with the casual brutality of those who wanted nothing but blood blood blood, medicinal blood for their antibodies and serums, blood they could drain from those who did not consent to it and then toss them back, used up, half-dead. Or quarter them and cut them up, stuff them into traps that would soon be crawling with thick slimy eels.

She had seen one of these traps being pulled out of the water once—the mesh bag reinforced with steel hoops that kept the trap open and barrel shaped, with a half-decomposed mass within it, unbearable to look at—it dripped and stank, and the fisherman who held the rope on which the trap was suspended seemed oblivious to the stench.

Vimbai had felt like gagging and looked at her classmates (it was a fieldtrip for her very first marine bio class, and they were doing a unit on fisheries, which meant fieldtrips and talking to the fishermen a lot, and going on their boats to check their nets). Those trips always made Vimbai so nauseous.

"And this is how you catch eels," the bearded old man said.

Vimbai had been peering into the trap, puzzled—there didn't seem to be anything in there, except the fishy organic rot and a few broken segmented legs tipped with pale pincer claws. And then the mass started to move—seethe, churn, roil, like a pot of stew left in the sun for a few days roiled with maggots—and Vimbai had to look away just as the writhing black eels started falling through the mesh and slithering across the wooden pier.

"I'm never eating eel sushi again," one of Vimbai's classmates muttered in her ear.

"These are usually not for sushi," the professor explained cheerfully, his stereotypically gray goatee shaking with glee. "These are used as bait for the large-mouth bass."

It was then that Vimbai had decided that she would work on horseshoe crabs, on saving them from the awful destiny of being bait for bait, so recursively demeaned.

And now, standing in the ruins of the Great Zimbabwe and faced with their accusing stalked eyes, she blushed and looked away. "I am sorry I could not protect you. I swear to you that I tried. I did my best."

She feared their accusations, but they remained silent, looking at her with an indecipherable expression in their beady eyes. Vimbai couldn't figure out if they had forgiven her, these crabs that were now doomed to forever remain undead, or if she should apologize further.

Maya broke the awkwardness. "Can you hear that?"

Vimbai listened to the distant sound—lapping of waves, she had thought initially. Rustling of leaves, pounding of surf, beating of wings. For a moment, her hope of seeing the people in winged boats once again flared up, but she soon recognized the thudding of a car engine.

"They are coming back," Vimbai told the crabs. "You better leave if you don't want to be fed to the catfish."

The crabs finally listened and skittered away, one wide glistening river of olive and gray and brown, and Maya's dogs followed them at Maya's command—there was no use for them, and no point in them trying to protect Maya from the rapidly approaching danger.

Vimbai and Maya were left alone again, with only the dead body as their protection from the *wazimamoto*. And Vimbai's scars—she almost regretted not having offered Maya to carve some protection into her skin, and simultaneously found this way of thinking horrifying and repellent, just like she found her grandmother's beliefs in mutilating her own daughters wrong.

The medical truck pulled up to them, squealing to a slow laborious stop by the largest of the slabs. The old-fashioned cab of the truck was filled with the faceless surgeons, and they also clustered along the railings, their hands mere pale latex gloves that looked as if they contained nothing but air. Their faces remained hidden behind the gauze masks that could not disguise the absence of human features beneath the draping of their folds.

They disembarked from their vehicle as it groaned under their shifting weight, its shocks raising it higher above the ground as its passengers stepped down from it. They gave the body of Maya's grandmother only a cursory glance, immediately pegging it for something that offered no drainage possibilities, and moved past it, toward Maya— they must've remembered that Vimbai was not accessible to them.

As they moved by the dead body, Vimbai saw thin wisps of rainbow-radiant energy start peeling from them, swirling into a complex geometric shape in the air right above the dead woman's forehead. The *wazimamoto* faltered in their tracks and grasped with their gloved hands at the dancing, laughing apparition—the soap bubble, the shining glassy skin stretched over the countless phantom legs, a teasing smile of ethereal dimensions.

The shimmering shape remained floating and suspended, and time itself seemed to slow down and hover, twining around it like a strange dimensional pretzel. The *wazimamoto* slowed their motions, and their gloved hands grasped at the apparition as it leaked out of them—rainbow and brimstone!—as if trying to force it back into their pale hollow chests.

And yet, Vimbai thought, it was not their fault—it was not their fault that they kept draining life out of everything they saw, like it wasn't their fault that now they were struggling, like ragdolls, against falling apart as the bright tongues of light exited them and filled the prostrate body of Maya's grandmother with their ghostly light. Was it just Peb's tongue? Vimbai thought. Or were there are other psychic energies, other dimensional body parts that the *wazimamoto* had collected somewhere along their dream travels—and now they were all unraveling.

Vimbai thought—or some uninvolved part of her did, as the rest of her mind alternately recoiled away from the spectacle and drew closer to it, not to miss a single spark, a single wisp—of how pretty it was, how reminiscent of Peb himself, of his shimmering misshapen glory. And she was reminded of the aurora borealis, which she had seen only once, on her class trip to Alaska; the shimmery stretchy wisps lifted the dead woman off the ground and filled her—they seemed to be wearing her like a suit, as if the dead flesh was just a mask to hide the terrible and glorious lights inside.

Vimbai pressed Maya's head against her shoulder, wishing she could hide her from the traumatic scene unfolding before them, protect her with embrace. The sigils on her arms glowed with a molten color of burning tissue and embers, and she kept hugging Maya closer. "Don't look, don't look," she muttered.

"It'll be okay, I promise you, I promise." Maya's tears burned through the thin cotton of Vimbai's t-shirt.

But Vimbai herself looked—she looked at the conflagration of plasma and earthly fire, at the sputtering sparks from her own unintentioned charms and the spirit lights, at the flames that were springing up to consume the surgical scrubs and the latex gloves—so obviously empty now. The facemasks and the gauze, the hats and the rubber hoses were all going up in a giant bonfire that sprang where the *wazimamoto* had previously stood.

The fire roared up, up, and it spread sideways, bathing Vimbai's face in a blast of hot air, like the lick of a tremendous tongue. Vimbai retreated behind one of the slabs, Maya still held securely in her arms, Maya's face turned carefully away from the fire and the shambling puppet of her dead grandmother who lumbered slowly away from the spreading flames, her white eyes wide open and pouring out the same tormented fire that spread on the ground.

The grass turned to ash and the saplings bent and sputtered sap, crackling and groaning, their green branches bending and twisting like thelimbs of contortionists. The fire circle spread until it reached the truck, and Vimbai ducked behind her slab, expecting an explosion, just like anyone who had ever seen an action movie would.

To her surprise and secret disappointment, the fire did little more than melt the metal tires—apparently, the vehicles of colonial vampires did not use gasoline; the paint on the sides burned and crackled, swelling up in blisters and bursting. The rails and the cab heated to bright red and then white, and then they buckled and melted, turning into a soft clay and then viscous liquid. As it flowed to the ground, covering the burned grass and whatever ash was left of the *wazimamoto*'s former shapes, Vimbai realized that the vampires and their truck were gone now, and whatever terrible essence had animated them was not trapped in Maya's grandmother's body, which stood silently in the clearing, unaffected by either fire or molten metal. The old woman looked quiet, pensive almost, and if it wasn't for the white light streaming from her wide-open eyes the color and appearance of boiled eggs, she wouldn't have warranted a second look from a passerby; just an ordinary old lady, wearing a hat and gloves as if heading to church on a Sunday morning.

Maya sobbed behind her. "Grandmother?" she whimpered, sounding disturbingly like a small girl. "Granma, is this really you?"

The old woman turned with a clockwork-like motion, and opened her arms to Maya. "How you have grown," she said by way of greeting, and Vimbai did not know whether she should've held Maya back as she rushed into her undead grandmother's embrace.

THE *VADZIMU* HAD MADE A POT OF *MATÉ*, AND EVEN thoughtfully filtered it through a cheesecloth (Vimbai did not even know they had any cheesecloth, let alone what to use one for). Vimbai made a small cry of relieved gratitude and poured herself a cup, for a moment abandoning the unpleasant thoughts that had been swirling in her mind all the way home. Was Maya's grandmother really herself, just animated by energies better not to be contemplated, or was it just a sham, the *wazimamoto* disguised to assume a new form? And, most importantly and most impossibly, if they were to return Peb his tongue (another matter the feasibility of which Vimbai could not possibly assess), would it mean the destruction of Maya's grandmother, be she real or illusory?

The *vadzimu* took the presence of another grandmother well. The two of them shook hands and engaged in some small talk about the best way of cleaning off residue from the inside of a coffee machine carafe, and Vimbai and Maya sat by the table, momentarily reduced to the age of twelve or thereabout, and drank their *maté* and listened.

Peb floated into the room, and Vimbai tensed as soon as he zeroed in on Maya's grandmother. He hovered up to her and started crying—a terrible wordless yowling, like that of a cat.

"He wants what's his," said Vimbai's grandmother, and reached for Maya's, reassuring. "Don't worry, dear. He can wait a bit longer."

As Peb wailed and whined, demanding, Maya turned to Vimbai. "We can't just give his tongue back to him, can we?"

"I don't think we have a choice," Vimbai said. "Look at him—he's so little."

Maya heaved a sigh. "This is my grandma you're talking about."

Vimbai patted her friend's hand; it looked so alone and weak splayed on the Formica surface of the kitchen table that Vimbai felt like crying. "I know. But Peb . . . he's been with us since the very beginning, remember? Sure, he looks weird and all, but he's our friend, like Felix."

Maya stroked some shallow cuts on the table surface, running her fingertips along their ragged ridges. Vimbai thought about the kitchen table back home—her parents' house, which she still considered home, no matter how much the house in the dunes grew on her. That table bore no cuts or irregularities of any sort, its surface smooth and polished daily by a soft cloth—it was so soft, in fact, that little Vimbai used to sleep with this cloth after she managed to liberate it from the kitchen cupboards.

"Do you think it will hurt her?" Maya said. "If Peb gets his tongue back, will my grandma go back to being dead?"

"I don't know," Vimbai said. "Ask her."

Maya gave her a tormented look. "I can't. What if she says yes?"

"Then we get the man-fish and beat the fuck out of that slimy bastard," Vimbai said and scowled, feeling rough and dangerous for once. "Then he would have to help us to sort things so that Peb gets his tongue back, and your grandmother can stay. Or at least—" Vimbai saw Maya's face, and didn't finish her sentence. There was too much hope mixed with fear in her dark eyes.

Maya drained her cup. The grandmothers had gotten acquainted by then, and chatted amiably, with Peb lolling and crying nearby, refusing to be ignored by the grandmothers.

"Grandma," Maya called. "Will you survive if you give Peb his tongue back?"

"Which one is his tongue, child?" the grandma answered.

"Oh damn it," Maya said. "We might need Felix again."

Vimbai clapped her hands over her mouth. "Oh, poor Félix! We left him all alone since last night!"

"Or longer," Maya confirmed. "Plus, that universe of his was drained."

"There's still some floating on the surface outside," Vimbai answered. "Maybe. Balshazaar poured it out. Let's go check."

"I would say that you're talking crazy," Maya said and stood, "if I wasn't used to all of us talking crazy."

On the porch, they stood a while, both surprised that the sun was so bright and large and real outside—and there were smells, familiar smells of the ocean and a new, coppery odor Vimbai could not immediately place. It didn't matter though—she thought that they were spending so much time indoors, in the constantly growing, mutating house, in its musty smell and its fake sky painted over the ceiling; with its sheetrock ridges and furniture mountains, carpet lawns and meat windows.

"It's nice to be outside," Maya said.

Vimbai nodded. She stared at the water, choppy with small stubborn waves, solid and angry. The waves butted against the porch, and there was no trace of Felix's remaining universe as far as the eye could see. "Damn it," Vimbai said.

Maya kneeled on the porch, peering between the boards—it wasn't too long ago, Vimbai remembered, that she imagined a nest of foxes under it, thought she observed a quick liquid movement of a long-tailed creature. "Look at this," Maya said.

Vimbai kneeled next to her. The water was dark under the porch, and until Vimbai's eyes adjusted to the shifts of light and shadow, to the narrow stripes of sunlight and sudden collapses of darkness, she wasn't sure whether she was seeing just water, or something else. Soon enough her eyes grew sensitive enough to discern the nuances, and she sighed with relief as she recognized the dark oily substance trapped under the porch. "How do we get it out?"

"I think I know," Maya said, and jumped to her feet. "You stay put, I'll go get Felix."

Felix was revived somewhat by the mention of his errant black hole, and he rushed outside, his lips, white as sheets, trembling with weakness and relief, a savage hope battling the familiar fears. He stuck his hands between the floorboards and wept as the thick oily fluid flowed up his pale arms and slopped over his neck and face and head, in an orgy of recognition and achieving completeness.

THERE WERE TIMES, VIMBAI THOUGHT, WHEN THINGS JUST came together—the constellations aligned and the world turned in such a way that the Coriolis forces of the world pushed all the disparate things and influences so that they came together in a beautiful swirl. Perhaps the house was too big to truly see that, but the kitchen was not—and Vimbai held her breath, wishing for this moment to stay with her as long as it could. There were Vimbai and Maya, standing by the sides of the screen door, their backs propping up the walls. They held hands in mutual support and anticipation, the jointed lock of their fingers hanging by the doorknob, as if it too was capable of admitting them somewhere else.

The grandmothers sat by the table, opposite each other,

their eyes locked—one ghostly and one undead, but grandmothers nonetheless, and one could not help but love them, love them in ways one could not love one's parents out of pride and embarrassment and too much baggage and adolescent arguments. Perhaps those resentments too would burn away in a clean spiritual fire, Vimbai thought; for now, grandmothers sufficed.

The horseshoe crabs Vimbai thought of as hers and Maya's dogs were not in attendance, with the crabs being under the ocean and industriously pulling the house along, and the dogs temporarily exiled to the porch, where they squinted at the sun and panted with their tongues lolling; neither seemed to mind much at not being included in the ceremony.

And then there was Peb, floating grandly over the kitchen table, and Felix standing nearby, somewhat less pale, somewhat more animated ever since he managed to collect the remnants of the oily universe from under the porch and reattach them to his skull. It wasn't anything like his old do—there was no magnificence left there, it was barely enough to cover his head with a thin film, but, as they all had observed in turn, it was better than nothing at all.

Felix swallowed a few times as he looked from Peb to Maya's grandma and back. His Adam's apple, suddenly large and fragile under the transparent skin like a porcelain egg, bobbed in rhythm with the swallowing. He licked his lips a few times. "Here goes," he said, and dipped both hands into his hair. Both came away covered in what looked like tar but Vimbai guessed at the gooey space of his former universe, and squeezed Maya's hand tighter.

Maya squeezed back. It was a bad time, Vimbai thought, but then again, is there ever a good time for anything? And just as Felix reached his stained fingers into Maya's grandmother's mouth, Vimbai whispered under her breath, *I love you*, looking straight ahead and addressing no one in particular.

She had been getting used to the otherworldly light shows; still, when Felix pulled out a writhing, rainbow colored fish, Vimbai gave a little gasp of surprise. The small thing flapped and strained against his fingers, ethereal, and for a moment Vimbai thought that Felix had extracted something he wasn't supposed to. But Peb reached out with seven or eight of his limbs and grabbed the brightly colored appendage and stuffed it in his mouth. He smiled then, and babbled happily about the ethereal dimensions and the deepest chasm filled with molten sulfur and black iron.

Vimbai's eyes turned to the grandma—the old lady gave Felix a disapproving look of her white eyes and coughed, delicately covering her wrinkled mouth with one white-gloved hand. She coughed for a while, as if clearing her throat from dust and grime accumulated over the years (and Vimbai suspected that was the case); grandma hacked and caught her breath and hacked again, with great inhales and sharp coughs reminiscent of the tearing of butcher's paper. When she was finally able to stop, she extracted a small white handkerchief demurely tucked away into her sleeve, and mopped the corners of her eyes and her mouth. "Good Lord," she said. "Maya, are you wearing cutoffs made from man's jeans? Have you lost your mind?"

Maya let go of Vimbai's hand then, and she rushed across

the kitchen floor elbowing Felix out of the way, and she gave her grandmother a great hug, crying and laughing at the same time.

And what was Vimbai going to say about that? Nothing, that's what—she kept her lips sealed, because she too had her grandmother who had no reason or way of being here, because sometimes hows and whys did not matter as much as the greatest gift in the world, the biggest privilege imaginable—the ability to look at someone whom one had lost, and to tell them all the things you always wanted to say but did not have a chance. The second chance, the greatest gift—and who was Vimbai to deny it to anyone, least of all Maya?

Chapter 20

VIMBAI WATCHED THE SUN RISING OVER THE OCEAN—STILL a thin silvery stripe, with the clouds just barely turning pink and golden.

Maya came out onto the porch and stood next to her. "Nice sunrise. I don't remember the last time I've seen one—properly, I mean. Driving home after the night shift doesn't quite count."

"Sunrise is a sunrise," Vimbai said. "You okay?"

Maya nodded. "Yeah. Just trying to get used to the idea that my grandmother is, you know, a zombie."

"Mine is a ghost," Vimbai pointed out.

Maya heaved a sigh. "Do you think ghosts are cooler than zombies?"

"No way." Vimbai smiled. "Zombies are way cool. Although the ghosts are too."

"And undead horseshoe crabs?"

"They are in their own category," Vimbai said. She pointed at the dark stripe on the horizon, something she had been trying to discern the shape of since it was light enough to see anything. "What does this look like to you?"

Maya looked, her hand shielding her squinting eyes, and grinned, wider than Vimbai had ever seen her smile. "This is land, Vimbai. This is land! We'll get us some milk soon."

"And afterwards?"

"I still vote for staying in the house and being queens of all we see," Maya said. "I don't think we'd get to keep our grandmothers in the outside world."

"I'm sure they'll be fine in the house," Vimbai said. "But we . . . you and I, we need to go outside now and again. I want to see my parents, and I would like you to meet them, and I hope they are not too mad at me—I mean, they would be mad, but they'll forgive me, I hope. And I want to go back to school, and I hope to get away with academic probation for such a long absence, and I worry that I won't be able to."

Maya smiled. "I know. Still, it's tempting to imagine what it would be like, to leave everything behind like that, and just explore and name things, wouldn't it?"

"Sure," Vimbai said. "Maybe we'll be able to—maybe the house will keep growing on the inside, and we can take weekend trips to its distant reaches."

"And we can go and visit the man-fish."

"Oh, damn it!" Vimbai clasped her hands to her chest. "I completely forgot that I promised him a spell—I better take care of it before he gets pissed off and starts walking around swallowing souls."

"I'll come with you," Maya said. "Do I need to bring the dogs with me?"

Vimbai shook her head. "Nah, let them be. I will need a knife, though."

Maya followed her in the kitchen and stayed close, as Vimbai rummaged through every drawer looking for the sharpest knife. "You think you know what you're doing?"

"Yeah," Vimbai lied, and shot a reassuring smile in the direction of both grandmothers. She headed for the door before the grandmothers got suspicious and started asking what they wanted with sharp knives. Maya followed, her expression alternating between giddy and doubtful.

Vimbai and Maya hurried to the man-fish's lake. The way was so familiar now, so ordinary that Vimbai barely paid any attention to the usual overnight terrain alterations—there was a small hill built of rolled up, twisted laundry, and on the other side of the path a freshly sprung puddle of Jell-O and rich mud. Weak and pale stems of rye fringed the path and brushed against Vimbai's bare calves, like stiff cat whiskers.

"Do you think that land we saw was . . . is really New Jersey?" Maya said. "I mean, could it be some never-never land or something?"

Vimbai shrugged. "I doubt it. The crabs know where they are going, and they know New Jersey. They would tell us if they were lost . . . wouldn't they?"

"Of course," Maya said. "Just wondering, you know? These past few weeks have been a bit—"

"Weird?" Vimbai interrupted.

Maya smiled and nodded. "Yeah. If you're aiming for the understatement of the century."

"You've been coping well." Vimbai sucked on her lower lip, considering her words. "I was getting an impression that you were rather . . . *reveling* in it."

"I never thought it would make sense to freak out or whine about shit," Maya said. "Roll with the punches, dontcha know. But this stuff, this . . . this house and the ghosts and my dogs—all this has been great. I like it, and sometimes you just have to stop worrying about what's possible and what isn't, and how it's all going to play out, and what will happen to you and if you're losing your mind."

"You thought that you might?" Vimbai said.

"And you didn't?"

Vimbai shook her head. "I would've, if it was just me. But with you around, being so cool about all this . . . I never really doubted."

The cattails and reeds fringing the man-fish's lake greeted them with sage nodding to the nudgings of a light gentle wind, and the sun reflected in a thousand facets on the lake's surface.

There was a movement, a splash by the small island of wild rice not too far off the bank. The man-fish waited for them, his wide mouth twisted in a grimace of acute displeasure that eerily reminded Vimbai of her mother. "Finally," he said. "Took you long enough to show up."

"Sorry," Vimbai said. "We've been battling blood-draining monsters."

"Successfully, I assume." The man-fish gave Vimbai a long measuring look. "Of course. You wouldn't be here otherwise."

"And you would." Maya shook her head. "You really know how to hedge your bets—you would be here no matter what."

"You don't seem to understand the man-fish," the man-fish said.

Vimbai nodded. It seemed impossible to understand such a creature, like it was not possible to understand the vampires.

There was that solitary drive, the terrible single-minded obsession that Vimbai lacked and yet did not envy. "I suppose we don't," she said. "Then again, what are you going to do?"

"You don't understand the survival." The man-fish crawled closer to the bank, his wet browned skin glistening in the sun as his humped back and the stiff dorsal fin breached the water surface. "You don't know what it is like, constantly thinking of not dying, and finding enough to eat so you can live another day."

"Maybe not," Maya said. "But you need Vimbai now, so you better be nice to her."

The man-fish grumbled and crawled closer still. "All right, all right. So what say you, witch-girl?"

"I'm definitely not a witch," Vimbai said, even as she doubted her own words. Her thoughts ran in so many directions at once now—was she really a witch, or was her magic born merely of love and desperation? Would her mother be mad at her if she knew? Of course not, Vimbai thought. She would be mad at Vimbai's long disappearance first of all, and if she was ever kicked out of school or even put on academic probation, she would be even madder. Magic was quite far down on the list of things Vimbai's mother would get mad about. "But I can cut you good. It's a pity I didn't bring a fish knife."

Maya snickered, and the man-fish rolled his beady eyes. "Very funny," he said. "Go ahead—less talking and more cutting, and I only pray that you're more proficient in the latter than in the former."

Vimbai eyed the wide expanse of the man-fish's flank and

back, brown and green like silt, like river mud. He swelled immense, and his eye still glimmered with malice he never bothered to conceal. And what sort of magic could she pour into such a creature? She could only rely on her vague understanding of how these things worked, and she reasoned that if her love, her unrequited desire fueled the protective spell she had somehow carved into her forearms, then to quench the insatiable thirst for souls she had to offer something the opposite of it—satisfaction, satiety, contentment. Vimbai smiled, since this was something she knew quite a bit about.

She turned to Maya. "I'm going to tell a story—it's a traditional *ngano*, and I'm a *sarungano*, a storyteller. You'll be the audience and you'll have to ask me questions when I stop, all right? And answer mine when I ask you."

"I'll do my best," Maya said, and looked puzzled. "Is it like a spell?"

"It's like a story," Vimbai answered. "*Ngano* is how children learn." She cleared her throat and started, the knife in her hand rising and falling in rhythm with her story.

"Who is the wisest animal in the forest?" Vimbai said.

Maya opened her mouth and laughed. Then said, "I don't know. Who?"

"Is it a jaguar?" Her knife fell, leaving a long thin mark on the catfish's smooth skin.

"No."

The mark swelled with blood.

"Is it a baboon?" Another cut, crisscrossing the first at a sharp angle.

"No, it is not." Even Maya fell under the spell of her rhythm and swayed along, and gave her answers in a singsong voice.

"Is it a hare?" The new cut fell, and the overall patter of crosshatching grew apparent to Vimbai.

Maya hesitated, and Vimbai shrugged at her, indicating the correct answer. "Maybe," Maya said.

"Is it a tortoise?" The skin of the catfish was now developing a pattern of blood-stained, elongated rhombi.

"Yes?" Maya offered.

Vimbai nodded and smiled. "Go on, ask."

"Why is it wise?" Maya asked.

"Because it does not chase after things." Cut.

"Because it is satisfied with what it has." Cut.

"Because it carries his house on his back and does not covet a new one." Cut.

"He is never aggressive and yet he gets his way." Nod to Maya.

"How?" Maya said.

The knife in Vimbai's hand trembled and paused, raised over the devastation it had wrought—the skin of the man-fish was a pattern of bloodied diamonds, a horrible jester's suit. "Because he knows that he already has everything he needs, and if he ever needs more, the creator will give him more. It is up to the *Mwari*, the creator, and the *mhondoro*, the tribal spirits, to give everyone what they need. Otherwise, the eyes grow greedy, the hands feel empty, and there's never any satisfaction and no one is ever sated and happy with what they have."

"Except the tortoise," Maya offered, sounding more confident.

"Except the tortoise," Vimbai agreed. "May the moon forever slosh in his belly."

At her last words, the man-fish's mouth snapped open—a dark tunnel of unquenched hunger—and he lunged, his jaws snapping shut just a hairbreadth away from Vimbai's nose. She screamed out and jerked away, the hand holding the knife lashing out in a reflexively protective gesture.

Maya gasped nearby and out of a corner of her eye Vimbai caught a blur of motion as Maya struggled to her feet, as the man-fish slithered and snapped, trying to get to Vimbai's soul, his evil reaching out in a final desperate gesture. Vimbai's knife caught him across the throat, and the last cut, ragged and cruel, traced the pale skin below his jaw, carved away a good chunk of his snout.

The fish fell back, exhausted, the bloodied chunk of his face in Vimbai's lap. She pushed him away, kicked his limp slippery body away from her, and struggled to catch her breath.

She dropped her hand with the knife down into her lap and looked at her handiwork. For a moment she worried that the man-fish would bleed to death, expire because of her incompetent magicking—and even he had tried to drown her not too long ago, even if he tried to steal her soul it would seem wrong to her, having killed someone who voluntarily went under her knife, preferring it to the needles of the *wazi-mamoto* and the eternal hunger of the cursed.

Then, the man-fish stirred, and the flow of blood stopped. The diamonds of his savaged skin glowed and silvered, and Vimbai and Maya could not quite believe their eyes and had to touch them with their fingers, to make sure that those were indeed scales—something no catfish ever had.

"Whoa," Maya whispered. "How'd you learn to do this?"

"I didn't," Vimbai said.

"And that story?"

"I just made it up." She tossed the knife to the ground and sat back, her weight pushing her heels deeper into the muddy soil. "I don't really *know* anything. I just make shit up, you know?"

"Seems to work just fine." Maya crouched low next to Vimbai, close enough for their knees to touch, and watched the man-fish's continued transformation. His skin was now covered in perfect silver scales with small shimmering white and green spots, and his face was changing too—the whiskers had disappeared and his upper jaw curved into a haughty beak, extending his face forward, covering up the disfigured lower one. His head and body did not look flat anymore, but acquired the graceful proportion of a fast fish that did not feed on the bottom but propelled itself with strong strokes of its lobed tailfin.

"That's a lake trout," Vimbai said. "I think."

"Is it good?" Maya dared to pat the fish's head, and it flared its gill covers in response.

"Hey, Mr. Fish?" Vimbai said. "Can you still talk?"

The fish opened its mouth as if in silent laughter, splashed its tail in the shallow water like an oar, and—one, two, three—it was gone, disappeared under water. In just a few moments, the surface of the lake grew smooth like silk again, and did not betray the presence of a large fish underneath anywhere.

THE HOUSE OF DISCARDED DREAMS

THAT NIGHT, VIMBAI COULD NOT SLEEP. THE THOUGHTS OF the previous day kept churning in her mind, and her imaginings of the day to come charged the air with great anticipation. She wasn't the only one—the previous evening, even though no one had said anything about it, had been taut with barely concealed excitement.

The two grandmothers in the kitchen argued about what needed to be done food-wise, seeing as how they only had some preserves and canned soups and ramen and a bag of flour left. They compromised on pancakes but barely spoke to each other afterwards. Felix retreated to his room, but seemed to be in high spirits—the universe around his head, drained and ravaged and discarded, had been growing again, and Vimbai supposed that soon enough it would resume its normal undulation—although without Balshazaar, whose demise in the hands of *wazimamoto* passed unlamented by anyone; only Felix was kind enough to acknowledge that he had ever existed.

Peb would not stop babbling now that he had his tongue back, and he traveled all over the house, his many limbs bristling like the fins of a lionfish, yelling cheerful nonsense about brimstone rivers and blue electrical storms, of the worlds made of ball lightning and fire and of black unfathomable chasms populated by creatures capable of swallowing entire galaxies.

Maya's dogs and Vimbai's horseshoe crabs remained outside—the former curled up on the boards of the porch, their bushy tails covering their glistening wet noses from the cold, their eyes looking up wetly at whoever ventured onto the steps. The crabs stayed hidden, but Vimbai could imagine the restless churning of their legs, the clusters of their soul shells waiting for them on the ropes, waiting for the day that it was warm enough for the creatures to become whole again.

Maya and Vimbai had left the kitchen with its squabbling old women and the overexcited Peb, and sat on the porch, under the stars, the hunk of land black against black sky, its outline only hinted at by the absence of stars. In the darkness of her room, Vimbai smiled at the memory, at the contentment she felt whenever she and Maya could be away from everyone else and sit side by side, listening to the quiet sluicing of the waves and talking in low voices, as if sharing secrets even though they discussed quite mundane topics.

"What will you do when we get back to New Jersey?" Maya had asked. "I mean, besides going back to school and freaking out that your mom would yell at you."

Vimbai smiled at the barb, at the fond familiarity of it. "I will start looking into horseshoe crab conservation. I mean, there are initiatives now—like they don't allow fisheries to use them as bait anymore, but I'm sure there are more things I could do. And no one thinks that the medical research is damaging them, but I know it does—you can't just drain away most of someone's blood and think that you're not harming them."

"I'll say." Maya's face was hidden by the night, but her voice was smiling.

"Anyway," Vimbai said. "Shouldn't you be spending more time with your zombie grandmother?"

"Not when you put it this way." Maya laughed softly. "No, I will. I'm just . . . it takes getting used to, you know? And then there are all these crazy notions that she would be disappointed in me for not finishing college, for not making more of myself."

"You still can."

"I know." Maya sighed. "Still."

"I'm sure she won't be disappointed." Vimbai continued.

"Well, maybe not. But it's strange for me too, having her back and yet not quite knowing if it's really her, you know? How did you cope with your grandma?"

"I barely knew her when she was alive." Vimbai stroked the wooden plank by her side. "I don't know if it's really her, but I can't know—I have very little idea of what she is supposed to be like. But you'll figure it out."

"I guess so."

"But again, does it even matter?" Vimbai said. "Isn't it better than having no grandmother at all?"

"You're right." Maya shifted in the darkness, petting the dogs, and stood. "We better turn in—we'll be there tomorrow. Need to get some sleep."

"Yeah," Vimbai said and rose too. "Good night, Maya."

And now she lay in her room, her mind racing. Occasionally, she drifted into brief snatches of sleep, and dreamt of the crabs coming ashore where Vimbai's mother waited for her, her hand shielding her eyes from the sun, forever vigilant, forever waiting. She dreamt of the sun rising and touching the silvery ocean surface behind her back, lighting the land outline in front of her. And as she dreamt, the house touched the beach softly, its porch sliding over the sand compacted by the surf, over the tops of the dunes, until it found its old foundation, left free of sand. The house sighed and creaked and stretched its roof corners and its wainscots as it settled into the familiar grooves—but carefully, as if afraid of disturbing the delicate contents that filled it to brimming.

The half-foxes, half-possums crawled under the porch, sighing contentedly, as they curled up in the familiar dark cave, the sand underneath still wearing the rounded troughs left by their bodies. They wondered if they would be allowed back inside, and if they would go hunting tomorrow, fording rivers and running across the great golden plains of straw and couch cushions.

The horseshoe crabs remained underwater, sleeping, soul-less for now, under the freezing waves, and dreaming of the days when the sun would rise high and warm the chilly waters, when the tides would rage high on the beach and they would put on their soul shells and perhaps fix them with the remnants of the souls still sluicing in these waters, become themselves again and come dancing through the surf, raising their legs high like chitinous ballerinas. They dreamed of the bygone days when wave after wave of spawning crabs flooded the beaches and crashed upon them in a frenzy of whipping tail spikes and burrowing legs, where the eggs of the crabs outnumbered the grains of sand.

The ghosts in the house slept too—unusual for the ghosts, but they welcomed the relief. Peb curled in the *chipoko's* lap as she nodded off in a living-room chair, and both dreamed of the branches of jacaranda trees. Maya's zombie grandma closed her terrible white eyes for the first time since she walked again, and she conjured up visions of downtown Newark and church service on Sundays, of the gospel choir whose singing reached through the honking, screeching traffic, all the way down the street.

And the human inhabitants . . . their dreams were more vague, more difficult to pin down—but they were the ones that filled the house with the forlorn memories of the past and the regrets of the present, they were the ones that gave the walls and the valleys and the ridges their shape. They were the namers and the creators, the wills that shaped the house so that it could remain itself, even now, when it was moored securely on solid land, in the forever shifting dunes.

PRAISE FOR
THE ALCHEMY OF STONE

A *Los Angeles Times* Summer Reading Selection

"*The Alchemy of Stone* may be ostensibly rooted in genre fiction and indeed be quite appealing to the genre fiction audience . . . But such is the alchemy of literary invention that it's quite clear *The Alchemy of Stone* explores our world within the confines of a world created with language alone."—*The Agony Column*

"The tale of a clockwork woman named Mattie whose heart is literally kept locked up by her maker, *The Alchemy of Stone* is set in a spy-ridden world of intrigue and class warfare. As a scientific revolution sweeps through the city of Ayona, Mattie discovers a secret that could help her lead a coup. If only she could figure out who to trust, and regain the key to her own heart. Written by the author of *The Secret History of Moscow,* this novel is beautifully strange."—*io9.com*

"Sedia's evocative third novel, a steampunk fable about the price of industrial development, deliberately skewers familiar ideas, leaving readers to reach their own conclusions about the proper balance of tradition and progress and what it means to be alive."—*Publishers Weekly*, starred review

continued

"*The Alchemy of Stone* is beautiful and strong, with images of wonder and strangeness to rival the Brothers Quay. *The Secret History of Moscow* marked her as a talent to watch. This one's better."—Daniel Abraham, author of *The Long Price Quartet*

"Ekaterina Sedia has once more brought her stunningly lateral view of the fantastic, this time to *The Alchemy of Stone*: a steampunk fantasy of creatures, cities and affairs of the heart."—Jay Lake, author of *Mainspring* and *Escapement*

"A gorgeous meditation on what it means to *not* be human. I haven't been able to stop thinking about this beautiful book, from its robot heroine to the Soul-Smoker and stone gargoyles that watch over the city."—Justine Larbalestier, author of *Magic or Madness*

"Strange and smooth, sweet and clever, *The Alchemy of Stone* is a deeply engaging clockwork fable with real mechanical heart."—Cherie Priest, author of *Not Flesh Nor Feathers* and *Dreadful Skin*

"Ekaterina Sedia goes from strength to strength, with *The Alchemy of Stone* a worthy follow-up to *The Secret History of Moscow*. This is richly detailed, steampunkian adventure." —Jeff VanderMeer, author of *Shriek: An Afterword* and World Fantasy Award winner

AN EXCERPT FROM
THE ALCHEMY OF STONE

Mattie, an intelligent automaton skilled in the use of alchemy, finds herself caught in the middle of a conflict between gargoyles, the Mechanics, and the Alchemists. With the old order quickly giving way to the new, Mattie discovers powerful and dangerous secrets—secrets that can completely alter the balance of power in the city of Ayona. This doesn't sit well with Loharri, the Mechanic who created Mattie and still has the key to her heart—literally.

Chapter 1

———

WE SCALE THE ROUGH BRICKS OF THE BUILDING'S FACADE. *Their crumbling edges soften under our claw-like fingers; they jut out of the flat, adenoid face of the wall to provide easy footholds. We could've used fire escapes, we could've climbed up, up, past the indifferent faces of the walls, their windows cataracted with shutters; we could've bounded up in the joyful cacophony of corrugated metal and barely audible whispers of the falling rust shaken loose by our ascent. We could've flown.*

But instead we hug the wall, press our cheeks against the warm bricks; the filigree of age and weather covering their surface imprints on our skin, steely-gray like the thunderous skies above us. We rest, clinging to the wall, our fingertips nestled in snug depressions in the brick, like they were made especially for that, clinging. We are almost all the way to the steep roof red with shingles shaped like fish scales.

We look into the lone window lit with a warm glow, the only one with open shutters and smells of sage, lamb, and chlorine wafting outside. We look at the long bench decorated with alembics and retorts and colored powders and bunches of dried herbs and bowls of watery sheep's eyes from the butcher's shop down the alleyway. We look at the girl.

Her porcelain face has cracked—a recent fall, an accident?—and we worry as we count the cracks cobwebbing her cheek and her forehead, radiating from the point of impact like sunrays. Yes, we remember the sun. Her blue eyes, facets of expensive glass colored with copper salts, look into the darkness, and we do not know if she can see us at all.

But she smiles and waves at us, and the bronzed wheel-bearings of her joints squeak their mechanical greeting. She pushes the lock of dark, dark hair (she doesn't know, but it used to belong to a dead boy) behind her delicate ear, a perfect and pink seashell. Her deft hands, designed for grinding and mixing and measuring, smooth the front of her fashionably wide skirt, and she motions to us. "Come in," she says.

We creep inside through the window, grudgingly, gingerly, we creep (we could've flown). We grow aware of our not-belonging, of the grayness of our skin, of our stench—we smell like pigeon-shit, and we wonder if she notices; we fill her entire room with our rough awkward sour bodies. "We seek your help," we say.

Her cracked porcelain face remains as expressionless as ours. "I am honored," she says. Her blue eyes bulge a little from their sockets, taking us in. Her frame clicks as she leans forward, curious about us. Her dress is low-cut, and we see that there is a small transparent window in her chest, where a clockwork heart is ticking along steadily, and we cannot help but feel resentful of the sound and—by extension—of her, the sound of time falling away grain by grain, the time that dulls our senses and hardens our skins, the time that is in too short supply. "I will do everything I can," she says, and our resentment falls away too, giving way to gratitude—falls like dead skin. We bow and leap out of the window, one by one by one, and we fly, hopeful for the first time in centuries.

———

LOHARRI'S ROOM SMELLED OF INCENSE AND SMOKE, THE AIR thick like taffy. Mattie tasted it on her lips, and squinted through the thick haze concealing its denizen.

"Mattie," Loharri said from the chaise by the fireplace where he sprawled in his habitual languor, a half-empty glass on the floor. A fat black cat sniffed at its contents prissily, found them not to her liking, but knocked the glass over nonetheless, adding the smell of flat beer to the already overwhelming concoction that was barely air. "So glad to see you."

"You should open the window," she said.

"You don't need air," Loharri said, petulant. He was in one of his moods again.

"But you do," she pointed out. "You are one fart away from death by suffocation. Fresh air won't kill you."

"It might," he said, still sulking.

"Only one way to find out." She glided past him, the whirring of her gears muffled by the room—it was so full of draperies and old rugs rolled up in the corners, so cluttered with bits of machinery and empty dishes. Mattie reached up and swung open the shutters, admitting a wave of air sweet with lilac blooms and rich river mud and roasted nuts from the market square down the street. "Alive still?"

"Just barely." Loharri sat up and stretched, his long spine crackling like flywheels. He then yawned, his mouth gaping dark in his pale face. "What brings you here, my dear love?"

She extended her hand, the slender copper springs of

her fingers grasping a phial of blue glass. "One of your admirers sent for me—she said you were ailing. I made you a potion."

Loharri uncorked the phial and sniffed at the contents with suspicion. "A woman? Which one?" he asked. "Because if it was a jilted lover, I am not drinking this."

"Amelia," Mattie said. "I do not suppose she wishes you dead."

"Not yet," Loharri said darkly, and drank. "What does it do?"

"Not yet," Mattie agreed. "It's just a tonic. It'll dispel your ennui, although I imagine a fresh breeze might do just as well."

Loharri made a face; he was not a handsome man to begin with, and a grimace of disgust did not improve his appearance.

Mattie smiled. "If an angel passes over you, your face will be stuck like that."

Loharri scoffed. "Dear love, if only it could make matters worse. But speaking of faces . . . yours has been bothering me lately. What did you do to it?"

Mattie touched the cracks, feeling their familiar swelling on the smooth porcelain surface. "Accident," she said.

Loharri arched his left eyebrow—the right one was paralyzed by the scar and the knotted mottled tissue that ruined half of his face; it was a miracle his eye had been spared. Mattie heard that some women found scars attractive in a romantic sort of way, but she was pretty certain that Loharri's were quite a long way past romantic and into disfiguring. "Another accident," he said. "You are a very clumsy automaton, do you know that?"

"I am not clumsy," Mattie said. "Not with my hands."

He scowled at the phial in his hand. "I guess not, although my taste buds beg to differ. Still, I made you a little something."

"A new face," Mattie guessed.

Loharri smiled lopsidedly and stood, and stretched his long, lanky frame again. He searched through the cluttered room until he came upon a workbench that somehow got hidden and lost under the pile of springs, coils, wood shavings, and half-finished suits of armor that appeared decorative rather than functional in their coppery, glistening glory. There were cogs and parts of engines and things that seemed neither animate nor entirely dead, and for a short while Mattie worried that the chaotic pile would consume Loharri; however, he soon emerged with a triumphant cry, a round white object in his hand.

It looked like a mask and Mattie averted her eyes—she did not like looking at her faces like that, as they hovered, blind and disembodied. She closed her eyes and extended her neck toward Loharri in a habitual gesture. His strong, practiced fingers brushed the hair from her forehead, lingering just a second too long, and felt around her jaw line, looking for the tiny cogs and pistons that attached her face to the rest of her head. She felt her face pop off, and the brief moment when she felt exposed, naked, seemed to last an eternity. She whirred her relief when she felt the touch of the new concave surface as it enveloped her, hid her from the world.

Loharri affixed the new face in place, and she opened her eyes. Her eyes took a moment to adjust to the new sockets.

"How does it fit?" Loharri asked.

"Well enough," she said. "Let me see how I look." She extended one of the flexible joints that held her eyes and tilted it, to see the white porcelain mask. Loharri had not painted this one—he remembered her complaints about the previous face, that it was too bright, too garish (this is why she broke it in the first place), and he left this one plain, suffused with the natural bluish tint that reminded her of the pale skies over the city during July and its heat spells. Only the lips, lined with pitted smell and taste sensors, were tinted pale red, same as the rooftops in the merchants' district.

"It is nice," Mattie said. "Thank you."

Loharri nodded. "Don't mention it. No matter how emancipated, you're still mine." His voice lost its usual acidity as he studied her new face with a serious expression. There were things Mattie and Loharri didn't talk about—one of them was Mattie's features, which remained constant from one mask to the next, no matter how much he experimented with colors and other elaborations. "Looks good," he finally concluded. "Now, tell me the real reason for your visit—surely, you don't rush over every time someone tells you I might be ill."

"The gargoyles," Mattie said. "They want to hire me, and I want your permission to make them my priority, at the expense of your project."

Loharri nodded. "It's a good one," he said. "I guess our gray overlords have grown tired of being turned into stone?"

"Yes," Mattie answered. "They feel that their life spans are too short and their fate is too cruel; I cannot say that I disagree. Only . . . I really do not know where to start. I thought of vitality potions and the mixes to soften the leather, of the elixirs to loosen the calcified joints . . . only they all seem lacking."

Loharri smiled and drummed his fingers on his knee. "I see your problem, and yes, you can work on it to your little clockwork heart's content."

"Thank you," Mattie said. If she had been able to smile, she would have. "I brought you what I have so far—a list of chemicals that change color when exposed to light."

Loharri took the proffered piece of paper with two long fingers, and opened it absentmindedly. "I know little of alchemy," he said. "I'm not friends with any of your colleagues, but I suppose I could find a replacement for you nonetheless, although I doubt there's anyone who knows more on the matter than you do. Meanwhile, I do have one bit of advice regarding the gargoyles."

Mattie tilted her head to the shoulder, expectant. She had learned expressive poses, and knew that they amused her creator; she wondered if she was supposed to feel shame at being manipulative.

As expected, he snickered. "Aren't you just the sweetest machine in the city? And oh, you listen so well. Heed my words then: I remember a woman who worked on the gargoyle problem some years back. Beresta was her name, a foreigner; Beresta from the eastern district. But she died—a sad, sad thing."

"Oh," Mattie said, disappointed. "Did she leave any papers behind?"

Loharri shook his head. "No papers. But, lucky for you, she was a restless spirit, a sneaky little ghost who hid in the rafters of her old home. And you know what they do with naughty ghosts."

Mattie inclined her head in agreement. "They call for the Soul-Smoker."

"Indeed. And if there's anyone who still knows Beresta's secrets, it's him. You're not afraid of the Soul-Smokers, are you?"

"Of course not," Mattie said mildly. "I have no soul; to fear him would be a mere superstition." She stood and smoothed her skirts, feeling the stiff whalebone stays that held her skirts full and round under the thin fabric. "Thank you, Loharri. You've been kind."

"Thank you for the tonic," he said. "But please, do visit me occasionally, even if there's nothing you want. I am a sentimental man."

"I shall," Mattie answered, and took her leave. As she walked out of the door, it occurred to her that if she wanted to be kind to Loharri she could offer him things she knew he wanted but would never ask for—she could invite him to touch her hair, or let him listen to the ticking of her heart. To sit with him in the darkness, in the dead hours between night and morning when the demons tormented him more than usual, and then perhaps he would talk of things they did not talk about otherwise—perhaps then he would tell her why he had made her and why he grew so despondent when she wanted to live on her own and to study, to become something other than a part of him. The problem was, those were the things she preferred not to know.

MATTIE TOOK A LONG WAY HOME, WEAVING THROUGH THE market among the many stalls selling food and fabric and spices; she lingered by a booth that sold imported herbs and chemicals, and picked up a bunch of dried salamanders and a bottle of copper salts. She then continued east to the river, and she stood a while on the embankment watching the steamboats huff across, carrying marble for the new construction on the northern bank. There were talks of the new parliament building, and Mattie supposed that it signaled an even bigger change than gossip at Loharri's parties suggested. Ever since the mechanics won a majority, the renovations in the city acquired a feverish pace, and the streets themselves seemed to shift daily, accommodating new roads and more and more factories that belched smoke and steam and manufactured new and frightening machines.

Still, Mattie tried not to think of politics too much. She thought about gargoyles and of Loharri's words. He called them their overlords, even though the city owed its existence to the gargoyles, and they had been nothing but benefactors to the people. Did he know something she didn't? And if he were so disdainful of gargoyles, why did he offer to help?

Mattie walked leisurely along the river. It was a nice day, and many people strolled along the embankment, enjoying the first spring warmth and the sweet, dank smell of the river. She received a few curious looks, but overall people paid her no mind. She passed a paper factory that squatted over the river like an ugly toad, disgorging a stream of white foam into the water; a strong smell of bleach surrounded it like a cloud.

From the factory she turned into the twisty streets of the eastern district, where narrow three-storied buildings clung close together like swallows' nests on the face of a cliff. The sea of red tiled roofs flowed and ebbed as far as the eye could see, and Mattie smiled—she liked her neighborhood the way it was, full of people and small shops occupying the lower stories, without any factories and with the streets too narrow for any mechanized conveyances. She turned into her street and headed home, the ticking of her heart keeping pace with her thoughts filled with gargoyles and Loharri's strange relationship to them.

Mattie's room and laboratory were located above an apothecary's, which she occasionally supplied with elixirs and ointments. Less mainstream remedies remained in her laboratory, and those who sought them knew to visit her rooms upstairs; they usually used the back entrance and the rickety stairs that led past the apothecary.

When Mattie got home to her garret, she found a visitor waiting on the steps. She had met this woman before at one of Loharri's gatherings—her name was Iolanda; she stood out from the crowd, Mattie remembered—she moved energetically and laughed loudly, and looked Mattie straight in the eye when they were introduced. And now Iolanda's gaze did not waver. "May I come in?" she said as soon as she saw Mattie, and smiled.

"Of course," Mattie said and unlocked the door. The

corridor was narrow and led directly into her room, which contained a roll-top desk and her few books; Mattie led her visitor through and into the laboratory, where there was space to sit and talk.

"Would you like a drink?" Mattie asked. "I have a lovely jasmine-flavored liqueur."

Iolanda nodded. "I would love that. How considerate of you to keep refreshments."

Mattie poured her a drink. "Of course," she said. "How kind of you to notice."

Iolanda took the proffered glass from Mattie's copper fingers, studying them as she did so, and took a long swallow. "Indeed, it is divine," she said. "Now, if you don't mind, I would like to dispense with the pleasantries and state my business."

Mattie inclined her head and sat on a stool by her work-bench, offering the other one to Iolanda with a gesture.

"You are not wealthy," Iolanda said. Not a question but a statement.

"Not really," Mattie agreed. "But I do not need much."

"Mmmm," Iolanda said. "One might suspect that a well-off alchemist is a successful alchemist—you do need to buy your ingredients, and some are more expensive than others."

"That is true," Mattie said. "Now, how does this relate to your business?"

"I can make you rich," Iolanda said. "I have need of an alchemist, of one who is discreet and skillful. But before I explain my needs, let me ask you this: do you consider your-self a woman?"

"Of course," Mattie said, taken aback and puzzled. "What else would I consider myself?"

"Perhaps I did not phrase it well," Iolanda said, and tossed back the remainder of her drink with an unexpectedly habitual and abrupt gesture. "What I meant was, why do you consider yourself a woman? Because you were created as one?"

"Yes," Mattie replied, although she grew increasingly uncomfortable with the conversation. "And because of the clothes I wear."

"So if you changed your clothes . . . "

"But I can't," Mattie said. "The shape of them is built into me—I know that you have to wear corsets and hoops and stays to give your clothes a proper shape. But I was created with all of those already in place, they are as much as part of me as my eyes. So I ask you: what else would you consider me?"

"I sought not to offend," Iolanda said. "I do confess to my prejudice: I will not do business nor would I employ a person or an automaton of a gender different from mine, and I simply had to know if your gender was coincidental."

"I understand," Mattie said. "And I assure you that my femaleness is as ingrained as your own."

Iolanda sighed. Mattie supposed that Iolanda was beautiful, with her shining dark curls cascading onto her full shoulders and chest, and heavy, languid eyelids half-concealing her dark eyes. "Fair enough. And Loharri . . . can you keep secrets from him?"

"I can and I do," Mattie said.

"In this case, I will appreciate it if you keep our business private," Iolanda said.

"I will, once you tell me what it is," Mattie replied. She shot an involuntary look toward her bench, where the ingredients waited for her to grind and mix and vaporize them, where the aludel yawned empty as if hungry; she grew restless sitting for too long, empty-handed and motionless.

Iolanda raised her eyebrows, as if unsure whether she understood Mattie. She seemed one of those people who rarely encountered anything but abject agreement, and she was not used to being hurried. "Well, I want you to be available for the times I have a need of you, and to fulfill my orders on a short notice. Potions, perfumes, tonics . . . that sort of thing. I will pay you a retainer, so you will be receiving money even when I do not have a need of you."

"I have other clients and projects," Mattie said.

Iolanda waved her hand dismissively. "It doesn't matter. As long as I can find you when I need you."

"It sounds reasonable," Mattie agreed. "I will endeavor to fulfill simple orders within a day, and complex ones— from two days to a week. You won't have them done faster anywhere."

"It is acceptable," Iolanda said. "And for your first order, I need you to create me a fragrance that would cause regret."

"Come back tomorrow," Mattie said. "Or leave me your address, I'll have a courier bring it over."

"No need," Iolanda said. "I will send someone to pick it up. And here's your first week's pay." She rose from her stool and placed a small pouch of stones on the bench. "And if anyone asks, we are casual acquaintances, nothing more."

Iolanda left, and Mattie felt too preoccupied to even look

at the stones that were her payment. She almost regretted agreeing to Iolanda's requests—while they seemed straightforward and it was not that uncommon for courtiers to employ alchemists or any other artisans on a contract basis, something about Iolanda seemed off. Most puzzling, if she wanted to keep a secret from Loharri, she could do better than hire the automaton made by his hands. Mattie was not so vain as to presuppose that her reputation outweighed common good sense.

But there was work to do, and perfume certainly seemed less daunting than granting gargoyles a lifespan extension, and she mixed ambergris and sage, blended myrrh and the bark of grave cypress, and sublimated dry camphor. The smell she obtained was pleasing and sad, and yet she was not certain that this was enough to evoke regret—something seemed missing. She closed her eyes and smelled-tasted the mixture with her sensors, trying hard to remember the last time she felt regret.